Praise for
LORI AVOCATO's
PAULINE SOKOL mysteries

"Sexy and sassy . . . a sure prescription
for outrageous sleuthing."
Agatha, Anthony, and Macavity Award-winning
author Carolyn Hart

"Hilarious."
USA Today bestselling author Merline Lovelace

"An outstanding mix of humor, family relationships,
unusual characters, and realistic detecting."
Ft. Lauderdale Sun-Sentinel

"Great fun."
Laura Van Wormer

"Lori Avocato just gets better and better."
Carla Neggers

"When the prescription is mystery, no one is any better
at serving up the cure."
Former FBI agent and *New York Times* bestselling
author Christopher Whitcomb

Books by Lori Avocato

DEAD ON ARRIVAL
NIP, TUCK, DEAD
DEEP SEA DEAD
ONE DEAD UNDER THE CUCKOO'S NEST
THE STIFF AND THE DEAD
A DOSE OF MURDER

LORI AVOCATO

Dead On Arrival

A PAULINE SOKOL MYSTERY

AVON BOOKS
An Imprint of HarperCollins*Publishers*

This is a work of fiction. Names, characters, places, and incidents are products of the author's imagination or are used fictitiously and are not to be construed as real. Any resemblance to actual events, locales, organizations, or persons, living or dead, is entirely coincidental.

AVON BOOKS
An Imprint of HarperCollins*Publishers*
10 East 53rd Street
New York, New York 10022-5299

Copyright © 2007 by Lori Avocato
ISBN: 978-0-06-083708-2
ISBN-10: 0-06-083708-X
www.avonmystery.com

First Avon Books paperback printing: July 2007

Avon Trademark Reg. U.S. Pat. Off. and in Other Countries,
Marca Registrada, Hecho en U.S.A.
HarperCollins® is a registered trademark of HarperCollins Publishers.

Printed in the U.S.A.

10 9 8 7 6 5 4 3 2 1

To my dear friend and fellow author, attorney Kimberly Peterson Zaniewski. Thanks for being you and for all your encouragement, input, and for calling me daily to wake me so that I can get up at a decent hour to write.

And many thanks to the real ER Dano, Daniel D. Mastropietro, for all his help.

Acknowledgments

It's a scary thing to be taken as a patient in an ambulance. Scary too, to send off a loved one in an ambulance. I know. I've been on both sides of the fence, along with riding with patients on helicopters and ambulances as a nurse in the Air Force.

So, to all those folks I dedicate this novel, in hopes that all turned out perfect and this story, Pauline's story, can add some humor to your lives. All of our lives. Nothing is better or healthier than a laugh (except, of course, maybe chocolate).

To all my readers: Thank you so much! Needless to say, without you all, there would be no Pauline Sokol Mystery series, and what would poor Goldie do without the gang?

To my fantastic agent, Caren Johnson, who has more energy than I had at her age—no, at any age—thanks so much!

To May Chen, my wonderful editor, whose input keeps making my work better and better: I'm thrilled to be on your team.

And thanks go to all the workers at Avon who weave their magic to produce fabulous, eye-catching covers and book-selling blurbs, and to the copy editors, who more than likely have a good laugh when I write *locks* for *lox*. Yes, I've done it . . . er . . . a few times.

To Cecile H. Custer, RN, real-life fraud investigator who has given me ideas along with helping with my research and being a dedicated fan: Thanks, Cecile!

And thanks to my family—Greg and Mario, my kids, who make life worth living and even hang posters of their author mom in their dorm rooms. Have you guys no shame?!

And a blanket thanks to anyone I've forgotten. You know who you are, or at least can claim to.

Dead
On
Arrival

One

I stared down at the handwritten Jagger note that said, "Case Number 6. Practice your driving skills, Sherlock. We'll talk in the morning—at our spot."

Our spot.

Suddenly the noise from Goldie's "nose-revealing" party at my parents' house brought me back to reality. My dearest roommate and second-best friend was celebrating the success (in his opinion) of his recent plastic surgery. Gotta love dear Gold. We all did, especially my other roomie, Miles. They were two of the best guys in the world, and although each had their own little quirks, I loved them dearly. The guys, not the quirks. I had to admit that I looked forward on a daily basis to seeing Goldie's outfits—especially when he wore Armani from the women's department. Then again, he looked handsome in men's Armani too, but when in his female mode, he always made some fashion statement that I later stole for myself.

Since knowing Goldie, I was looking better and better. Maybe there was hope for me yet.

I stared at the note again and decided I had to forget that Jagger had called Dunkin Donuts "our spot," as if he thought we really were an "our" (be still, my foolish heart), and forced my mind back to Case Number 6. That was my sixth medical fraud insurance case to investigate.

Practice my driving skills. Hmm. Okay, I'd be the first to admit I was no Mario Andretti, and, okay again, I admitted to closing my eyes when driving but only if something bad was about to happen. So what could case number six be about? Me and Jagger racing in the Grand Prix?

I had started to laugh, when I felt a presence behind me. My hormones ready to explode, I turned to see Jagger, but unfortunately—very unfortunately—saw Fabio Scarpello instead. My boss. A definite misnomer.

Then the recent revelation by none other than Jagger that he was, in fact, a Tonelli, making *him* my boss, hit me. Hard.

I grabbed Fabio, subsequently startling him. "Is Jagger the owner of Scarpello and Tonelli Insurance Agency? Does he own it? Do you? Is he my boss?"

Normally Fabio would have called me "doll" and brushed off any of my questions with a curse or two, but he looked directly at me. Damn. Was that fear in his eyes? No one had ever been able to say who Jagger really was. What was his last name? Or first name, for that matter? And whom did he work for?

Until now.

However, I always figured Jagger intimidated Fabio.

"Well?" I yanked on the lapel of Fabio's dark brown polyester suit. "Wel-l-l-l-l-l?"

"Ha!"

"Ha? That's all you have to say? Ha doesn't explain shit, Fabio. Tell me the truth!"

Finally he reached both hands up between my arms

and pushed me until I lost my grip. While he tried to straighten out his always-wrinkled suit, he said, "*I* own it."

With that he turned and walked down the steps, out to his car and drove off, with me standing there—back to square one.

And here I thought I'd had some information on Jagger.

Not to mention that I thought he was my boss!

What a fool! No one got any information on Jagger—unless *he* gave it to them.

The next morning I pulled into the parking lot of the local Hope Valley Dunkin Donuts. Hope Valley was not exactly a booming metropolis, but it was where I was born, raised and lived my entire life.

As a tiny, very ethnic town with a green in the center and bordered by Hartford, Connecticut, one of the largest insurance capitals, Hope Valley was the center of my existence—which said a lot. Sad but true.

After burning out of a very successful nursing career, I decided to throw that profession out of the proverbial window and landed (through my roomie, Miles, who had connections all over town) this job. Pauline Sokol, ex-RN, medical insurance fraud investigator.

I smiled to myself as I watched Jagger's black Suburban pull into the spot next to me.

I licked my lips. Only because they were dry!

I couldn't eat a thing if my mouth went as dry as the Sahara each time the guy appeared. And appeared he did. Mostly when I least expected him, but I will say, he'd taught me a lot of what I knew about investigating medical insurance fraud.

Limited amount, sure. But when he gave me his standard "Atta girl, Sherlock," I melted—and knew I was learning and growing in this profession.

I rolled down my window. "Hey."

Once he got out of his SUV, he nodded and paused, and when I got out of my Volvo, we both walked in to get our coffee.

Jagger did the ordering—as usual. The thing about that was, it always gave me a jolt that he knew exactly what I'd want. Hazelnut decaf, light and sweet with one Splenda, and either a Boston cream donut or a French cruller. Today I was in the mood for French.

"Give her a French cruller," I heard him say to the clerk—and I didn't even blink my eyes.

However, there was no denying the little hormonal surge inside me.

Yikes.

It was always a "yikes" kinda moment, whenever Jagger just about read my mind. I turned my flushed face away from him so he wouldn't read *those* kinds of thoughts.

After we got our order, I followed Jagger to the last booth by the window.

Our spot.

Sometimes though, our spot was out in the parking lot—in his SUV, which was big enough for a family of four to vacation in. I actually debated about whether Jagger lived in the Suburban that wanted to be an RV.

But even if I asked as a direct question, there was no telling if he'd answer.

He was just that mysterious.

And I loved it. Damn.

He sat down and took a sip of his coffee. Black. Natch. Nothing pretentious about Jagger. "We start today on your sixth case, Sherlock."

He used that little nickname for me in jest—at first—since I started out in the profession knowing nothing. But now he used it more as a term of respect for my learning the job.

At least that's how I chose to view it, and I was going with that permanently.

"Yeah, six." I took a sip of my coffee, licked my lips and broke off a piece of cruller, but before I shoved it into my mouth, I said, "What the hell did you mean about driving?"

He leaned back and looked around Dunkin Donuts as if half expecting some spies to be nibbling muffins and sipping coffee and listening to us.

When he looked back at me, my hand shook, so I shoved the donut into my mouth. The shaking wasn't only because of him looking at me—that was normal. This time it was how his eyes grew concerned that made me shake and eat. Jagger was going to fill me in on my next case—and it troubled him.

Yikes again.

You didn't want Jagger troubled. Although I had to say, I always felt safe with him.

I chewed and swallowed. "Come on, Jagger, tell me about my case. The driving bit. Etcetera."

He sipped his coffee very slowly. Very deliberately. Very Jaggerlike.

"Reports are that there is some suspicious activity going on that is costing the insurance companies money. Big money."

"Then you're not talking about my case."

He chuckled.

"Actually I was serious. You know I never get the big money cases."

Over his cup he said, "You have to start somewhere, Sherlock."

And I had. From Worker's Comp fraud to plastic surgery fraud, and now what? What kind of fraud involved driving?

"Oh wait. Does this have to do with visiting nurses or something?" I looked at the rest of the cruller, thought about unbuttoning my size 4 jeans—but only for a deeper breath—and while looking at Jagger, stuck the rest of it into the napkin, which I methodically folded up to save for my pup, Spanky. He was a doll and I shared custody of him with my two roommates.

"So," I said, still looking at Jagger. "You are telling me that my case number six is a big one? A costly one?" My heart started to pound when I thought I could make a killing on this case if the bonuses were in conjunction with the wins.

No one needed money like I did after cosigning a loan I got burned on and giving the term "shop until you drop" new meaning. I really couldn't swing a place of my own yet and although I loved living with Miles and Goldie, as a thirty-something, I yearned for my own place.

"I'm telling you we start tomorrow on your case and it's the biggest one Fabio has given you yet."

Ugh. Fabio. "So why are you telling me about it instead of Fabio doing the deed?" I still couldn't figure out Jagger's place in all of this. Then again, I'd learned over time not to even *try* to figure him out.

"He gave me the info, since I had filed the report."

I leaned forward. "*You* filed the report? What report?"

Jagger leaned back (no doubt to get out of my face or make me get out of his face) and gave me a Jagger look. You don't even want to know. "It was brought to my attention that TLC Air and Land is making way too much dough, and may not be on the up and up."

"TLC? The ambulance company that has the market locked in on the northern side of Hope Valley?"

"Yeah. Apparently it's not exactly Tender Loving Care Express, Sherlock."

"Wow. Uncle Walt has used that ambulance service a few times as have numerous friends of his. It's not safe?"

"Relax. It's safe enough, but someone is making money on it—"

"Off the insurance companies," I said, worrying about my favorite, eighty-something uncle.

Jagger smiled.

My heart warmed like a puppy's (okay, I was thinking man's best friend, but not exactly a canine).

"So, TLC Air and Land is bilking the insurance companies—"

"For millions," he said.

"Mill . . . ions? I'm getting a case to investigate medical insurance fraud in the millions?" Gulp. My mouth went dry again.

Jagger shook his head. See, when he did that once, he was perturbed. Twice meant exasperated. Three times and—well, I'd better get the hell away from him.

He leaned forward, drained his coffee cup, set it down and looked at me. "Someone inside TLC reported billing fraud. Claims of charging for oxygen that was never used, and the law only allows a flat rate charge anyway; billing for advanced life support that was never given; air ambulance charges for statute miles rather than air miles—"

I wrinkled my forehead.

"Statute: on-the-ground miles. 5,280 feet. Twists and turns on streets add plenty of mileage, which adds up. In the air would be a lot less."

"Makes sense. Wow. How crooked."

Jagger merely looked at me, as well he should. Every suspect I'd investigated was crooked. Duh.

Suddenly it hit me. Jagger knew way too much about my case. Jagger talked way too much about my case.

Jagger thought he was going to be part of my case.

"You're not helping me with this one." The words actually came out sounding very sensible (to me), logical and firm.

Jagger smiled.

I groaned.

"Tomorrow you report to TLC."

"Oh good. You're not going with me." Phew. I really didn't want to work with him. "Am I going to be doing the receptionist job or—"

Looks really do say everything. I figured that out in seconds when I stared at Jagger.

He *was* working with me on this one.

He'd gotten me to don my nursing scrubs and head back into a profession I'd burned out of yet again.

He *was* working with me!

Oh great, Jagger and me probably riding in close quarters for an entire case . . . on the old Tender Loving Care . . . or should I say "Tough Luck Charlie Ambulance Company" after we got through with them?

Two

Scrubs. Ick. I hated wearing them, and yet I had on my bright pink ones today. Reminded me way too much of my past career—the one I wanted nothing to do with now yet kept getting thrown back into.

This I blamed on none other than Jagger.

Okay, it wasn't always his fault, but the guy had broad shoulders (sigh) and could handle anything. Sure it made sense that I would investigate the cases involving medical fraud.

That didn't mean I had to like it—or the damn scrubs.

I headed out of my bedroom and down the stairs.

Lying on the couch with a cold pack on his forehead was none other than my darling Goldie.

"Hey, Suga," he mumbled.

"Sinuses acting up again?" I thought about all the suffering he'd recently gone through for the "new" nose, and how maybe that caused him more sinus problems. "May is always a bad month for you, Gold. You taking your daily local honey?"

He peered out from under the ice pack.

"Gold, you have to take it! It's like desensitizing yourself to the pollen!"

"Why you dressed like that?" he mumbled, ignoring my sage advice and more than likely expecting me to give him the horticultural lesson that bees pollinate the flowers and when the pollen gets into the honey and we take it in small daily doses, it's just like getting a shot at the allergist's office.

I sat on the edge of the white couch Miles so lovingly picked out for our snowy-decorated living room. Sometimes I needed sunglasses, but the guy had exceptional taste in décor.

And roommates.

"Shit, Gold. I'm back to work already. Newport is barely a distant memory—"

Goldie shrieked, but not too loudly. Guess he didn't want to scare Spanky, who was nestled beneath Gold's arm. "Please don't remind me of that debacle. Let it fade into the sunset."

"It was only a few weeks ago, so I'm guessing fading is going to take some time. Either way, Gold, I start work today at TLC."

He dropped the ice bag to the side and it landed smack on Spanky's paw, causing him to spring up and jump off the couch before Goldie or I could catch him. I waved my hand at Goldie, who was apologizing to the absent pup.

"He's afraid if a paper falls. Don't sweat it. And—" I leaned forward, inches from his perfect nose. "—what's *that* look for? What do you know about TLC that I need to know?"

Goldie knew something about everything, but not in the same way that Jagger did. Let's just say, Goldie was always on the side of the law—while Jagger walked a fine line between right and wrong—but never got caught.

Gotta love both of them.

"Come on, Gold. Spill."

He lifted the ice bag to his forehead. "Word on the street is they've been in much better shape financially since the nephew and his sister took over." Leaning back into the white softness of Miles's silk pillows, Goldie sighed. "Payne Sterling."

"The nephew? I'm guessing he is going to be a pain to deal with and is not exactly sterling." I laughed.

Goldie glared at me with a perfectly mascaraed eye.

"Okay. Okay. That was lame. I know. But, Gold, I'm going back into *nursing*! (To my ears that last word came out like something out of *The Exorcist*.) Cut me some slack, here."

"Nursing on ambulance runs will be different, Suga. Especially flying in those air ambulances . . ."

I knew Goldie was talking. His mouth kept moving, but my mind wandered down the air-ambulance road. Just exactly how many near fatal or . . . eeks . . . fatal helicopter crashes occurred per year? Weren't those air ambulances caught up in telephone lines pretty regularly?

"Suga. Suga!"

I jumped. "Hmm?"

"You're as white as this freaking room. Stop worrying. The cruise ship didn't sink in the Bermuda Triangle and the helicopters are not going to crash."

He knew me so well. I did shiver at the thought of the cruise ship we'd taken a few months back when I was assigned a case on it. Actually it turned out to be great fun.

"Gold, Miles and I had a nursing friend named Hilly Wentworth. She joined the Air Force after leaving Saint

Greg's Hospital. All I remember from her e-mails to us was that there was an Air Force regulation that said the fire truck had to be called to the helipad each time the helicopter was going to land."

"Wow," Goldie mused. "Wouldn't make me feel very safe."

"No," I mumbled.

Goldie grew serious.

Yikes. I was not liking this. Not liking it one bit. "Gold?"

"You're correct. Payne really is not exactly sterling. Took over the business and—well, no one likes him. Now I know that's not reason to give the guy a bad name, but there is something about him that begs for dislike. Almost hatred."

"Wow."

"Yeah. Nephew Payne makes money, but I'm not sure how much on the up and up he is. Anyway, that's the street talk, and you know how reliable that can be."

Suddenly the pit of my stomach knotted. Yikes again.

"What do you mean you are not flying?" Jagger asked, looking at me from his SUV. Well, not exactly "asked." More like threatened, although I'll never know how he could turn a question into a threat.

Then again, I was talking Jagger here.

I leaned closer to him before we got out of his Suburban. "I'll do the ambulance runs, but I'm not setting foot on any helicopter. They're not safe."

Until my dying day I'll never really know if the look in Jagger's eyes was pity for me (my best bet), fear that I'd get hurt or worse (okay, also a best bet) or accusing me of being a wuss (oh-so very Jaggerlike), but whatever intent he had, I was standing firm.

"Come on, I'll introduce you to the pilot you'll be flying with." With that he got out of the SUV, didn't wait for me, and walked into the main building of the TLC property.

Three gigantic garages bordered the place while ambulances and vans sported the TLC slogan, RIDE IN STYLE AND COMFORT, on the sides.

I couldn't help but wonder if accident victims even cared about comfort or style, and why the heck would an ambulance company advertise that? I was thinking more along the lines of "speedy delivery," but the late Mr. Rogers only came to mind. I loved him!

On the north side of the complex (and it was large enough to call it one) was the helipad with two copters sitting at the ready.

I shivered.

When I turned back, Jagger was staring.

"I'm not riding in them," I said and walked in front of him to the door marked entrance. The way my cases usually went, I was certain they were expecting me for my first day of duty—and that Jagger had all the kinks ironed out of the plans.

At the door, I grabbed the handle but Jagger's hand covered mine before I could yank. "What?" I said, turning. "Are you suddenly turning into a gentleman and opening doors for me?" I laughed. Sounded more like a snort. To ignore my burning complexion, (yeah, he still had the power to embarrass the hell out of me) I pulled my hand from beneath his, ignored the fact that I wanted to rub it, and stood there speechless but with my shoulders straightened to show it was my choice.

He opened the door, walked inside and over his

shoulder said, "If the case calls for it, you'll fly on them or you'll drive an ambulance if necessary."

Speechless was an understatement.

I followed him inside, biting my tongue although I really had no snappy comment other than, "No I won't," but felt it would have come out sounding like a kid—and my foot would stomp all on its own.

The room hummed with phones ringing and air-conditioning clicking on and off. Sunlight streamed in through bay windows that overlooked a fountain (of Cupid—geez) and the rest of the complex. All in all a nice office.

They really must have been raking in the dough.

Before I could turn to see whom Jagger was talking to, I heard, "*ça suce!*" The French-Canadian version of "That sucks!"

I knew this just as I knew who'd said it, because Lilla Marcel was sitting directly before me—behind the reception desk.

An obvious Jagger plant—probably working there illegally, since she was Canadian.

I didn't even want to go there, knowing Jagger had finagled something to get Lilla working on the inside for us. Her mother was Adele Girard, who was Fabio's receptionist and an ex-con. I curled my lips at the thought. Adele was like a second mother to me—which would make my first one gasp if she saw the "hooker" attire that dear Adele wore. After getting her hands burned in prison (this after she'd committed fraud to get money for her mother who was dying of cancer), Adele always wore gloves. White ones. Looked great with her spiffy, usually black-and-white, skintight polka-dotted outfits. And very fifties.

I loved Adele.

And after recently meeting her daughter, Lilla, I had taken to her too. I pushed past Jagger. "Lilla! Great to see—"

Before I could finish, I was yanked away toward the doorway. Jagger leaned into me and said, "Are you nuts, Pauline?"

When he called me by my real name, Jagger was dead serious. Suddenly I realized he was correct though. I should have pretended not to know Lilla. Damn. Sometimes I sank back into Nurse Pauline instead of Investigator Pauline.

I pulled free of Jagger and rubbed my arm as if it hurt. That always got a look of concern from him. "Sorry. I slipped. I'm human, ya know."

As I turned to go back to "meet" Lilla I heard him mumble, "Don't I know it."

Of course that could be what I imagined I heard, but I was going with it. See, with Jagger, I had to sometimes take leeway with interpreting things—to sway them in my favor.

The guy was a veritable closed book.

I walked up to the reception desk and tried to ignore Lilla's beauty (sometimes that could be very intimidating) and the fact that she wore some kind of Victoria's Secret outfit all in black (which, in fact, was even more intimidating).

Jagger too, usually wore black.

It dawned on me that Lilla was a bit of a female Jagger—but when we'd first met, I immediately liked her.

"Hi, I'm Pauline Sokol." I held my hand out to her. "And you are?"

"Lilla," she said.

I noticed her nails, the length of some heroin-addicted Asian warlords', as she shook my hand and, without a beat, pretended not to know me.

"Nice to meet you, Pauline." She held up a clipboard with several sheets of paper on it. In her thick French-Canadian accent, she said, "Please to fill these out."

I smiled, winked and took the paperwork. New hire. Eeks. I wanted to shake my head and run. How the hell was I getting back into nursing again?

Out of the corner of my eye, I could see Jagger approaching—with another fantastically gorgeous guy in tow.

Perhaps I'd died on the way to work here and this was heaven—where males outpopulated the females two to one. Wait—surely there couldn't be that many men in heaven.

Where Jagger's hair was jet-black, this other guy's was light sunshine—and nearly shoulder length. All right, it fell below his eyes and had some fantastic waves that any woman would envy. Deep brown eyes matched Jagger's, but where Jag's were mysterious, this guy's were friendlier. Sparkling. He stood about six foot two.

I swallowed hard and told myself to cool off or I'd never make it on this case. I said a silent prayer to my favorite saint, Theresa, that this guy was not going to be working here with me.

"Sky Palmer, Pauline, the pilot of one of the choppers," Jagger said, his voice sounding as if in a dream.

I was hung up on the closeness of the two hunks, my hands shaking, my knees knocking and my hormones on speed dial (with a busy signal).

I had to get . . . you know . . . soon.

Slowly I held out my hand, since the guy next to Jagger had his in front of me. I felt a nudge on my left arm and heard a "What the hell is wrong with you?"

Jagger had pulled me back to reality. Delicious reality.

"I'm sorry. I didn't get your name?" Proud that I'd managed a logical sentence as our hands were still touching, I smiled like a fool.

"Sky. Sky Palmer," he said in a Texas drawl that had me nearly drooling, as if I'd just bitten into a juicy rib eye. He let go of my hand.

I tucked mine into my pants pocket and was about to reply when Jagger cut me off: "And don't go joking about Sky being a pilot. He's heard it all. Sky is his real name."

I bit back the joke I'd had ready, turned to Jagger and mouthed, "No kidding," and then looked at Sky. Who the hell named a bouncing baby Sky? "Great to meet you. Texas? Huh?"

"Yes, ma'am." He winked and smiled—I think at the same time, which had me nearly in a pile of liquid like the melted Wicked Witch in Oz.

"Oh, no need for the 'ma'am.' Just call me Pauline. I'm so looking forward to flying with you, Sky." Quickly I turned to Jagger and mouthed, "Shut up."

Three

Thank goodness Jagger didn't argue with me, I thought as I sat on the chair near Lilla's desk. She fiddled with the paperwork, and I also thought anyone who'd survived four husbands, two of whom were abusive, sure fit into this investigative job pretty well. She looked as if she knew exactly what she was doing.

I, on the other hand, sat there thinking of Sky, Jagger, Sky and Jagger, until my mind was nearly mush. Damn. Why couldn't I get a job with less-attractive guys around me? Way less attractive. Something about that Texas drawl had piqued my interest.

Then it hit me that I'd openly agreed to fly on a helicopter.

I rested my head in my hands and thought for a few seconds, and then I prayed the rest of the time that I wouldn't get assigned any helicopter runs. After all, I wasn't an EMT or a trained nurse in airovac.

"Pauline. Pauline."

"Hmm?" I looked up to see Lilla looking at me. "Sorry. Did you say something?"

"I have some paperwork—release forms, *chéri*—for you to sign so you can do a ride along."

"Ride along?" I figured that meant a test drive in an ambulance, since Jagger and I were obviously going to do our investigative work as if on orientation. Surely we weren't going out alone? I laughed at the stupid thought.

"With *Monsieur* Sky." She leaned back in her seat with the paperwork in her hand.

I got stuck on *Monsieur* Sky until it hit me—the ride along was a fly along!

"No way!" flew out of my mouth just as Sky and Jagger approached from the office behind Lilla.

"No way what?" Sky asked.

Lilla started to say, "Pauline does not—"

Damn that drawl. "Thanks, Lilla. I'll explain." I chuckled to fill in the gaping hole in the conversation and to buy myself time to make up a lie. I stunk at lying. When I looked at Jagger, I saw that he knew very well that I was trying to come up with a fib.

And damn it all, but he just stood there—*silently*.

I decided to wave my hands, as if that would erase everyone's current memory and said, "So, this should be fun. A ride along, I mean," as I got up, pushed past traitor Jagger and stood next to Sky. "You are going to be careful, aren't you?" I did my best hooker eyelash fluttering and turned back in time to see Jagger shaking his head. Once. Thank the good Lord; however, once was bad enough.

I couldn't help but glare at the metal container I was about to enter and wondered if there was more than one bolt that held on the blades sticking out of the top. I'd heard there wasn't.

Sky and his buddy pilot, who'd been introduced as Mario Fortunato, were doing some kind of preflight check of the chopper. I held my breath and prayed they wouldn't miss a loose bolt or *the* loose bolt, but since Jagger sat inside as if nothing bothered him (and it didn't), I didn't want to sound girly scared.

"It's a go," Mario said and winked at me.

I laughed. "Tell me, Fortunato, are you going to bring good luck our way?"

He laughed. "None needed with Sky at the controls."

I let out the breath I'd been holding since signing my life away on Lilla's release form and let Mario guide me toward the open door of the helicopter, which sat so innocently on the helipad.

Jagger had obviously set this up. The guy pulled more strings than a marionette operator.

I ignored the bright red color of the helicopter (originally thinking blood here), telling myself it would be easier for other aircraft to see us in the sky. On top were the blades. Two blades—actually it looked like one really long one. I'd have felt better with about six instead, and again prayed that more than one bolt held them on.

The chopper was much shorter than I'd imagined and had what looked like three tails (one could only hope three tails offset one blade). All in all, not exactly a menacing figure—until I thought about getting inside.

As I readied to turn and run, Mario reached inside and pulled out a helmet, which he handed to me without even asking my size, then ran through instructions like walking low so the blades wouldn't . . . you know . . . and that there were earphones and a microphone inside the helmet to communicate with the pilots.

Great. I'm sure my soft, shaking voice would

come out loud and clear over the roar of the swirling blades.

Then again, at least with the microphone off they might not hear me screaming.

Before I knew it, I was strapped into a seat next to Jagger (good if we had to evacuate) and with my eyes shut (figuring he couldn't see because of the helmet) we were above the ground.

Above the ground.

And, not on a smooth direct flight path. Oh no. Sky, obviously living up to his birth name, was maneuvering through Hope Valley as if in a video game and we were the targets.

Today's breakfast rose up my throat.

I grabbed Jagger's arm. Then let go as quickly as the idea flashed into my head that I seemed like a real "girl" doing that. Wouldn't set right with him.

I blinked, thinking that might help and knowing it wouldn't do shit, until I took several long, slow, deep breaths—and reminded myself that vomiting next to these three hunks would not be in my best interest professionally or sexually.

Sitting much straighter, I refused myself any more feelings of nausea (as if that were some mental luxury) and took several deep breaths. The phrase *I am a professional* became my mantra. I heard some static and that soothing, sexy Texas drawl. "So, ma'am, how you doing?"

"I love flying!" I shouted, and then promptly bit my lip. Really. What the hell was I talking about? I looked out the window and the ground was a gazillion miles away. I held so tightly onto the handlebar next to me, my fingers went numb as we zoomed around.

I caught a look at Jagger out of the corner of my eye—not easy to do with the damn helmet on—and there he sat, eyes closed and, I think, snoring.

Nothing bothered the damn guy!

I sucked in some air and sat straighter, all the while telling myself that I could do this without vomiting, screaming or passing out. In other words, I had to be professional, both as a nurse and investigator. After all, I'd be transporting patients and had to devote my attention to them and not myself.

What seemed like hours flew by (pun intended since I couldn't ignore that I didn't have any feet on the ground) and before I knew it, Jagger was standing next to me.

Standing?

We'd landed back at the helipad and he was already out and waiting for me to come back to reality. At least my reality hadn't involved airsickness.

I unhooked myself, stepped out and lifted the helmet off my head. Had to weigh a ton. Then I caught my reflection in the window. Geez. Ghost pale and helmet hair, and three hunks within inches.

That had to be the story of my life.

Sky stepped out and came closer. "So. How'd I do?"

I smiled, figuring he wasn't talking to Jagger. "You did great, partner," I said in a John Wayne cowboy accent. My attempt at Texas.

Jagger shook his head and walked toward the building.

I curled my lips at him, and then turned to Mario and Sky. "Really, it was fantastic. Do you work for TLC?"

Mario stepped closer. I felt like an Oreo. "We work

for them, but since Hope Valley isn't a budding metropolis, we cover nearby areas and transport to several of the big trauma centers in Hartford and New Haven if need be. Sometimes to New York City or Boston for private transportation. Cost a bundle in air miles."

"Oh. I see." I did see. TLC was making more money with this venture. Usually hospitals owned the helicopters, but in this case, it was privately owned. I couldn't wait to meet the Sterling twins. Oh yeah, the TLC/Sterling twins.

Normally I'm not a mean-spirited person, but standing there glaring at the owners of TLC, I wanted to ask, "So which one of you is the female?"

The twins were identical. Well, *identical* was a misnomer, but they might have been clones and, when dressed (not that I saw the twins undressed), they were exactly alike right down to the short, cropped blonde hair, green eyes and smile that appeared painted on—kind of like a clown's.

Since my thoughts were so uncharitable, I decided to stare at something else, but when I looked around Payne's office, there was nothing I could look at with a serious face.

The place was like something out of the fifties, but in no way similar to my mom's house. That at least had character. This office was a mismatch of old furniture—but brightly colored in oranges, reds and purples, as if the old psychedelic TV show *Laugh-In* had exploded all over Payne Sterling's office.

But on one wall were all religious paintings (copies I assumed) that appeared to have been done by one Leonardo da Vinci.

Trying not to notice the place, I looked to my left

where the door was open to the sister's, Pansy's, office.

Black and white. That was it. Apparently Payne had gotten the color gene. Well, at least décor was one thing they weren't cloned in.

I heard, "Nice to meet you, Ms. Sokol," and swung my head around. Pansy was holding her hand out to me. Short nails, more wrinkles than my Uncle Walt and bright white nail polish. I didn't know they even made white nail polish. I mean, what was the point?

I shook her hand, thought of what a weak grip she had and said, "I'm thrilled to be working here," hoping like hell that I sounded sincere. 'Cause looking at these two weirdos, I sure didn't mean it.

"Since you are a registered nurse, Pauline, you'll be assigned to our most experienced employee, who's been here longer than us. We are a private company and may run things a little differently. Nurses are only needed on certain trips as it is expensive for the patients, but I'm sure you are aware that paramedics cannot give some medications or maybe do a treatment that is needed. When not flying, you'll help with the ambulance runs." The siblings looked at each other and smiled.

Ick.

Not that it was a sexual smile, but it sure was weird.

Like they cared about the patient's wallet. The only thing these two cared about was money. I could just feel it in my intuitive brain, which had always served me well in my nursing. Often I could tell if a patient was going downhill and notified the docs ASAP. Now I was learning to trust that intuition.

"Welcome back, Jagger. You've been missed. The

other paramedics are thrilled you're here to help out,"
Payne said.

Wait a minute! Jagger? Paramedic? Why was I not
surprised? I knew he wouldn't be pulling one of his
chameleon charades at the expense of people's lives
and pretend to be an EMT or paramedic. Nope. Jagger
really was a trained paramedic. Maybe from his past
military days. I'd ask him later.

He wouldn't tell me later or ever.

Pansy looked at Jagger (I think she winked at him!)
and said, "Everyone around here calls the guy you'll
be with ER Dano." She laughed. "It's been so long, I'm
not even sure what his real name is."

Brother and sister broke out into hysterical
laughter.

Jagger shook his head.

And without thinking, I said, "Dan?" then swallowed back anything else that might pop out of my
mouth while I contemplated the two of these jokers
committing fraud.

No way.

They obviously were too stupid.

Pansy's eyes darkened. She stepped closer to me
and in a deep, husky voice said, "*No* kidding."

Gulp. Okay, I took it back. My intuition said: *She*
could be lethal.

As if holding court, darling ER Dano sat in the only
comfortable chair in the room, where he managed to
garner everyone's attention—except maybe Jagger's.

I sat across the coffee table from ER, staring. We'd
settled in the lounge area where the staff of EMT and
paramedics waited for calls while—I'd learned earlier—some sat in satellite stations around the town

and some in designated parking lots to be ready for 911 calls nearby.

The room had a somewhat homey atmosphere, if you liked royal blue and red, but also a dreary atmosphere that said the twins were not interior decorators, to be sure. Magazines were strewn across the glass top of the coffee table, the TV was attached to the wall (as if someone might want to take the old thing home) and there were decks of cards on the tables by the window along with a Mr. Coffee machine on the counter nearby.

And ER Dano sat there as nonchalant as could be while eager EMT newbies and experienced ones hung on his every word—which seemed to annoy him.

One of the newest (obviously because of his crisp new uniform) EMTs, whom ER called Buzz Lightyear—probably because the kid looked as if he'd just stepped out of a brand-new toy box—turned toward ER. "When do you think we'll get our next call?"

Oh, boy. Suddenly I wanted to put my arms around the kid, whose name badge read JEREMY BUTTMAN (poor thing).

Without looking around, or at Jeremy for that matter, ER said, "Eleven fifty-eight in the morning."

"Really?" I think Jeremy bounced in his seat when he spoke.

"You think I'm a freaking clairvoyant?" ER asked.

Jeremy shook his head, and I wondered if he even knew what that meant.

"No, sir, it's just . . . I'm anxious, is all."

Yikes.

ER's grip tightened on his mug. He didn't look at Jeremy, but more at all of us—at the same time—and said, "It's not about the lights and sirens . . . it's not about drivin' fast . . . and it has *nothin'* to do with what you want or think you might know about medicine . . ."

Then, when he had all of our attention he leaned back, slowly took a sip of coffee and paused dramatically.

The room hushed.

My heart beat faster, and I wondered if everyone could hear it. Poor "Buzz" looked as if he'd pass out.

ER then took a long Barney Fife kind of sniff and said, "It's about freaking savin' lives."

ER Dano sipped again at his steaming black coffee from a mug with an insignia of a red devil on it, and didn't look as if the liquid burned his mouth in the least.

Somehow that didn't surprise me. Intrigued? Yep. Surprised? Nope.

No one made a sound. I couldn't help but stare at him.

The guy was tall. About an inch over Jagger. I could still tell by the way he lounged in the chair. Hair a bit shorter than Jagger's and a deep brown. More slender than Jagger, but not too thin, and ER Dano definitely worked out. A lot.

"As a nurse, Nightingale, you'll be assigned to patients that need the special care. Mostly on transport," ER Dano said, and I sat at attention immediately. "For now, you're just a ride along."

"Fine," I mumbled. I had to chuckle at his term of endearment for me until I looked at Jagger.

He looked pissed!

My chuckle turned into a grin—a naughty grin that wanted Jagger to notice. "This is all new to me," I said, "so riding along for orientation will work fine. I'd also like to get a feel for how the company works." I watched him to see if there was any indication that he might be involved in any fraud, but so far, all I got was attitude. A bad attitude. The longer I listened to him talk to Jagger, the more I was convinced that ER Dano was a lifer here—but burned out worse than I'd been from my nursing career.

Clearly Dano had gone up in flames a long time ago.

"You sit here, Nightingale," ER said, pointing to the bench in the *back* of the ambulance.

My first thought was of motion sickness, but when I looked at the cocky paramedic, I refused to let myself even entertain that nauseous thought. I would sit in the back and *not* get sick.

From the corner of my eye, I could see Jagger, grinning. He was enjoying this so, again, I had to be "big" about it and not complain—even though I'd kill to sit up front.

And believe me, between the cockiness of ER Dano and good ol' Jagger, I'd be glad to "off" at least one of them, if not both.

I sat on the bench directly across from the empty stretcher, said a silent prayer to Saint Theresa for the power of antinausea and strapped myself in.

Suddenly the ambulance zoomed out of the parking lot and all I could think of was the ones you see in cartoons—balanced on two wheels!

ER Dano was some character.

This case might be fun . . . if I lived through today.

Four

I leaned over the sink in the staff's washroom of TLC Air and Land and splashed cold water over my face. Had to in order to settle my stomach, which ER Dano's driving had managed to slosh up into my throat.

"Ugh," I muttered.

"Hello, *chéri*?" Lilla said, coming in the door.

I looked to the side to make sure no one followed her in. "That ER guy is a pip."

She grinned, winked and said, "That he is."

Oh, boy. Maybe Lilla could be useful in getting info from him, since he was the longest-term employee around here. Dano was pretty hot, and it seemed as if Lilla thought so too. Then again, so did I, and Lilla'd had four husbands already! I mean, fair is fair.

Maybe I wouldn't suggest Dano to her.

Slowly I lifted my head toward the mirror. "Geez. I look like crap."

Lilla remained silent. I looked closer at myself. Oh, well, I was right.

"Do you have plans for lunch, *chéri*?"

I groaned. Lunch? Who asks a vomiting woman if she wants lunch? Then again, Lilla didn't know about my ride—very similar to a Disney roller coaster where you have to be a certain height, follow cardiac guidelines and not be pregnant.

"*Chéri?*"

I eased myself around toward her—to avoid any kind of quick motion. "Soup sounds comforting."

She laughed. "*Chéri*, you are too funny. Comforting? I would have said delicious or something similar. Meet me by the employee door in about five minutes. Okay?"

I nodded. Ick. Motion.

I leaned against the sink. Yet another case where I was miserable, back to nursing, but working with Jagger.

Suddenly I felt much better.

"Hurry up, Sherlock, we don't have all day," Jagger said as I approached the employees' exit to look for Lilla.

"We? Oh, no. Don't include me. I'm meeting Lilla for lunch. I'll see you back here," I said.

Suddenly his hand was on the small of my back, his other was pushing the door open and out we went.

There in the parking lot sat Ambulance #456—with ER Dano at the helm, and Lilla riding shotgun.

For a few seconds I tried to comprehend the situation, but before I knew it, Jagger had me—no, us—strapped into the back of #456, and Dano hit the gas.

I made a mental note to take Dramamine with my daily vitamins until this case was closed.

I looked at Jagger thinking that if we talked about anything, I'd forget that the front of the ambulance seemed to sway one way while the back the other. "So, any progress?"

He glared at me. "You all right?"

Geez. The guy was so astute. "Fine. Just hungry. My blood sugar is probably low. The case? Anything on it?"

"Seems the billing in this place is way out of whack. Dano showed me the daily run sheets and how the paramedics chart."

"You didn't know that? I mean how to chart?"

He looked at me. I thought he was about to accuse me of something, but he merely said, "I worked paramedic at a different company. They're similar but different."

"Apples and oranges?"

Jagger bent his head and looked at me. Had to want to shake his head, but he held steady. Well, as steady as one could riding with ER Dano.

Just then several packages of gauze sailed off the shelves as Dano made a right. I'd hate to think of what it'd be like if we were going to a 911 call.

"Anyway, we need to get into billing to check things out," I heard Jagger say. "Lilla can't do that for us. We need her to run interference."

"True. She'd be good at that too. Good mind."

He didn't look up, but nodded. Then he leaned back and shut his eyes, falling asleep from the life-threatening motion.

I watched him for a few seconds and told myself that surely Jagger would have enlightened me if he knew anything more I should know. Surely.

Dano bit into his roast beef sandwich while a drop of horseradish dripped out the other end. He didn't even flinch. Not only was this guy hardened about his job, but also about life in general. He was a fun study though, I had to admit.

"So," I said to him. He didn't look up. "Are either of the Sterling twins married?"

ER Dano kept eating.

Lilla gave me a shrug.

Jagger took a sip of his black coffee and looked at me over his mug with a what-the-hell's-the-difference expression on his face.

"Dano, are they?" I persisted, not even sure why I cared.

Dano took another bite, looked at me and shrugged too. Only his shrug looked like he knew, didn't give a shit and wasn't about to tell me anything.

Lilla started to ask him about how long he'd worked at TLC and when he perked up and answered "years," I decided I was spinning my wheels at this meal. I excused myself to leave for the ladies' room.

No one said a word.

When I got near the front door, I looked at our waitress, who was now sitting at the counter eating a hamburger, and decided I really didn't need to use the ladies' room.

"Excuse me. Please tell my friends I have to leave." I started to dig into my purse for money for my bill.

She motioned her head toward our table. "You with those two hunks? Man, if I were twenty years younger." She cackled. "That one drinking his coffee. Yum. 'Course, the other one ain't bad. He could put his shoes under my bed anytime, sweetie!"

I laughed and pulled my empty hand out of my bag. "The hunk drinking coffee will pay my tab."

With that I was out the door and hailing a cab, which was not an easy feat in Hope Valley. However, obviously by some divine intervention a yellow cab zoomed around the corner just as I raised my hand.

Thank you very much, Saint T!

* * *

Except for the dispatchers, who were on call 24/7, TLC's offices were pretty empty. I took the opportunity to "acquaint" myself with my new employment surrounds.

I made my way through the reception area, into the filing area, and down the corridor. I found myself at Payne's door.

His open door.

"Payne? Mr. Sterling?" I stepped inside and walked to Pansy's adjoining office. Geez. Pansy. Some name. Shaking my head, I knocked, opened the door after no reply and ran my gaze around the room.

Empty.

There is a God.

I withdrew from the room and shut the door as quietly as I could and walked toward Payne's desk. If I got caught, I had already decided I'd say that since Lilla wasn't there I was trying to find the employee forms she'd given me this morning, because I thought I'd put down the wrong phone number.

Maybe I was getting better at this lying stuff.

Quickly I looked over his desk. Payne was not the neatest guy in the world, but he wasn't a Fabio either. I reached into the pocket of my scrubs and took out a pair of gloves.

Jagger had taught me well.

They'd become a staple in my wardrobe now, much like a tissue and clean underwear (a la Stella Sokol).

I pushed the desk chair back and tried to open the top drawer. No such luck. The others opened without any problem, so I helped myself to the documents that were inside.

Daily run sheets. The ones Jagger had been talking about. Each EMT or Paramedic had to fill them out. I glanced through them with my nursing eye, weeding out any unnecessary information.

Old Payne was pretty organized when it came to his files, which made my job easier.

Several had oxygen listed. Two had charges for ALS, which I knew stood for advanced life support and was more expensive. I sat down and read through the entire pile, glancing at the clock every once in a while.

Suddenly I heard footsteps outside the door. Gulp. I started to stick the files back, remembering the exact order they'd been in. That, I was very good at—I had an almost photographic memory.

The hallway quieted. I swallowed and decided there was no need to rush off. I had to find his billing information to cross-check it against the run forms.

Behind his desk, and below the Mona Lisa, who suddenly gave me the creeps the way she seemed to be watching me, was another file cabinet.

Locked.

Hmm.

Piqued my interest. So, I dug around the cabinet, the one behind Mona, until I found a set of keys. Two didn't work. "Bingo!" I whispered as the lock clicked open on the third key.

Copies of bills for the last three years. Could life get any better? I found the matching bills to the files, and indeed, TLC had charged the patients for oxygen when it wasn't even used (not to mention the fact that the law didn't allow for individual charges like that), and the ALS was really a BLS—basic life support, which was a much cheaper ride.

An eighty-year-old guy had fallen while mowing his lawn. His wife called 911, but since he'd fallen in the grass, there wasn't a scratch on him, nor was he in any distress to the point where he'd needed oxygen, according to the paramedic's run sheet—of one ER Dano.

If nothing else, I just knew in my gut that Dano was a fantastic, crackerjack paramedic.

I leaned back after checking out several more bills.

"So, you are bilking the insurance company out of millions, Mr. Sterling. Aren't you?"

"Yes. For a new employee, Ms. Sokol, you *are* perceptive."

I dropped the files and swung around to see Payne Sterling with a knife aimed at me.

A knife!

I had this real phobia of knives and always said I'd rather be shot than stabbed.

However, right now, I was hoping for neither.

Five

Payne Sterling eased closer to me, the knife blade mocking me with its sparkle.

"Oh, hey, Payne. I mean, Mr. S. Somehow I got lost and was looking for the forms Lilla gave me this morning." I mumbled and rambled so that suddenly Payne looked confused. This after he'd heard me accuse him of insurance fraud—and he'd admitted it.

So, I took that opportunity to cut and run (forgive the pun again!). I kicked at his groin, stayed around only seconds to hear him groan, then grabbed the stack of files from the desk and threw them in his face, buying me only nanoseconds.

By the time I got to the door, his hand was on mine. I started to scream like a girl—hey, we're talking life and death here—but he had his hand on my mouth faster than I could take a breath.

"Shut up or you'll end up needing 911 called for you." Wow. His voice had grown eerily *threatening* in a few hours.

Gone was the *"Laugh-In"* guy. Replaced by a threatening maniac who had a knife at my throat.

Payne knew his anatomy. I'd give him that as he

pressed the blade into the area of my carotid artery.

Big-time bleeder when cut, that ol' artery was. I was talking pumping out the entire ten pints of blood that the average human being has in their circulatory system in a *very* short time.

"Payne," I mumbled. "Please. Let me go, and we can make a deal."

He'd slowly eased his hold so I could talk. Or make that money could talk. When he let go and started to ask what I meant, I kneed him again, used a few self-defense moves Jagger had taught me, and before I knew it, I was running like hell down the corridor, through the empty reception area and out the door.

In my haste, I wasn't sure, but it didn't sound as if Payne was fast on my heels, and I wasn't stupid enough to turn to look.

I pushed at the front door so hard, it swung out with a thud—and I banged smack-dab into Jagger and Lilla.

I screamed.

Jagger shook his head.

Lilla pulled back as if she was afraid of me, and I started to chatter on and on.

Jagger grabbed my shoulders. "Calm down, Pauline. What the hell are you talking about?" He'd grown serious and with the use of my name, yanked me out of my hysteria long enough to tell him what I found out and how Payne tried to kill me.

Jagger pushed me to the side so hard, that I stumbled into Lilla, knocking her down.

"*Chéri!*" she shouted.

"Sorry!" I yelled as I pulled her up, and we ran after Jagger—although my first instinct was to run in the other direction. I couldn't let him face a knife-wielding Payne all by himself. I know Jagger would smirk at that, but still, I meant well.

We got to the office door and found Jagger standing there.

Standing there?

I figured Payne had hightailed it out the back door—until I got side by side with Jagger.

Lilla screamed and slithered in a faint, very sexy-like, down to the floor with one hand running along the wall.

I grabbed Jagger's arm and my first words were, "Damn, there goes our suspect."

The two of us stood staring down at Payne Sterling with the aforementioned knife sticking out of his chest. Heart level.

And we both knew calling 911 was out of the question—because ambulances didn't carry dead bodies.

Ambulances didn't carry dead bodies, I thought over and over to take my mind off the scene in front of me.

Lieutenant Shatley, Hope Valley homicide and close friend of Jagger's—although I had no idea how they knew each other—gave orders to the police staff while I stood behind the yellow-taped area—trying to think of anything else but . . . a dead body.

Pansy had been notified, or make that heard the commotion, and hurried over. To this very minute, she was still wailing in grief.

I wondered if losing an identical twin hurt more than a regular sibling and then told myself that was crazy. However, I do think it was *different*, as they were way too close. And now that I thought about it, her wailing was eerie and strange and—I was ashamed to even think it—almost . . . fake.

I looked at her. She stood with one of the other secretaries holding her by the shoulders and glaring down at the body of her brother.

I realized I couldn't do that if it were a sibling of mine. I couldn't just stand there looking. Hmm. Maybe it was me, and I shouldn't let my personal feelings get in the way.

Deciding to have a more Christian attitude, I felt a bit better, until I saw Pansy wiping her face.

No tears.

Had she cried herself out already? Or was it something else? Then again, she could have had some condition that dried up her tears. That was a reality for some people. But she acted as if she was crying.

And made me wonder if *acting* was the operative word here.

Once the lieutenant said to clear the scene, we all started to move about, and before I knew it, the undertaker was taking out Payne's body.

And Pansy nowhere to be seen.

I knew, just knew, I'd be following the stretcher along, not ready to let go of a loved one so easily.

Lilla walked past me with a solemn look on her face. "*Chéri.*" She nodded.

For some reason I needed a bit of confirmation on my thoughts, and I touched Lilla's arm. Before I let her startled look stop me, I asked, "If that was your brother, would you just let them—"

"Wheel him away like that?" she finished while shaking her head. "Never. I'd be clutching onto their shirttails to not take him." She shrugged. "Guess we are all different."

"That we are," I said, making a mental note to observe dear Pansy much closer. Hopefully I wasn't shifting suspicion onto her just because my number-one suspect was now deceased.

I hated when that happened.

Although a gloomy air now filled the TLC Land and Air halls, work resumed. No one joked around, but phones rang, clients came in and 911 calls never stopped.

Before I knew it, I heard, *"Number Four five six, Code Eighty-three at 114 Buckingham Place."*

ER Dano rushed out of the lounge, grabbed me by the arm and said, "Get going!"

Not able to protest, I remembered why I was here—or make that what my cover was—and obediently followed him. Jagger was nowhere to be seen, and Dano didn't seem to notice or care.

"Where's Jagger?" I asked as Dano nearly shoved me into the *front* seat of #456.

He shrugged and said, "Breathing difficulty. Can't wait."

With that I fastened my seat belt, said a fast prayer to Saint T for the patient and myself (the driving, you know) and we were out onto East Main Street, siren blaring and Dano leaning back and driving as if in a kid's bumper car.

I swallowed hard, refusing to let my lunch even near my mouth again.

After several deep breaths, we pulled into the driveway of a dilapidated house on Buckingham Place—not exactly the ritzy section of Hope Valley. Dano grabbed the bag of supplies, muttered something to me, and we ran up the stairs to the front door, which wasn't locked.

For a fleeting second I thought, *How convenient*, until we ran down a long hallway into the kitchen.

Lying on the floor was a rather attractive woman dressed in tight jeans and a slinky black top—with a phone cord wrapped tightly around her neck.

Difficulty breathing?

Her coloring was pale, but her eyes were still open if not watery, and her lips were a bit cyanotic—that horrible grayish blue of someone in need of oxygen.

Dano immediately began unwrapping the phone cord while I dug into the bag for the portable oxygen and a mask. We worked for a few minutes until the woman looked a tiny bit better.

"How'd this happen, ma'am?" Dano asked.

She turned toward him and in a raspy voice said, "Er . . . I tripped. I tripped and got tangled in the cord."

Dano and I looked at each other and I controlled the urge to shout out, "*Are you kidding us?*" Due to the seriousness of her condition, I only raised an eyebrow to Dano.

"Really?" he said, while taking her blood pressure and adjusting the oxygen mask on her face.

I assisted him with whatever he needed until I felt something. Something behind me.

Gradually I turned around to come face to knees with a pair of jeans.

I heard Dano mutter, "Shit."

And I looked up into the barrel of a shotgun—aimed at my face.

Six

The barrel of a shotgun looks more like a cannon when it's aimed at your head in such close proximity.

The guy holding it was gigantic, at least from my angle, with a huge potbelly, a red plaid shirt, and a beard that would rival Rip Van Winkle's. He seemed to growl a bit, then clearly (as if we were morons) said , "If I'd wanted her to live, I wouldn't have strangled her."

I only wished that I lived long enough to repeat those words in a trial testimony against him.

Dano looked at me and then the guy. "You know what? You're right, buddy." As he spoke, he grabbed my arm and we stood. "She shouldn't have called us. Fell and got tangled. Ha!" With that, he hustled me past the shotgun, which the guy now pointed at the woman.

I wanted to run and grab it before he shot her right then.

"We can't leave," I protested to Dano.

He gave me some kind of look. A dirty look one might say, but I had no idea what it meant. "Nope. She shouldn't have called."

"Dano, we can't leave that woman!" I tried to push at his arm, but, even though I believed in equality of the sexes when it comes to ... well ... everything, there are things that some women (like *moi*) are physically not strong enough to do.

Right now, I couldn't get away from ER Dano if I tried.

Continuing to push me, he said to the gunman, "We're outta here. Have a nice day."

"Have a nice day!" I said, as he shoved me out the front door.

I turned to give him a piece of my mind, but he slid into the dining room before the door shut.

"Dan—" If I said anything, he'd get caught. I stopped myself.

I ran to the ambulance, grabbed my cell phone out of my purse and called 911. If I didn't have to wear stupid scrubs, I would have on a TLC uniform and a phone on my shoulder. "Give me the police!" I shouted, and then told them the situation. I ran around to the back of the house. I couldn't leave Dano and that woman in there alone.

I peered through a window, which, although covered in dirt and whatever, looked into the kitchen.

Dano had the guy in a choke hold, the shotgun lay on the floor and the poor woman was kicking the guy's legs. But before I could blink, the guy did some kind of maneuver—looked like ex-military—and now Dano was on the floor next to the patient.

I ran into the house on a surge of adrenaline and not much common sense, and when I got to the kitchen, the guy had picked up the shotgun.

"No!" I shouted and pushed the barrel as a *crack!* filled the air. A loud *crack*!

The scene became a madhouse of screaming (me), shouting at me (ER Dano), longshoreman-type cursing (the guy) and the woman on the floor kicking at him with her shoeless foot. When Dano grabbed my arm to shove me to the side, the guy took the gun and aimed straight at Dano's chest— and I suddenly thought of Jagger.

Not really thought about him. In reality it was more as if I felt him, his *presence*, and I reached beneath my scrubs and yanked out the pink locket Jagger had given me a few cases back.

This time I shoved my hip into Dano's side to get past him, aimed, pressed the pump dispenser and let the pepper spray do its job. The guy screamed and cried like a girl.

Despite Dano telling me to get the hell out of there, I grabbed the gun from the guy and pointed it at his legs . . . despite the fact that I had no idea how to shoot.

"Oh, shit," Dano murmured as he stepped back and leaned against the counter, more nonchalant than I think Jagger would have been.

Thank goodness I didn't have to shoot, because what seemed like hours had passed before the sirens blared and the guys in blue stormed into the hallway, aiming their guns—at *me*.

Dano knew all the cops and made it clear that *I* was not the whacko, even though I held the shotgun, but I could swear he *hesitated* first.

Dano called TLC's dispatch after we'd safely dropped the poor phone lady off at the hospital and the rest of the trip was silent. A few times I turned toward him to say something, but I only got the cold shoulder and decided to keep my mouth shut. I wanted to say that was a rude way to treat someone who had just saved his life—and then it hit me.

ER Dano was pissed that I, a *woman*, had saved *his* life!

I couldn't help smile.

At a stoplight, he turned and glared at me.

Yikes.

I bit my tongue so as not to ask, "What?" which I would have done to Jagger. Although a hunk, ER Dano was a bit more . . . frightening . . . to me than Jagger ever was.

We pulled into the driveway of TLC and directly into the gigantic garage that housed the ambulances. Dispatch had cleared us for the day, and I couldn't wait to get home.

Dano pulled into a space, shut off the ambulance, opened his door and turned to me. "Hose her out and replace the supplies," he said.

My mouth often dropped to near chest level when I was surprised, shocked or merely astonished.

This time it almost made it past my waist.

I shut my mouth faster than Dano could spin around and pop out of the driver's side.

Shoving my door open and jumping out, I ran after him—and made the mistake of grabbing his arm.

He swung around and I knew, just knew, if I were a guy, I'd be splayed out on the floor beneath Dano's feet right now. Instead he yanked free and said, "What?" in such a gruff voice that I jumped back.

But I recovered quickly, straightened my shoulders and said, "What? What? It's my first day! I'm not cleaning out the ambulance!"

He leaned really close.

Oops.

I swallowed and ran self-defense maneuvers through my mind even though, in reality, I never felt a second of fear for my life. "Yeah, I'm not doing it, Dano. Not alone," I added, using my smarts to avoid letting him get the upper hand. Or at least that's what I was telling myself.

He moved closer, looked closer and said, really closely, "Hose is on the wall, scrubbers next to it, soap's on the shelf, stocking is self-explanatory for a nurse."

My mouth went dry and my brain froze at the same time, and not like when you eat ice cream. For some reason—and help me to understand this, Saint T—having Dano so near and talking that way had some kind of mesmerizing effect on me.

Hot was the first word that came to mind.

Damn, the second.

And third, I came back to reality and said, "Fine, but you owe me a drink then." With that, and as if some foreign power overtook me, I turned and walked away—all the while *feeling* ER Dano staring at my butt—which I unashamedly wiggled.

When I came out of the locker room, where I'd cleaned up after my "extra" duty with the help of darling Buzz L, I ran into Jagger in the hallway. "Where the hell were you?" I said.

He looked at me from head to toe. "You all right, Pauline?"

"Guess I should be honored that you are concerned I didn't get my head blown off with a shotgun, but yeah, I'm fine."

He grinned.

"Dano told you everything." It wasn't a question

and Jagger didn't look as if he was going to answer. "Any news on the demise of Payne?"

Jagger shook his head.

"Great. Why is it that I never get the proverbial open-and-shut cases? How come no one ever hands *me* a suspect?"

He shook his head again, but this time it was the typical Jagger shake that said he was annoyed with me. *Who cared?* I thought as I walked toward the employees' door.

Just then the door to the men's locker room swung open. Out swaggered Dano, all decked out in jeans and a navy tee. Over his shoulder he said to me, "Boz's Bar and Grille on Dearborn, two blocks from Saint Greg's."

I knew it well, since that's where all the hospital staff hung out, not to mention my dear Uncle Walt and his cronies. The seniors, however, stuck to the front room, while the younger crowd cavorted in the back.

Not that I planned to cavort with ER Dano.

He pushed open the back door while Jagger looked from Dano to me.

"I'll be there," Jagger said.

I'm not sure whose eyes were larger, Dano's or mine. Wait. Mine.

Dano actually squinted.

"What'll your one drink be?" Dano asked, looking at me—I mean, nearly through me.

Damn. The guy had gorgeous deep brown eyes and a way of using them that made a girl notice. And, for some reason, I just knew Dano used them to his benefit on more than one occasion.

"Cosmo, please," I said, pulling the stool next to him

from near the bar. He remained seated, not offering to help. *Shades of Jagger*, I thought, and looked around to see where he was. Maybe he'd changed his mind.

"He's in the head," Dano muttered then turned toward the bartender. "Give her a Cosmopolitan, Patty."

The bartender winked at me. "You'll probably need something sweet to balance his effects," she said, and then laughed as she gestured with her head toward Dano.

As if I didn't know whom she was talking about.

I laughed and then caught him staring at me and stopped. "What? That was funny."

"What's funny?" Jagger asked from behind me. Suddenly I felt like a sandwich—only the two pieces of bread were different kinds. Wheat and rye. And they really didn't go together too well in my opinion.

"Nothing," I said, taking a sip of my drink as soon as Patty put it down. Actually, it was still sloshing about, but I *needed* it quickly. When I took the napkin to wipe my lips, ER Dano turned to look at me, but remained silent.

Jagger eased himself next to me on the other side, and I knew I should get the hell out of there—'cause it was going to be one heck of a night!

A couple of EMTs came into the place, and I quickly realized it was a hangout for the TLC crowd, plus—by the looks of some of the other uniforms—several other ambulance companies. I'm sure with the stress of the job and the equal stress of competition, they all needed to unwind.

Buzz Lightyear walked in with Lilla, and I knew she probably made his night by even walking next to him. The kid was so fresh and new—his patches actually stood out straight on his sleeves instead of being molded to the shape of his arm as ER Dano's were. Poor Jeremy. Now I could only think of him as Buzz.

He came closer and said, "Hi, everyone!"

ER Dano turned. "You old enough to be in here, kid?"

Buzz laughed, and I knew he had a fondness for the experienced paramedic—although why, I couldn't figure out. Actually, I figured beneath the rough exterior, ER Dano was a softie.

"Don't sit next to me, kid," Dano said, "Your new EMT smell is ruining the taste of my Coors."

Buzz laughed hysterically. "New EMT smell! You mean like a new car smells. Right, Dan?"

Dano turned to him.

I was about to intervene before he embarrassed the hell out of Jeremy, but ER Dano merely rolled his eyes.

"That is what I mean, Buzz. That is what I mean," ER said, then took what I thought was a very long, slow sip of his beer.

Jagger leaned nearer and touched my shoulder.

Wow. I wondered if I was going to make it out of here alive, or at least in decent condition. I swung around to him. "What?"

He gestured with his head to follow him and stood up.

I got up, said, "Excuse me," as if ER Dano would care, and followed Jagger toward the pool table, all the while wondering if he wanted me to spend time with him alone—or, more likely, to discuss the case.

"Pick out a stick," he ordered, and then racked up the balls.

I was not a very good player, and he probably knew that, but at least it gave us time to be alone and talk.

From the corner of my eye, I could see Lilla doing her job of keeping ER Dano and Buzz busy.

She impressed me with how fast she had learned the PI business. I figured Lilla was going to be helpful on this case and, hopefully, future ones if immigration didn't deport her back to Canada.

"You're solid, Sherlock," Jagger said.

I looked over to see him standing oh-so-nonchalantly Jaggerlike with a cue stick at his side. "Hmm?" Solid? Was he telling me I was hot and solid? (Please, God!)

He looked at the pool table. "Solid."

Solid-colored balls. Duh. What on earth made me think that Jagger had complimented me?

I took a cue stick in my hands then noticed the square of blue chalk sitting on the end of the table. Uncle Walt sometimes watched pool on television, and I'd joined him on more than one occasion. Being a quick study, I stopped, picked up the chalk and rubbed it on the end of the cue stick as I'd seen the pros do many times.

Jagger raised one eyebrow.

Buzz Lightyear got off his stool and walked over, more than likely thinking he was going to see some spectacular shot, and ER Dano looked at me and then turned back to his drink.

But I could see his reflection in the mirror—and he could see me.

Great. An audience, and me not exactly a pool hustler.

I shut my eyes for a second to picture the pros' hands when they shot. Even if I didn't get any ball in, I'd at least look good.

I set the chalk down, leaned over, placed my fingers in position and aimed the white ball at a lovely shade of green ball that was near the corner pocket, realizing

I had no idea how to hit it. *Just give me this first one, Saint T*, I prayed in my head and before I knew it, I'd hit the white ball, it sailed down the felt concourse and hit the lovely shade of green ball directly into the side pocket!

I looked up at Jagger. No expression.

Ha! That, in and of itself, meant I did well—I believed that and was sticking to it. Slowly I stepped back and leaned against the wall, hoping I looked hot or sexy or at least not stupid.

"Still your turn," Jagger muttered.

Damn. "No kidding. I was taking a break." With that I looked over the table, found a darling red ball near another pocket—and landed that sucker right in!

After one more I missed, and Jagger took over, sinking five balls in a row.

Well, at least I'd lose with my dignity still intact, since he didn't cream me right off the bat. Actually, I played on, holding my own, all the while praying and visualizing the pros.

"Good job, Sherlock," Jagger said right after I sank the eight ball—after all my solid ones.

Of course, Jagger only had one left, so I didn't cream him by any sense of the word, but I did beat him.

I beat Jagger!

"Thanks," I said, smiling. Couldn't help it. Maybe it was more of a cocky grin, but beginner's luck had given me a gift tonight.

Suddenly ER Dano was standing right next to me. "Five bucks." He looked directly at me.

I swallowed. "Five bucks for the winner?" Geez, that sounded so stupid. By the look on Jagger's face and his head shakings, he thought so too. But Dano remained stone-faced. "Oh. Okay," I said. "But, you know, I should get some points spotted to me since I've already played a game."

"How you figure that out, Nightingale?"

Did Jagger just flinch?

This was getting to be more and more fun!

I walked toward the bar, took the last few sips of my Cosmo and turned back. "I mean, kicking Jagger's butt took some energy out of me. Not sure if I have enough left to kick yours."

Jagger really glared at me now.

Lilla and Buzz gasped behind me.

And ER Dano gave me a delicious smile.

Suddenly I felt as if I had a phone cord wrapped around *my* neck—and it was tightening.

Seven

"Okay, so it was beginner's luck with you," I said to Jagger after ER Dano kicked my butt—three times. Fifteen bucks. I owed him fifteen bucks.

Jagger pretended as if he didn't care as he took my arm—make that *grabbed* my arm—and pulled me toward the back of the bar and out the emergency door. No alarm sounded, and I'm sure he knew it wouldn't. Out in the alleyway, he turned toward me.

"I could give a shit about pool, Pauline. We need to talk about the case, since we haven't had a chance to yet."

I'll just bet you don't give a shit—since you lost! I thought.

"Okay, what the hell are we doing out here?" I asked. "What? You want some pool playing tips from a pro?" I started to laugh, and he gave me a look.

Oops.

Silenced me right up.

"What did you find in the files before Payne was . . . before Payne came in?" he asked.

"How'd you know I even found anything?"

At first he looked at me as if I were nuts. Maybe I

was, for asking *him* that question, when Jagger seemed to know all. Or maybe not.

"Payne wouldn't have tried to kill you for no good reason."

Hmm. That was probably true. If he had simply caught me there and wasn't worried, he wouldn't have pulled a knife. After all, that would have blown his scam. A knife. Eeks.

My knees weakened.

I leaned forward.

Then steadied myself on. . . Jagger's chest.

"I was nearly killed," I mumbled.

His finger touched just beneath my chin, lifted my head a bit until we met eye to eye, and before I could contemplate what kind of outfits souls wore up in heaven, Jagger's lips were on mine.

Well, not exactly *on* mine, but over, inside and . . . yum.

He pulled me closer, and I let him. Strong arms held me so tight, I could barely breathe, but knew—just knew—that if he held me tighter, I'd be in Nirvana. Very gently he ran a finger around my face, encircling me with his touch.

After a few moans (mine) and a few sensual animal sounds (his), I reached my hands up to run my fingers through his hair.

Jagger eased to the side enough that his lips touched near my ear. "I don't know what I'd do if . . ."

As his words trailed off (no way could I fully comprehend *anything* in this position), I ran my hands down his neck, around his shoulders and just leaned into him.

If there was safety in numbers, I felt very safe with this *one*.

He ran his hands along my spine, sending warm

sensations throughout my body. If I'd had to walk, I would have melted into a puddle of desire. Slowly his hands ran across my shoulders, arms and settled on my breasts. With the very gentle touch, I sighed and wished my clothes would melt into a puddle.

Jagger's lips continued to explore mine, his tongue touching my mouth. We both sighed and held tighter.

Before I could run my hand across his chest, he was holding me at arm's length and looking oh-so-very Jaggerlike. "We need to get working more on this case, Sherlock."

Suddenly my safe, sensual little harbor of love was interrupted by the question, Did Jagger mean he couldn't live without me cause I was fantastic and he was madly in love with me—or did he mean that I was a decent partner?

"Yeah," I said, pulled back and ran my hands down my clothing as if taking out any Jagger-induced wrinkles—as if that could erase what I felt right now. "Yeah, we do." I swallowed, hoping that would bring me back to reality.

Reality? Reality that Jagger and I were coworkers and nothing more? Or that we really had feelings for each other, but couldn't pursue that avenue or it'd ruin our partnership? In my book, love was thicker than a paycheck. But then again, there was so much about Jagger that I didn't know at this point, I had to tell myself that we were merely coworkers and that people's lives might depend on us working platonically.

That was what I tried to convince myself of, but in reality, I sensed there was something more. Something Jagger was keeping to himself (surprise, surprise). Something, maybe, from a past relationship—because he certainly reigned in his feelings with me.

With us.

"So? What did you find before Payne came in?" he asked again—thank goodness, because I didn't like where I was going in my head. "I assume he came in and found you."

"Yeah. He came in, all right." I proceeded to tell Jagger about the files that I found, which convinced me that Payne Sterling was a criminal—but an empty feeling nagged at me all the while.

Jagger took a step back.

A step back physically . . . and a step back from my heart.

After Jagger's kiss and our discussion of the case— which still had us stymied at square one—I made it back home in record time. Had to, or I'd have stalked Jagger for the rest of the night. Funny thing was, I had no idea where he lived and often thought the guy just "disappeared" into thin air when not around.

Made him so damn mysterious.

The living room was quiet when I opened the door, and I figured Goldie and Miles were out. It was a bit too early for anyone to be asleep, so I called Spanky, who came running like an obedient dog—now that Jagger wasn't with me.

I bent down and rubbed Spank's tummy. "Hey, buddy. How you been?"

After a few more rubs, I let him out and got myself a glass of warm milk. I stuck a pat of butter in it and watched it slowly melt. This was Stella Sokol's old remedy for us kids when we couldn't sleep. Of course she'd die if she knew Jagger's kiss was what I envisioned was going to keep me awake like a gallon of caffeine would.

Then again, there was that time she changed all my undies to thongs while I was away on a case.

Maybe I misjudged my mother.

I laughed and took a sip of the concoction, all the while ignoring the gazillion cholesterol grams that floated before my eyes.

Spanky was taking his good old time, so I went to the phone to see if anyone had called. The red light blinked three times, so I pushed PLAY.

"Pauline? Pauline Sokol?"

I rolled my eyes at my mother's voice. She always talked to the machine as if it were alive. Make that as if it were me.

"Pauline, this is your mother. I want you to come for dinner tomorrow night. Be here at six sharp. Bring the boys. You know what I mean. The homosexual men."

I groaned and let Spanky back in. "She's going to drive me insane, Spanks." He looked as if he agreed. He knew her very well. "Guess there's no trying to get out of it though."

Spanky nodded.

I waited for the second message. "Pauline Sokol, this is Nancy at Banker's Holding Company—"

"Damn!" I poked at the DELETE button, silencing Nancy. No point in hearing her *remind* me that my car payment was due. Past due. I'd send it in tomorrow. I would!

I looked at Spanky. Not sure if dogs even had eyebrows, but he seemed to raise one in disbelief. "Shut up. I will send it in. I'll postdate a check and get paid soon." This should be a fast case, with Payne already dead.

Spanky gave me a "yeah sure" look and walked away. The little creature of habit knew when it was bedtime, and I figured he was headed upstairs. I started to turn and the last message began in a garbled, almost robotic voice. Reminded me of the device patients who had suffered cancer of the larynx used.

"Two plus two equals four. Then if four plus four equals eight, what does that mean, Pauline? What does eight mean for you? For your *life*, Sokol? Wanna find out?" Sick laughter filled my kitchen. I dropped my glass of milk, the contents splashing across Miles's immaculate white kitchen floor. "Get the hell out of TLC."

That last part came out so clearly, so threatening, so menacing, that I gasped.

"Do you have to listen to that again?" I asked Jagger as Goldie and Miles both made little sounds of shock.

"I'm guessing you didn't call me over here to chat, Sherlock. Just listening for clues." He gave a sympathetic look to Goldie and Miles, who were huddled at the kitchen table, both holding my hand. Same one. "Maybe you guys want to wait in the living room?" he asked.

I had to smile at that thoughtful suggestion. Jagger was such a dichotomy of personalities, but I loved that he cared about my dearest friends in the world.

"We're fine," Miles said, tightening his hold.

"I'm gonna take this to Shatley and have his boys analyze it." Jagger lifted the tape out of the recorder and all I could say was, "Glad we have the old-fashioned kind of machine instead of the tapeless one."

Everyone looked at me.

No one smiled.

Amazingly enough, I slept a few hours that night. Of course, knowing Jagger was sleeping on our couch downstairs had something to do with it.

He really did represent safety for me.

When my alarm went off, I got up, not in the mood to lounge around, although I always thought the best feeling in the world was waking up and staying in bed while still in that glorious restful state.

I couldn't even pretend last night was restful.

Who the hell was that on the tape? Who knew my number? What did the damn riddle mean? And, more important, why me?

After showering and dressing in my blue scrubs—which I hated but thought today was a day I should wear them, for some strange reason—I headed downstairs, inhaling maple syrup and coffee aromas coming from the kitchen.

I pushed open the kitchen door. Jagger sat at the counter, reading the newspaper. Spanky was nestled at his feet, with traces of maple syrup on his whiskers, and Miles and Goldie ate solemnly at the table.

I wanted to hug both of them. No, all three . . . four of them.

"Hey, why so gloomy?"

"Suga?" Goldie squealed.

"Okay, I know why, but stop it, you two. What a great breakfast," I said, taking my teacup and putting water in it. The decaffeinated green tea bag was already in it. A dish, with aluminum foil covering it, sat at my place, and I turned to Jagger. "Thanks. Breakfast smells great."

He merely nodded. We all ate in silence and then Goldie and Miles kissed my cheeks simultaneously (and held me way too long, as if they knew this was my last day on earth).

I said a quick prayer that my darling roomies were not clairvoyant.

* * *

"Stop following me around, Jagger," I said close to his ear so no one else in the employee lounge would hear.

Buzz Lightyear sat at the ready, with a newspaper in hand but not reading. Two other EMTs watched the *Today* show and darling ER Dano sat in the corner by himself, drinking steaming coffee. Damn, he made it look so delicious.

Jagger said nothing but took a step away from me. He'd been following me all morning since we left the condo, as if the threatening phone caller, whom I nicknamed "Robotman," was right on my tail.

Usually having Jagger so close would be fun. Sexy. Sensual. Pheromonally intoxicating.

But today he annoyed me.

That, in all reality, was because I was on edge—but didn't want him to know it. When he was so protective, I interpreted that as him fearing for me. I didn't much like Jagger being afraid for anyone or anything.

"Four five six, we have a possible Eight ninety-two at 24 Chester Drive," came over the intercom.

Jagger looked at me, dumped his coffee cup on the nearest table and headed toward the door. Buzz jumped to attention, so I figured he'd be riding with us. Great. That put me in the back. And ER Dano took the last sip of his black coffee, set the mug down and sauntered to the door.

Once outside, ER got into the driver's seat, although I could tell Buzz was dying to drive. He looked like a puppy wildly wagging his tail in anticipation.

"Get in, the bunch of you!" Dano ordered, cranked the engine, and before Jagger and I had seated ourselves on the bench in the back, we were flying out of the parking lot.

Flying might have been too mild a word.

Suddenly, I think while ER was making a left-hand turn, I found myself sliding toward Jagger. "Oh! Sorry!" I yelled as the siren tended to drown out any sounds in close proximity to the ambulance.

"Hang on." He pointed at the railing on the wall near me.

I nodded and grabbed the wall handle. "You know what an Eight ninety-two is?"

As soon as the words came out, I shook my head. Jagger knew something about everything.

"Attempted suicide."

One of my hands flew to my face in shock, and my grip slipped. Dano jammed on the brakes, and before I knew it, I was in Jagger's lap.

I pulled myself back to a sitting position, inhaled to clear my head and got up—then hurried out the doors without a word.

"Yowza," Buzz Lightyear said.

Dano grunted at him.

Jagger remained silent, with an indistinguishable look on his face.

And I had to grasp the doorjamb as I watched the young woman in the bed.

She writhed about like a stripper. Had to be only about mid-twenties, dressed in a thin—very thin— white nightie that might as well have been hanging in her closet instead of trying to cover her.

Buzz cleared his throat.

Dano turned to him. "You got this one."

"She's nuts," said a woman who looked as if she might be the patient's sister, edging into the room.

In spite of the harshness of the comment, I had to

agree; although I also thought the patient looked a bit pale. For a second, I figured these three guys could handle this babe and maybe I'd sneak out and get back to TLC to snoop, but then she started grabbing onto the headboard—as if it were a pole.

The three guys took a step forward.

I wasn't going anywhere.

Buzz asked, "Um, ma'am, can you hear me?"

The girl looked at him with disgust. "Why the hell wouldn't I be able to?"

"Oh. Good. Great." Sweat broke out on his forehead and he wiped a finger across it. "So, ma'am, uh," he looked at the sister.

"Virginia," her sister said, while ER Dano threw a sheet over the girl.

Buzz nodded. "Ms. Virginia, why are we here today?"

She just about spit the words at him as she kicked at the sheet until it flew off. "I didn't call you, handsome, but if you wanna f—"

"Virginia!" Her horrified sister said, making the sign of the cross.

I looked around the room. Statues of the Blessed Mother, Jesus and a few others I didn't recognize—other than they had to be saints—covered the walls. Virginia had to be Catholic. A set of rosary beads hung off the doorknob. Yep. Catholic school too.

Virginia glared at her sister. "So, why the hell are these pseudo docs here, Margaret? You called them . . ." She started to drift off.

Virginia must have taken a whopping dose of some medication. Despite her maneuvers, she looked semi out of it and her nail beds were cyanotic instead of bright pink. Not enough oxygen in her system.

Buzz diligently opened the supply bag, got out a

mask and hooked it up to the oxygen, then tried to put it on Virginia. I'm not sure how it happened, but I blinked and then saw the oxygen mask hanging off of ER Dano's left ear.

He grabbed it, pushed Buzz to the side and said, "What'd you take, Virginia? And—" he undid the mask from the tubing, took out a nasal cannula from the bag —"I'm not leaving unless you put this on. It's not confining like the mask. I'll just stick it into your nostrils."

She let him but grabbed his arm and said, "You can stick something else into—"

"We're gonna take you on a little trip to the hospital, Virginia," Dano interrupted.

Since she didn't look in any immediate danger, other than mental health-wise, I had to smile.

Virginia wiggled and jiggled in the bed. "Why? Why? Why?"

"Just to make sure you are all right, ma'am," Buzz interrupted, standing at attention.

Dano turned to him.

"Uhn, sorry." Buzz kinda faded into the background of the shrine-room.

I felt sorry for him, but intrigued that Jagger stood so silently near the doorway. Was he merely letting them do their job, or was a sexy, gorgeous nut like Virginia hard for him to deal with? Interesting.

Virginia took a tissue from under her pillow and started to wipe her hands. She rubbed at each nail as if taking polish off, although there wasn't any on. The compulsive behavior continued while Buzz went to get the stretcher, Jagger offered to help him, and ER Dano and I stayed in the room, listening to Virginia, who was now chanting something.

Sounded like a Gypsy Rose Lee stripper tune.

Dano leaned over her. "What'd you take today, Virginia?"

I was amazed at his gentle yet firm tone. *Even I would have answered him,* I thought as she turned to him.

"La, dee, da," she said, then stopped. "Vodka."

"And?"

"What makes you think there's an 'and,' handsome? You are one hot guy, buddy." She reached up to him, grabbed his tie and pulled him near enough to give him a kiss, but Dano was apparently on the ball at all times. Before she could, he'd taken her hands and firmly released them.

"Let's keep to ourselves, Virginia. What'd you take with the Vodka?"

"You married, handsome? Kids. Good sex?" she asked.

I found myself leaning forward to hear better, and then caught myself.

"Gin?" Dano asked.

For a few seconds she looked like a child. Her eyes grew watery, her lips pouted and she took a few deep breaths. "He broke up with me. He broke up with me."

Dano rolled his eyes, but not until after he'd turned his head away. "Yeah, sometimes life sucks. Maybe it's for the better. Look, kid, no guy, or anyone for that matter, is worth dying for." He gazed around with a "Where the hell is that stretcher?" look. "So, pills?"

"Pills. Pot."

"What kinda pills?"

She looked toward the bedside table, which was so crowded with statues that none of us had noticed a prescription bottle hidden amongst them. I walked toward it and lifted it up. "Xanax. Anti-anxiety drug."

ER looked at me. "No kidding." He turned back to her. "Whose pills are they?"

I looked at the bottle and saw that the name was scratched off. Dano was one sharp guy. I wished he wasn't involved in the fraud. We could probably use his help.

Buzz and Jagger appeared at the doorway.

Virginia started to chant in some kind of tongue. Everyone ignored her as they covered her and re-covered her each time she threw off the sheet. They got her safely on the stretcher, where she promptly spit out a pill, most likely Xanax, which landed on Buzz Lightyear's crisp new shirt.

I don't think I've ever seen the kind of horror that was on poor Buzz's face right then.

Then Virginia said to Buzz, "You look like shit, buddy. You should be down here, not me."

While she laughed, I felt sorry for Buzz, but Dano shook his head as if that wasn't the first time a patient had said that to Buzz Lightyear.

Virginia started to chant a Hail Mary.

Now her sister shook her head and looked at me, "We're Jewish."

In a sitcom, that would be funny. I merely touched her arm and smiled.

"You drive," Dano said to Buzz, who beamed with delight, once we were outside.

I knew Buzz just couldn't wait to turn on the lights and sirens.

"Back for you, Nightingale." Which meant Jagger was up in front with Buzz.

Jagger looked pissed.

I smiled to myself as we quickly took our places and Buzz drove out of the driveway.

And damn but I didn't even shift in my seat.

Eight

The ambulance ride went smoothly with Buzz Lightyear driving, considering Virginia vacillated from crying to wiping her nails, to chanting and stripper maneuvers. Occasionally she'd say an Our Father, which, I might add, she did damn well for a Jewish girl—except for saying "who *aren't* in heaven" instead of "who art in heaven." I had to wonder what that said about her beliefs.

Dano seemed to ignore her while he wrote on his daily run sheet, but did occasionally stick the nasal cannula back in her nose so she got her oxygen.

I leaned back to rest and contemplate my job.

Suddenly she bolted up on the stretcher.

"Get down, Virginia, before you get hurt," Dano ordered. "What the hell are you doing, anyway?"

She leaned toward him, "I'm waiting for the Immaculate Conception."

I bit back a smile and said a quick prayer for some type of mental-health recovery for the girl. How the heck did a Jewish girl even know about that?

"Fine. Good. Lie back down," Dano said, barely looking up from his clipboard.

She lay down. "I'm a virgin, you know."

Dano and I looked at each other. "Of course you are," he said, in what I thought a very professional tone.

He'd almost convinced me.

Virginia remained still.

Amazingly enough, riding in the back of an ambulance wasn't anywhere near as motion sickness inducing with Buzz Lightyear driving. "How sad about Payne," I said to Dano. Not sure where that came from—other than the fact that I needed to pump him for fraud info. Being stuck back here with self-proclaimed Virgin Virginia seemed like an opportune time, since she wasn't in critical condition or requiring us to be working on her en route.

"Sad. Yeah, but not surprising."

Bingo. Had to be a "Bingo" with that statement. "Not surprising?"

Dano never looked up. "Come on, Pauline, I'm sure an intelligent woman like yourself has figured out that Payne Sterling was a weirdo and not well liked. Not only was Payne nuts, he was hated."

"By?"

Dano started to open his mouth, and before I could move, Virgin Virginia was trying to stand up on the stretcher.

"Oh!" I shouted.

"Get down!" ordered Dano, who looked as if he was trying to get up, the clipboard still at his chest. In seconds, Virginia was on top of said clipboard—and said *Dano*.

The way she straddled him said she was *not* a virgin.

Dano tried to struggle free, but Virginia had long nails, which she dug into the back of his neck.

"Aye!" he shouted. "A little help here, Nightingale!"

I started to get up to help. Suddenly a sharp pain centered on my abdomen, sending me sailing back toward the wall, down the side of the bench and into the corner of the ambulance, only to realize Virginia's leg had been aimed straight at me. The drug-crazed vixen had kicked me!

Now the pain came from the back of my head, and stars danced around both Dano and the proclaimed virgin.

He kept trying to get her off, but she was like Velcro, the way she kept sticking to him, all the while her nightie bunching up around her thighs from what I could see with my blurry vision. Nausea sped up my throat from the smack on my head, and I couldn't move if I wanted to.

"You all right, Pauline?" Dano shouted, as he tried to break Virginia's death grip on his neck.

"Mentally ill people are very strong," was all I could manage.

Dano turned toward the window to the driver's area. He couldn't reach it, but leaned over far enough to kick it with his black boot.

Jagger swung around, his eyes wide open, while he shoved the glass to the side. "What the hell. Dude, cut it out! Pauline? Stop the ambulance! Dano, cool it! Help Pauline!"

Virginia yelled, "He's mine!"

And Jagger countered with, "Trust me, I don't want him."

Dano growled. "Get her the hell off of me, but don't piss her off. Those nails are lethal."

Buzz must have been confused, but we all sloshed about as he pulled over to the side of the road. My head throbbed like the dickens and my vision hadn't cleared.

I tried to take a few deep breaths and leaned to the side when suddenly the back doors opened—and I landed in Jagger's arms.

"Jesus, Pauline!" He held me for a few seconds. "Get her off of Dano," Jagger ordered a very confused-looking Buzz.

In a few minutes, I was sitting on the bench with an ice pack on the back of my head. The virgin was nestled all snug in her stretcher—with restraints to hold her in place, after ER called in the "problem" and got orders from the ER doc—and Jagger was sitting next to me.

I vaguely remember he and Dano arguing about who would sit in the back for the rest of the ride.

I smiled at Jagger, squinted from the pain, and looked at Virginia, who grinned at me and said, "He left me. Aren't there eight ways to leave your lover? Eight?"

Eight? Eight?

Was that coincidence or something to do with the threat against me and my case?

Because Robotman had used that exact word.

Dano ordered me to sit in a wheelchair and Jagger pushed me into the ER following the stretcher containing Virginia, who was now chanting in tongues.

"She banged her head," he said to a male nurse who hurried over to me.

"Hi, I'm a nurse here. Ted. Ted Grosch. How you feeling?"

"How do I look?" I asked.

He chuckled. "Gorgeous."

I laughed, grabbed my forehead and said, "Ouch."

Jagger stepped forward. "Come on, buddy. Cat-scan

her or MRI her or something. Could be internal bleeding."

Ted paused and glared at him. "You a doctor?"

Jagger ignored the dig and said, "Do something fast!"

This time I had to chuckle, no matter how much it hurt.

In a short time, Ted had me in the exam room (who wouldn't, with Jagger standing guard?), seen by the doc and off for a scan, which—thank the good Lord— came back negative. Once the doctor pronounced me just bruised with a prize-winning egg-sized bump, I was released.

When I was rolled out to the waiting room, I smiled—to myself, since it hurt less than the real thing. There sat Buzz, wiping at the spot on his shirt. I think Virginia had spit on his sparklingly crisp top. ER Dano leaned against the wall with his eyes shut, but opened them when Ted said my name, and Jagger, who looked the worst for wear, straightened up.

"What a pathetic-looking crew," I said.

Dano stood up and grabbed Buzz by the shoulder. "Back to work. She's all restocked."

I knew he meant the ambulance was restocked with supplies from the ER but he didn't go out with Buzz. Oh, no. There seemed to begin a challenge between him and Jagger as to who would sit in the back—to watch me.

How cute.

In a few minutes I was sitting on the bench next to ER Dano.

Hmm. Jagger seemed to have lost his grip on that one. I guessed Dano was king in his ambulance, and no one, not even the mysterious, infamous Jagger, could knock him off his throne.

Did that mean Dano had a stake in the company? He had been there a very long time. Being so burned out, one would think he'd have quit and moved on in life to something less stressful.

I leaned back, shut my eyes and sighed.

"What?" I heard him say.

I opened one eyelid. "Hmm?"

"You made a sound." He leaned forward as if expecting me to pass out.

"Oh. I'm fine." I sighed again, just on principle. "It just feels good to be all right. My head is better." It really hurt like hell, but if I told him, he'd probably insist I lie down on the stretcher or something.

Dano leaned back again. "Good. Good."

I smiled to myself. Sitting next to him was not unpleasant at all. For some strange reason (and I was blaming it on hormones) I wanted to touch him. Anyplace. His arm. His hand. His thigh. Yikes. I wanted to touch ER Dano!

Get a grip, I told myself, rationalizing that the knock on my head was causing strange reactions in my libido.

However, ER Dano was one hot guy. Even Jewish, pseudo-Catholic Virgin Virginia had thought so.

Then again, she was whacko. I looked at Dano, told myself to change the subject in my head and asked, "How long have you been working at TLC?"

He looked surprised at the question, and I was guessing, if I hadn't been injured earlier, he wouldn't have answered. But he did look at me and say, "Long time."

I forced a chuckle. Sounded pretty damn good to me. I wondered if I should take some acting courses to help out with this career. "What's a long time?"

"It'll be twenty-one years pretty soon."

"Wow. Twenty-one years at TLC. I'm impressed." I really was, along with wondering how the heck old he was.

"Started at nineteen, Nightingale," he said as if he'd read my mind.

"So this has been your only job?"

He nodded. "I started at TLC right after taking courses." He looked off into space and said, "Hadn't really thought about it being my only job."

Dano sounded a bit melancholy, which was certainly out of character for someone so tough, so rough around the edges and so . . . edgy.

Still looking into space he said, "Twenty-one freaking years. No one should have to go through this that long."

Wow. I should have remained silent, but I said, "Through this? What is this?"

Without looking at me he said, "Everything we see. Everything that can happen to a human body. Everything that can be done to a human body."

"It is a tough job."

He swung around toward me. "Tough? You don't know tough." He leaned back and sighed. "Every night. Nightmares. Bodies. Parts. The ones you know won't make it. The ones you know won't make it and there's no freaking thing you can do about it."

I touched his hand. He barely acknowledged me, but at least he didn't push me away.

"It's like a bucket. Keeps getting filled with pain, dying, death. But there's holes in the bucket so the shit filters out." He turned, looked me in the eyes and said, "But it *always* gets refilled. Always."

I patted his hand very gently and then took mine

away. "I guess it never would get any easier no matter how long you work at it."

"Nope."

Time to lighten the mood, I decided. "Oh, yeah. TLC. How'd it start doing so much better?" I asked also to see if his story jived with what I already had heard.

Dano proceeded to tell me about Payne and Pansy's uncle, who had started the company after owning a gas station near the interstate. His wreckers were often forced to be used to take patients to the hospital, since Hope Valley didn't have its own ambulance service. It was serviced by a few companies from Hartford and surrounding towns like Bloomfield and Glastonbury.

"When he got sick, his . . . nephew took over."

"That'd be Payne?"

Dano didn't look at me. "That *was* Payne."

A chill raced up my spine. Suddenly I pictured him dead on the floor and the knife . . . sticking out. I swallowed in order not to get nauseous. "Who do you think killed him?" flew out of my mouth.

Dano froze.

Yikes.

For some reason I looked toward Jagger. Even the back of his head gave me some comfort. Dano really shouldn't scare me. *He was not a killer*, I told myself without a shred of evidence other than my gut instinct— which had served me well in my nursing career.

But did I want to trust it when the issue was *murder*?

Well, I had nothing else to work with other than my gut instincts and very little evidence, so I looked directly into his eyes and waited.

Dano squinted at me. I wondered if that was so I couldn't read his pupils. Never could remember if constricting pupils meant someone was lying—or was it dilating ones? What the hell good was looking into his eyes, then?

"If I knew that, Nightingale, wouldn't I have already told the police?" He turned away—so I couldn't see his eyes?

I sat still for a few seconds, contemplating the ever-confusing ER Dano. On the surface, he was hot, gorgeous, all man. On the inside, he was beginning to be as mysterious as Jagger. But at least with him, I knew it was always on the up and up. Jagger was the cowboy who should have worn the white hat.

I mentally looked up to heaven and mouthed, "What did I do to deserve this?" Had to be to keep me on my toes and not become bored. "Of course I know you would have, Dano."

He looked at me as if confused.

"Told the police. I know you would have told them. Actually, I'd have no way of knowing if you told them or what you told them, since I'm only a nurse and new employee to boot. Well, even if I wasn't new. I mean, even if I was a longtime employee like you, the police wouldn't share any investigative information with me."

I actually bit down on my own tongue.

What the hell had just happened? Dano had me spewing out words in a ramble by merely sitting next to me. I reached up and rubbed my head to make him think I was going insane from the fall.

Obviously Dano was used to dealing with crazies, since he ignored me and said, "But if I had to speculate as to who offed Payne—"

The ambulance stopped, most likely on a damn dime, 'cause I flew toward Dano. Then the doors opened and Jagger stood there, with me . . . in Dano's arms.

Nine

Lilla handed me a fresh ice pack. "So, *chéri*, nothing yet on the case?"

I took the ice pack, held it to my head, and said, "Thanks. Damn it. No. ER Dano was just about to spill his thoughts to me, and we got interrupted."

Lilla grinned. Damn, she looked hot like that. If I were a guy, I'd be all over her.

"Not like that!" I chuckled, and grabbed my head. "Ouch."

"I put you down as sick for the rest of the shift, *chéri*. You should go home and rest."

I started to nod and then realized that would hurt like hell. I also realized what an opportune moment this could be. The powers that be around here would think I was still working, and ER Dano and Jagger would (hopefully) think I'd gone home.

But Pauline Sokol had other ideas.

Lilla was a peach, I'd decided, as I walked toward the administrative section of TLC Air and Land. She had signed me out as sick so I'd still get paid, and then she told Pansy about the incident today.

Obviously, grief-stricken Pansy was also the legal eagle in the family, as she insisted I go home for as long as needed—paid, I might add. I figured she'd made the offer in order to avoid any lawsuit I might conjure up. Hmm. I could pay off a lot of bills. . . .

But that wasn't me.

I went to the office of Pansy's receptionist and stopped at the door and waited. A few seconds later, a French-Canadian accent sounded over the intercom. "Mrs. Dawson, please report to the main reception area."

Thank you, dear Lilla.

Mrs. Dawson hurried out, and I only wasted a few seconds wondering what lie Lilla was going to give for paging the woman. Lilla really was a peach.

Looking around, I noticed the door to Pansy's office was still open even though she'd told Lilla that she had to go meet with the undertaker right after she'd told me to go home. I shuddered, said a prayer for Payne's soul—which by the sound of things might need a bit more than a "few" prayers. I walked nonchalantly into Pansy's office . . .

And nearly passed out from fear!

In the center of the room was a life-size cardboard figure of Payne Sterling.

I grabbed the desk to steady myself since I could almost picture the knife in . . .

After a few mental shakes, I told myself this was probably for the memorial service—although weirder than anything I'd seen so far. There was an odd expression on Payne's face—almost a grimace—and I couldn't help but wonder if he had the last laugh.

But he couldn't have known he was going to die when this picture was taken.

Okay, Sokol, compose yourself, I ordered. Gawking at an eerie cardboard Payne was not getting me anywhere. I tried to ignore it, easing to the side to get around it. No way in hell was I going to *touch* the damn thing.

I figured Pansy would be gone for a bit, if not the rest of the day, so I needn't hurry. Then again, who knew how long Lilla could keep Mrs. Dawson busy?

After taking my gloves from the pocket of my scrubs and pulling them on, I walked to the door and eased it closed, hoping that would buy me time if I heard someone coming. I hurried to the other door and opened it. Good. Payne's office door was unlocked. A perfect escape route.

I said a quick prayer that I wouldn't need it, went to Pansy's desk and started snooping.

After what seemed like hours, I flopped down in her black chair that went with the monochromatic décor and sighed. Nothing. She had nothing left for any evidence—consequently, I had nothing on her. Could twins like Payne and Pansy not be in cahoots? Was it really possible that Payne had been scamming the insurance companies and she never knew about it?

I didn't buy that.

There had to be something fishy going on here . . . wait! Pansy must have cleaned out her office of any evidence. That's why she was here instead of mourning at home.

My gut was talking to me again, and once again, I agreed.

"I'll get it for you, Miss Sterling."

Mrs. Dawson!

And, yikes, she was talking to Pansy. I hoped it was on the phone. Before I could find out, the doorknob started to turn . . . and I got myself through the door to Payne's office in a flash.

But I kept the door open a crack and watched as the dear woman walked in, hefted up Payne's picture into her arms, sniffled, shook her head—almost in disgust—and carried him out the door.

Maybe his presence was requested at the funeral home now.

Phew. I leaned against the wall, took in a deep breath and blew it out while looking at the room. Eerie wasn't quite strong enough of a word. The kaleidoscope-colored room gave me the feeling someone was watching me. I shook my head and ignored the nonsense as I silently walked toward the door.

When I went to grab the handle, a hand covered mine. . . .

My eyelids fluttered. I sucked in some air and tried to remember where I was. Why was I lying on the floor? I looked up to see the colorful room and remembered I was in the late Payne Sterling's office. "Right," I muttered. "What the hell made me pass out?"

I heard a soft chuckle and swung my head around to see Sky near the doorway. "I went to get a cold compress. So sorry I scared you, Pauline." He knelt down and gently set it on my forehead.

As if I'd feel better from a wet cloth. Okay, it was soothing. "What happened?" I held the cloth with one hand and pushed myself to a sitting position with the other. A girl did not want to be lying prone beneath a hunk like Sky Palmer.

"You passed out."

I raised one eyebrow. "No kidding."

"Yeah." He chuckled. "I'm so sorry that I scared you, Pauline. I—" He chuckled again. "This is going to sound so stupid. I came in here to get some log forms for a flight I did a few days ago, and you . . . you scared the shit out of me!"

I scared *this* guy?

Then again, maybe that idea wasn't so far-fetched. I was in the office of a dead man—and obviously Sky hadn't been expecting to find anyone in here.

"I knew I should have asked Mrs. Dawson to find the logs for me." He took the cloth from my head. "I'll go make this colder."

"No," I said, even though it would have felt wonderful, but I had to get out of there. Hopefully Sky was so shocked seeing me that he'd forget to ask what *I* was doing there.

"So, Pauline, what the hell were you doing here?"

So much for my shocked pilot theory.

"Oh, that." I stood up and wiped at the back of my head. "I hit the back of my head during an ambulance run today. Fell. Well, actually kicked down by a virgin patient." I rubbed my head a few times. "So Pansy, the generous darling—"

Sky's eyes darkened.

Interesting.

"Well, she was so sweet to let me go home for the rest of the day." I rattled on the entire story of Virgin Virginia until poor Sky's gorgeous, sexy eyes were glazed over.

Not one word that I said explained his original question of what I was doing here, but I'd finagled my way out of answering that with all the bullshit rambling.

Geez. This investigator stuff was getting easier and

easier, and now I had to wonder if Sky was involved—or how.

After Sky fell for my long-winded explanation of nothing, we said goodbye and I headed out the back door while he went toward the reception desk. I thought for sure his seeing gorgeous Lilla would confuse him more and make him forget me instantly.

Once seated in my car, I looked at my watch and groaned. Nearly six. The hour of doom.

Dinner at 171 David Drive. Michael and Stella Sokol's house.

Well, I told myself, worse things could happen to me. Sky Palmer could have ratted me out today. Instead I proudly drove to my folks' house and pulled in the driveway with a smile on my face—until I noticed the black Suburban parked out front.

Jagger!

Mother had done it again. She had his cell number, which was more of a secret than a sealed envelope holding an Oscar winner's name. But she managed to get it, call him more than I cared to have her do (which would have been zero), and now he was going to be eating Mom's tender beef dinner tonight—I already knew the menu because it was Tuesday and my mother made the same meal on the same day of the week *every* week.

Oh well, I felt like crap after the time I'd just had, and Mom's home-cooked comfort food would be soothing if nothing else. Today also, I ashamedly admitted, was going to be a spritz-of-pine-scented-Renuzit kinda day. My mother hoarded the stuff for years and sprayed every inch of our house, so much that its Christmassy pine scent became very nostalgic to me. It said home.

Safety. Love. And, of course, food. Very comforting. I needed comfort now and a spray of it had fewer calories than the beef dinner.

I'd hurry into the bathroom, inhale a whiff or two and be ready to enjoy—make that *tolerate*—the meal with Jagger sitting across from me. Plan A was a go.

When I opened the front door, I froze. *What the hell was Plan B?* I wondered as I saw my parents, Uncle Walt, Goldie, Miles, Jagger, Buzz Lightyear (sitting next to Lilla) *and* ER Dano, all sitting in the living room.

Even my mother didn't stock enough Renuzit to get me through these kinds of moments.

I sat on the hamper, leaned against the wall, sprayed the Renuzit and inhaled. It wasn't as if it were a drug and I was really inhaling, but more like it was a breath of home—Mom and Dad.

Knock. Knock.

"Just a sec," I said, stuck the Renuzit on the back of the commode and opened the door. "What?"

Jagger looked at me and sniffed.

"Shut up," I said and started to push past him.

He grabbed my arm.

I sighed before pulling away. Actually, I hesitated before I pulled away. "What are you doing here anyway? And why the crowd?" I said.

"Your mother invited—"

I waved his words away. "No nonsense. Just stop. What are Dano and Buzz doing here?"

Jagger looked at me. I knew he'd never answer a direct question to my satisfaction. He said, "You should be glad I brought them. They might help your case."

Hmm. "What do you know?"

"Nothing."

"Then why tease me with—"

Jagger's lips touched mine, taking my words away. Then again, who cared? Words were cheap and flowing, but a kiss from Jagger was special and rare.

I savored every second, until I heard someone clear their throat and turned to see Goldie coming down the hallway. "Sincere apologies, you two, but nature calls," he said as he whisked past us, shut the door and, I think, giggled.

Jagger stepped back. "Where were you before? I thought you were supposed to be home resting."

"I was." He looked at me. Damn it. Why did I even try? "Okay. Okay. I got into Pansy's office and then Payne's again."

"And?"

"And she's cleaned everything out, if there was anything, which I highly suspect there was."

"And in Payne's? Anything new?"

Suddenly the vision of waking up with Sky Palmer leaning over me, dripping a cold compress on my head came over me. "Er . . . no. She must have cleaned that out too. Where do you suppose she took it all?"

"I'd say her home."

"Damn it. Now we need to find out where she lives and get into her place? That could be more than I'm capable of or at least willing to do."

Jagger chuckled. "It's not as if you've never committed breaking and entering, Sherlock."

I smiled.

He smiled back.

We smiled together, and suddenly I felt something. Some kind of bond with Jagger.

Could life get any better?

"She and Payne had apartments in the Tudor-style house on the northern part of the TLC property."

Leave it to him to know that. "Wait! That means it'll be easier to get into it, since it's on the property."

Life did just get better, until Jagger shook his head.

"What?" I said. "What?"

"Why does that make it easier? It'll still have to be B and E."

I punched his arm, said, "You are always so freaking negative," and walked away, all the while knowing full well that I had no idea why I'd said it'd be easier—other than the fact that I *hoped* it would be. Wait! After the memorial service. Great timing. Yeah.

Back at the dining-room table, I sat down, ignored looks from everyone—who I'm sure was wondering what the hell was wrong with me that I was gone so long—and picked up my knife and fork.

"You can cut my beef with a fork, Pauline," my mother said in a chastising tone.

I looked up. Yes, everyone was staring. "Force of habit. Guess I'm just used to eating my own cooking." I forced a laugh.

Goldie returned and joined us.

"Where's Mr. Jagger, Goldie?" Mother asked.

"Oh. He said he was sorry, everything was delicious but he had to go." Goldie sat down and picked up his fork, cut his meat and took a bite.

Damn it.

And where the hell did Jagger go? If he went to snoop at Pansy's by himself, I'd cut *him* with my fork.

"You boys sit still," Mother said to ER Dano and Buzz. "Pauline and Lilla will help clean up." She gave me the "mother eye".

I sat mesmerized for a few seconds as if in a trance. She tended to do that to me. Then I came to—obviously the change in my career also included a change in personality—and said, "Why? Why do women have to do all the work?"

Goldie and Miles gasped.

Buzz remained silent, although he looked frightened. Obviously he'd gotten to know my mother in a very short time.

Lilla mumbled that she didn't mind helping.

And ER Dano grinned.

I looked him square in the eye. "How about it? A little help?"

He got up, gathered up a stack of dishes and started toward the kitchen.

"Payback for me cleaning the ambulance," I whispered as he passed me but fully not intending for him to hear.

"Touché," he said over his shoulder.

Yikes. I had to keep my thoughts to myself around this guy. He was a sharp one.

Sharp enough to commit fraud?

I leaned back and watched him walk through the doorway.

Great butt.

Geez, I hope he wasn't involved . . . in the fraud . . . or *with* anyone!

Thank goodness I had the job of cleaning up, I thought. It at least kept me from continuing to ogle ER Dano and his great butt.

How pathetic.

Once the dishes were cleared, I took the salt and pepper shakers—Mickey and Minnie Mouse, which

Mother had since the fifties I'm sure—into the kitchen. Lilla was wiping the counter.

Daddy had gone to the living room to read—an all-night affair. Uncle Walt excused himself to go out—a date with Old Lady Wimple, he'd whispered to me with a wink.

Eeeeeeyew!

"I'm beat, Mrs. Sokol," Miles said. "Gold, you ready?"

Goldie looked horrified.

My mother touched his arm. "Not to worry, dearie, I'll put a slice of chocolate cake on a paper plate and you can take it home. Okay?"

He looked like one of my nephews on Christmas morning.

Gotta love Goldie.

Buzz watched my mother cut the cake, and I think he started to drool.

I had to laugh, until I noticed ER Dano—staring at *me*.

I wanted to say, "What?" but held my tongue so as not to get into an argument in front of everyone. What the hell was he looking at? When I peeked at him again, he nodded his head toward the back door. Toward the back porch door.

Did he want me to follow him?

When he turned and hesitated, I nearly pointed to my chest and mouthed, "Me?" but it was clear, so I said, "I need some air after all that work," and before my mother could ask what work, I headed out the door. I heard Dano say, "Good idea. Save me a piece, Mrs. S."

The moon's glow shone rays of light onto the porch. In the distance the peepers chirped and a gentle breeze bathed the porch in comfort. The neighbors were their usual quiet selves and only the din of traffic could be heard in the distance.

How very romantic, I thought, until I turned around. Romantic is not the term I'd use to describe ER Dano's glaring at me.

"What the hell were you doing in Payne's office today, Nightingale?"

Oops.

Ten

I was never a good liar, but standing out on my parents' porch with ER Dano interrogating me in an almost threatening way, I decided I had to give it a shot. Lying that was. And, oh yeah, that sure was a threatening way.

"I got lost." Even before the words came out, I heard myself scream inside my head, *"Are you nuts? That's the worse excuse I've ever heard, Pauline!"* However, the stupid words still came out. And now I *felt* stupid.

And you didn't want to feel stupid in front of Jagger or ER Dano.

Nope.

He took a step forward. I told myself, as I backed up, that it was his way of intimidating me and I shouldn't let him. My butt touched the railing. Nowhere else to go but leap over. And that I couldn't do, or I really would feel like a fool when I landed on my butt in Mom's hydrangeas. Besides, I had to stand up to Dano or forever face his chauvinistic attitude.

"You got lost?" His tone was almost sympathetic now—as if he thought I was some moron.

Moron? Well!

"Yeah," I said and pushed past him, with every fiber of my being trying not to notice that I'd touched his chest. Solid, rock-hard, works-out-four-or-five-times-per-week chest, by my best guess. Geez. I had to find a guy soon.

Dano turned and followed me, getting closer and closer until his hand was on my arm. Not as if he grabbed me. Nope. More as if he just wanted to touch me. I looked up into his darkened eyes.

Touch away, buddy.

In seconds I reminded myself that I was a professional and pulled back. "Excuse me? *Excuse* me?" Not sure even what I meant, I looked to see him just as confused.

"Why? What did you do, Nightingale?"

I faltered. The damn nickname. Then I pulled my shoulders straight and gathered up every ounce of hormone-free sanity that I could muster. "I didn't *do* anything." This time I pushed him enough to get myself to the other side of the porch. "Nothing. I got lost and you sound as if I did something . . . something wrong. And don't touch me like that." Okay, that last bit was overkill, but I knew if he touched me I might crumble.

Now, mind you, I was not some namby-pamby weak female. Nope. But any female would crumble around a tower of testosterone like ER—and she'd probably love it.

Suddenly ER Dano was no longer appearing as a threat.

Damn it. Nope. Now he stood a few feet away, looking oh-so-handsome and delicious in the moon's glow. How romantic. The only thing was, Dano might be a criminal, a liar and . . . a killer.

Naw.

My gut was denying all of that as nonsense, and I had to mentally agree. So, I took a step forward and said, "If you're so burned out on your job as a paramedic, why stick around TLC?" I needed to get to know him, spend some time around him—okay, make time with him. Yum.

Even he looked surprised at my candor—which, by the way, came out sounding very professional and intelligent.

At first he paused for a few uncomfortable moments.

To think of a lie?

Then he stepped closer and took both of my arms into his hands. "Good question, Nightingale. As I said, my bucket has holes in it."

"Hmm?" His sincere tone had me speechless.

"You know. My bucket of all the crap that I see, have to deal with and have to do something about. It has holes. As each day's work filters out, it's inevitably replaced—and often with things that are much worse."

ER Dano's eyes darkened more and tears formed—which had to be killing him to keep from flowing.

My old nurse's nurturing nature kicked in—as usual against my will—and before I could think logically, my nursing nature had me turning the tide, and now *I* was holding ER Dano in my arms.

At first he tensed. A sympathetic guy. Wasn't that an oxymoron? One thing about Dano I was certain, he never wanted anyone's help. The guy was a powerhouse of self-investment. Clearly he didn't want to feel beholden to anyone or as if he needed anyone.

He appeared so strong, and yet, I'd bet my paycheck (much-needed paycheck) that he had a teeny, tiny streak of softness in him.

I wondered what Dano's past relationships were like because I surmised that he definitely didn't want to be leaning on a woman.

But I held him closer.

His warm breath breezed across my neck. Ah. Suddenly I thought it might be hard to comfort him—if my damn mind couldn't keep this Platonic? . . . His lips were on mine and the word no longer had any meaning. Pla . . . what?

Dano's mouth covered mine. I sighed.

Then he eased his arms around me. I felt secure in his hold, and leaned into him. Oh, my.

I sighed.

When I reminded myself that I was on Stella Sokol's porch, I snuck a peek past Dano's shoulder. Good. No one. No one was in the doorway, in the window or within listening distance.

So, I stretched up and returned Dano's kiss.

Oh, my was right.

Dano's hand ran down my back and a hitch in my breath filled the air. Not caring if anyone hurried outside to find out what the hell that noise was, I ran kisses along his cheek while running my hands through his hair.

"You smell good, Nightingale." His voice was rough in an ER Dano sort of way, but an underlying tenderness, sensuality, in fact, made my knees weak.

I couldn't think of the words to express my appreciation of the comment. I was way too busy.

And it'd been way too long since I'd been kissed like this. Jagger's kisses had been specifically Jagger kisses—wonderful, delicious, confusing and mysterious. And not that I'd trade them for these, but right now, ER Dano's said reality.

And I sure as hell wanted/needed reality.

* * *

"We should go inside." ER Dano eased back from me, and I walked in a semi-trance into my mother's house.

The guy had class and concern. I'm sure he didn't want to take advantage of me out on my parents' porch—no matter that I *wanted* him to! Hey, Stella Sokol would probably celebrate that her only single daughter was getting some. *Getting some*? Surely my mother would not use that phrase, but then again, she did change all my undies to thongs once when I was out of town working a case.

We nonchalantly walked back into the dining room, me with Dano's hand on the small of my back.

Everyone in the room stared at me with that look of "Pauline just had sex" on their faces.

Or so I imagined.

Actually, only my mother had that look, and I wasn't sure if she was internally applauding me (her thirty-something, only single offspring) or giving me the evil eye—igniting my Catholic school-induced conscience.

"What's for dessert, Ma?" I asked, using the nick-name she hated, then feeling like a jerk for using it, since everyone glared at me.

"We had chocolate cake before, Pauline," my mother said in a very condescending tone.

I was about to argue—okay, with nothing to ar-gue about—but smiled weakly instead, and ER Dano stepped forward. "I have to rush off now. Fantastic meal, Mrs. S. Thanks so much for including us." ER Dano poked Buzz on the shoulder, who must have been on his fourth piece of cake, and walked toward the front door, mumbling his thanks with Lilla right behind.

I leaned against the doorjamb watching them go for a second, then remembered who the heck I was, ran back to my chair and grabbed my purse, blew a kiss to my mom and followed them.

"Good night, Daddy," I yelled, passing the living room.

Once outside, Dano gave Buzz a dirty look when he followed suit. So after Buzz said 'bye to me and went to his car, and Lilla left in hers, Dano turned to me and said, "Dinner tomorrow night. Around seven. After the memorial service and get-together at Pansy's place."

My jaw dropped but I managed a nod, not sure if the idea that he'd kinda ordered me on a date with him was so shocking, or if I was thinking about how the memorial service would be a great time for me to snoop at Pansy's place.

Next morning, I opened the front door of my condo and nearly passed out.

Now I knew what the term *swooned* meant.

Jagger stood there in a black suit—a classy one that said Armani, though I was no fashionista to be able to tell the difference. He looked more like we were heading to some fancy-schmancy restaurant for a candlelit dinner than a memorial service.

He looked *that* delicious.

And what really made my day was how he looked at *me*. As if I were a tasty morsel too. Not that I was aiming for sexy at a memorial service, but the only little black dress that I owned was a slinky Jones New York with three-quarter-length sleeves and a V-neck that allowed a sampling of cleavage.

I did look tasty.

Jagger stood there for a second, brushed past me and said, "Ready?"

I smiled. "I'm ready, and the car is that way." I pointed behind him.

Without a word, he walked toward the kitchen. "Any more phone messages?"

Damn. I'd nearly forgotten it. "No. Maybe that was just a fluke. Someone playing a joke."

"Murderers don't joke, Pauline."

"Gee. Thanks for that." I followed him into the kitchen, where I found him petting Spanky.

I think Jagger actually looked forward to seeing the dog. Maybe Spanky was the only thing that could ground Jagger in reality. Give him a sense of family. Pets were amazing.

"We need to go, or we'll be late."

He patted Spanky on the head, turned and walked past me again. As I followed him out to his SUV, I thought of what an odd scene that had just been.

Jagger had seemed so down to earth. So un-Jagger-like.

Maybe he was softening.

Jagger pulled his Suburban into a space in TLC's parking lot, which was full since, I figured, all the employees were there to pay their respects. Coincidentally, the funeral home was just across the street, so parking at TLC was logical, since there was a get-together at Pansy's after the service. No trip to the cemetery, thank goodness, since Payne had been cremated.

Jagger took me by the elbow and guided me across the busy intersection. Waiting outside the door was ER Dano, who looked as if he cared that Jagger held my elbow.

Two guys showing interest in me. Two!

What a great feeling, I told myself as I walked under the green-canopied entryway. "Morning," I said, smiling slightly since I didn't want to seem jovial at such a solemn event.

Dano nodded.

Jagger tightened his hold.

And I raised one eyebrow, moved away from both of them and walked inside, where I found Lilla, who had saved us a few seats.

I nodded to her, tried to ignore the huge cutout of Payne and sat directly in front of Sky and Mario. Buzz was on the other side of Lilla, sitting, I thought, much closer than necessary. Cute. Talk about opposites attracting.

Maybe he was vying for slot number five in the Lilla Marcel wedding bliss department.

I had to smile to myself, because that was not a bad idea. Buzz—geez, now I was calling him that and had to remind myself that his real name was Jeremy—might be just what Lilla needed for happiness, even though he was a few years younger.

She leaned toward me. "Isn't that cardboard thing eerie?"

I wanted to say, "You should have seen it in Pansy's office when I was snooping," but remembered Jagger's sage advice that one never knew whose ears were tuned into you and would hear stuff about your case. I nodded as a man I assumed was the minister took the podium, and performed the ceremony.

After several people had gotten up and spoken kind words about Payne—and most of the staff seemed to raise an eyebrow or shake a head at the falsehoods—Sky guided Pansy up to the front. She looked at her cardboard brother and then at the crowd. No tears, I noticed, but her face darkened to a deep crimson color.

Then she glared and pointed at Payne's image and began cursing like a sailor.

Between the gasps of the mourners and the high pitch of her voice, the place took on a creepy, almost surreal atmosphere.

Pansy accused her brother of just about everything under the sun except the fraud, although she alluded to his "unhealthy business practices." Then she looked above all of our heads and offered a halfhearted apology of some sorts.

I could barely make sense of her rambling, but Sky and ER Dano finally got up and took her back to her chair. Before she sat, she turned to us and yelled, "Everyone come to my place after this fiasco and celebrate!" Then she seemed to catch herself and added, "His life. Celebrate my brother Payne's life." In a very unflattering, unbelievable tone she said, "He would have wanted that."

She pushed Sky's arm from hers, nearly knocked ER Dano down in her haste, and hurried from the room.

The two guys stood speechless, the minister cleared his throat over and over, and the crowd hushed. Jagger got up, took my arm and led me toward the door, which got everyone else moving.

"Wow," I murmured.

Jagger looked at me and shook his head—this time not at me though. "Just shows you that it takes all kinds."

"How prophetic," I said and this time his hand was on my lower back, so I immediately felt safe and could care less about Pansy's nutty eulogy.

Okay, I'd relive her whacko words over and over to see if it would help my case—but later. I mean, Jagger's hand was on my back.

We crossed the street followed by the crowd of mourners, who were now laughing and chatting about Pansy—and, I might add, agreeing with everything she'd said.

"Seems as if finding Payne's murderer is going to be difficult if one considers motive," I said.

Jagger looked at me. "Sure is. Feels like a mob mentality. And they are all in agreement."

"Well, maybe Pansy will now have a staff of dedicated workers. She certainly didn't need to convince them of anything." I stopped and took Jagger's arm. "Hey, you think she did that on purpose?"

"Did what?"

"You know. Said those horrible things about her brother because, one, she knew how they all felt. Two, she figured she'd earn their undying loyalty, since her brother isn't coming back. And three, she's a damn good actress, *or* maybe she killed her own brother!"

Jagger looked at me for a few seconds while the others got closer. He leaned near and said, "Hmm. I hadn't thought of that."

I slugged his arm. "You're full of shit."

I knew that I never would think of anything case-related before Jagger did, but I was thrilled and proud of myself for thinking of something that he already had.

Baby steps. Baby steps to a successful career as an investigator.

Before anyone walked past us, Jagger led me to the front door, which was opened as if Pansy was welcoming everyone into her home for a real celebration.

"Pansy," I called out, while Jagger nudged me inside.

We walked through the beautiful Tudor-style entry-way and on into the living room—and Jagger grabbed my arm, which was a good thing. Because when I looked at the scene before us, my screaming kept me from rushing forward to do something about it—or passing out and breaking something important.

Eleven

"Oh, Lord. Talk about déjà vu," I said as Jagger held me by the shoulders. Amid the other mourners' gasping and screaming I looked at Pansy, sitting in a lovely hunter green brocade armchair—with a knife sticking out of *her* chest. Her lap formed a kind of catch basin for her blood. There was an enormous amount too.

Ashamedly, all I could think about was how she and her twin sure were alike, like clones.

One of the newer EMT women stepped forward, checked for a pulse, looked at the crowd and shook her head.

Lilla said, "Oh, my. I shall call 911."

I wanted to say don't bother, since there were plenty of paramedics and EMTs here to do something, but again, an ambulance could not transport a dead body, and by all appearances, Pansy fell into that category. So, the cops were the next logical step.

"Everyone just leave," Sky said. He, Mario and ER Dano tried to clear the room.

The morbid rubbernecking continued as nearly everyone had to take a look at Pansy, make a comment (usually negative, like the ones about her brother) and turn and walk out, most of them shaking their heads.

"Working here is starting to scare me," I said to Jagger.

"It is getting a bit odd. I'll see what Lieutenant Shatley has to say. I'm guessing he'll take this case, since it will tie in with Payne's murder."

I said a few "eternal rest grant unto her, oh, Lord" prayers in my head, and then grabbed Jagger's arm. "That is the same kind of knife," I muttered, "that was used on her brother. I'm not a cutlery expert, Jagger, but I vividly remember the other one, and that is the same handle, as if it came from a set."

He looked at me and smiled. "Good job, Sherlock."

Despite the dead body in the room, I was thrilled. Hey, Jagger compliments were few and far between.

He started to walk toward the door, and I took one more look at Pansy's body.

And her eyelids fluttered!

Now, being a nurse I knew that a dead body still sometimes twitches, but Pansy's eye fluttering was not a twitch.

"Jagger! Dano! She's still alive!" I shouted and rushed toward her.

They hurried over, along with Sky, Mario, Buzz and even Lilla, who was mumbling in French.

Dano grabbed her hand. "Still warm."

Wow. Even though that EMT had checked for a pulse (and it must have been so weak that she couldn't feel it), and with Pansy's gray pallor and rigid posture, we all thought there was no point in trying to treat her. And now this.

Pansy Sterling had appeared dead!

Either she was a damn good actress or some miracle had just occurred—and it simply wasn't her turn to die.

Before I knew it, the crackerjack staff had her on a stretcher, started an IV, and had placed packing around the knife so as not to jiggle it on the way to the hospital. We all knew not to pull it out, or she could bleed to death.

Jagger was on the phone to Shatley, who said he would be here in minutes. Everyone was to vacate the crime scene, so when Jagger got off the phone, he led me to the porch.

"Could be the break that we need."

We needed to get the case solved soon, before someone else was stabbed, I thought—

Make that before *I* was stabbed, since I'd already been threatened. Then I had another thought: Since Pansy had been stabbed, too, then she wasn't involved in Payne's death. Being a sibling of five kids, two sisters, two brothers, I was relieved to think that a sister hadn't killed her brother.

I nodded at Jagger. "Hopefully she can tell us who did this to her."

Before Jagger could answer, sirens filled the air as ER Dano and Buzz drove off with Pansy in an ambulance, and the police showed up simultaneously. Sky went with Dano and Buzz, even though he was a pilot. I figured he was doing his part.

Never a dull moment in this business, I thought.

Out in the parking lot, I said to Jagger, "Hope we make it to the hospital before she . . . you know."

He merely looked at me, and I guessed he was thinking the same thing that I was. Pansy might have "dodged a bullet"—but would it ricochet back and get her? She really didn't look all that good when they shipped her off.

I jumped into Jagger's Suburban and slammed the door. He took off before I could even fasten my seat belt. I said a silent prayer that Pansy lived. And not just because I needed her.

Jagger drove faster than usual, and for some reason—maybe because he was Jagger—I wasn't worried we'd get pulled over by one of Hope Valley's finest. If we did and they saw Jagger, I'm certain they would have nodded, smiled and let him go.

I just knew it.

When Jagger pulled into the hospital parking lot, I noticed Ambulance #456 still in the driveway of the ER.

We parked and got out, hurried to the emergency-room entrance and went inside.

Staff bustled about, running in and out of Trauma Room #1. Pansy. Had to be. There was a blackboard on the far wall, which listed patients, their conditions, time of arrival and a few other needed tidbits. I was thrilled to see her name there instead of erased off.

"Think they'll let us talk to her?" I asked, knowing full well Jagger would get us in somehow. I saw several police in the hallway near the room and figured they'd get first crack at questioning, but we wouldn't be far behind.

Because, of course, Jagger was Jagger.

Nurse Grosch hurried past us with a "hey, Pauline," and headed into Room #1. The few times I'd been here with ER Dano, I did get to meet several of the staff. Maybe that would help. I noticed one of the EMT women, Jennifer Shelton, who had been on duty during the memorial service. She stood near the main desk, talking to one of the nurses, Kim Gonzalez. I remembered her from when we'd brought in the phone-cord-around-the-neck lady.

"Excuse me," I said to Jagger, who looked a bit surprised. Good. At least he'd realize I had a brain and could work my cases alone too. I walked over to the two women, who were now talking with the receptionist. Her name badge read NANCY PRINGLE.

The receptionist looked up. "May I help you?"

She probably didn't recognize me in my little black dress as part of the TLC ambulance team. "Oh, hey, Nancy. I'm Pauline. A nurse. I was here with ER Dano the other day."

Kim looked up. "Hi. Sorry to hear about Pansy."

Hmm. According to that segue; my prayers were answered pretty darn quickly today. "Yes, a real shock. How is she?"

She and Jennifer, the EMT, looked at each other. Wow. What the heck? Was there something going on here, or was Pansy already gone?

"I'm not working that room, but the staff is still in there. So, that's a good sign," Kim said.

I nodded and leaned toward her. "Look, is there any chance that I can get in to see her?"

All three looked at me as if I were nuts. Jagger was standing near the desk, and his expression wasn't far off from theirs. I ignored him and tried to think of a lie. Again, that was not my forte. Nothing. I had nothing. What could I say that wouldn't cause suspicion of my asking?

"Why?" Nancy asked.

Oh, well. That was not unexpected, I thought. "I . . . er . . . ah . . . just want to see how she is. I mean, I work for her, you know."

They looked around the bustling ER. No one else from TLC was there other than Jennifer and her partner.

"I know no one else is here to check, but Pansy is a wonderful woman."

Jagger grabbed my arm and yanked me to the side, managing to shake his head at me while pulling me down the hallway. Over my shoulder I said, "Give her my regards," and turned to push Jagger's hand off my arm. "What the hell are you doing?"

He looked at me, and I knew he wanted to ask the same thing of me—and understandably so.

"Okay. Okay. Can't you give a girl kudos for trying?"

"Trying? How many employees of TLC do you see here? And how many would actually come here, with the reputation of the Sterling bosses? None, Pauline."

He was correct. I knew it. In all the shocking happenings of today, I wasn't really thinking clearly, but telling that to Jagger would be a mute point. He didn't do sympathy very well and that was the *last* emotion I'd want from him anyway.

"I get it." I refused to say I was sorry though.

"Let's go get a coffee," Jagger said, walking toward the sign for the cafeteria.

"But what if. . ." I paused. If Pansy died, we would miss our chance, but the cops surely would find out something if Pansy ever came to enough to answer. "Never mind," I added, even though Jagger wasn't even paying attention to me.

Glancing out a window in the hallway, I noticed a male figure in the parking lot that looked an awful lot like Sky. Hmm. Could he have remained here only to make sure his boss was all right, or was there more to it?

* * *

In the cafeteria, we found Buzz waiting in a short line. "Hey," I said. "How was she when you brought her in?"

At first he looked at me as if he didn't know me. Had to be the damn black dress. Why was it that no one knew me unless I was decked out in my hated scrubs? Had they all only related to me as Nurse Pauline? Damn!

Finally recognizing me, he started to answer, but I found myself looking around for Dano. Oh, geez. And with Jagger only feet away. Then again, I shared a few kisses with him, but he'd never made any attempt at asking me out, so no way was I beholden to him.

No way.

Jeremy sighed. "She was in bad shape. Great deal of blood lost. But when they hooked her up, she did have normal sinus rhythm, although also tachycardia."

"I'd certainly imagine her heart would be pumping faster with a blood loss." Jeremy knew this, but I figured my simple explanation would help him relax with me and realize that I knew medicine.

"Yeah. Blood loss." He turned to the girl behind the counter. "Hot-dog platter."

Suddenly I realized none of us had eaten. There was probably a huge buffet of sorts at Pansy's house. Maybe the cops would eat it. I smiled to myself and looked around for Jagger . . . who was gone.

Things like that didn't even faze me any longer.

After more chitchat, and with the departure of Jagger, I followed Jeremy to his table—where Dano sat.

My hands started to tremble.

My heart started to beat a bit faster, although not in tachycardia.

And my voice came out in a husky tone when I said, "Hey, Dano." Even I was impressed with it, and by the looks of him, he was too.

Good, since Jagger was gone.

"May I join you?" I asked.

Jeremy said, "Of course," at the same time Dano said, "No need for an invitation."

Hmm. Did that mean I was always welcome to sit with him 'cause of our kiss or 'cause I was an employee of TLC?

I was going with the kiss.

"Have you heard how she's doing?" I asked, sitting.

Dano shook his head. "We usually don't get reports from the ER staff." He sounded a bit pissed, and I wondered if that was because Pansy was an employer, or if Dano had another reason why he wanted to know if she was going to make it.

Hopefully that reason was because she was a human being and deserved to live, like everyone else.

And nothing dreadful.

I hung around the ER until the looks of the staff indicated they wanted to throw me out. After way too much small talk, Nancy even tried to look busy instead of talking to me. When Ted Grosch came out of Pansy's room, I asked how she was doing. He said, "She'll be off to surgery soon. Still alive, but barely," and then hurried off.

But barely. Damn.

Two of the cops standing by the doorway started to look at me suspiciously. Of course they didn't know who I was and Shatley was nowhere to be found, so I figured I'd better hightail it out of there before I was questioned as a suspect. Only Shatley knew I worked with Jagger. That was my cushion to fall back on and keep me from possible incarceration. There was that breaking and entering time. . . .

When I got to the exit, I realized Jagger had abandoned me without a ride. Damn it. Pulling out my cell phone, I stepped to the side while another ambulance company brought in an obviously "in labor" woman, who was cursing at her husband nonstop.

I winked at her and punched in Goldie's number. "Hey. I need a lift from the ER."

First, in his usual way, he shrieked, until I hollered into the cell to calm down. "A case, Gold. I'm fine."

"Oh, good. I'll swing by to get you, but I'm meeting Miles for lunch at Madelyn's. You'll of course join us."

I couldn't even use the excuse that I was not dressed up enough for the swanky—the only swanky—restaurant in Hope Valley. Sitting by the Connecticut River and having a Coors Light might be just what the doctor ordered right now. "I'm in," I said, to Goldie's delight, and I leaned against the wall to wait.

Miles hugged me as if we were long-lost buddies instead of roommates who had just seen each other that morning. "I'm thrilled you can join us."

I always felt as if I were interrupting a romance with these two, but that was my take on it, not theirs. I knew that much but still always wanted to give them some space. But I was famished, dressed to kill, and had nowhere else to go but home to flop on my bed and contemplate a horrible day.

"This turned out perfect," I said, following the hostess as she made small talk with Goldie, who just about everyone knew, and showed us to a table with a water view, since Goldie had insisted on as much for his "Suga."

The woman set the menus down on the table, turned and stepped to the side, holding the chair for Goldie.

He smiled, began to sit and gasped.

Miles looked in the direction Goldie had and said, "Shit."

Confused, I turned to see what the big deal was—and froze.

Sitting across the room was Jagger, still in his fantastic suit. Still looking like a *GQ* model from Testosterone Heaven, and still not noticing me.

Thank the good Lord, since across the table from him was the most gorgeous woman I'd ever seen.

Gorgeous with a damn capital "G."

Twelve

"You've got it all over her," I heard Goldie say as if in the distance.

Maybe that was because I was in shock, jealous as all get out, although I tried to tell myself I had no right to be. I was still staring.

Long black hair touched her shoulders. A mint green skirt suit with snakeskin shoes, of matching green and black, ivory skin set off by the darkened locks and no wedding ring blurred in the distance. My damn vision cleared enough, unfortunately, to notice teeth whiter than Pansy's pallor. Okay, bad analogy, but someone that looked so perfect as this chick deserved a bad/ morbid analogy.

Plus, she was with *my* Jagger!

She looked at him several times and smiled—like a freaking magazine model, airbrushed and all. She made "flirt" the word of the day.

He looked in her eyes and returned a smile. I had to think, though, that it wasn't too genuine-looking and maybe should be classified as a half smile. I felt my complexion turn a lovely shade of green while I told myself that I was trying to manipulate the image for my own satisfaction. Honest Abe that I was. I really knew little to nothing about Jagger's life outside of our investigating together and that he vacationed in Newport, Rhode Island, once a year.

Maybe he was making it perfectly clear that we were only coworkers.

I looked at my roomies. "Guys, I'm not really hungry," I said, and turned and walked away despite their protesting.

I yanked my cell phone out of my pocket. After I punched the buttons with much more force then needed and had to redial three times, I heard a voice that made me feel oh-so-much better.

"Hey, Nightingale."

Ah. . .

Earlier I'd only had to swallow a teeny, tiny bit of my pride to invite myself out to eat with ER Dano, I thought, as I looked at him across the table of the Dew Drop Inn diner, Hope Valley's famous.

Although I'd made the call to him on a whim and telling myself that if Jagger was spending time with the likes of Airbrushed Lady, then I shouldn't be pining for him. I had to have a love life of my own—it had only dawned on me after the fifth ring that Dano might refuse.

I smiled at him.

He smiled back.

Thank goodness for not refusing. Seems as if dear Dano was my saving grace today. He'd eaten with Buzz earlier, but graciously offered to meet me for coffee, which I took as a good sign.

"I feel a bit overdressed for this place," I said, knowing it was stupid small talk, but Dano—make that *most guys*—didn't do small talk very well. Actually, they didn't talk nearly as much as women, and when there was a lull in the conversation, I always felt obligated to fill in the dead airspace.

Dead airspace. I was full of lousy analogies today.

He looked at me. His eyes drifted down toward my hint of cleavage. Actually, when I bought the dress under Goldie's impeccable taste and guidance, it fit differently. There was no cleavage. At least that's the way it was after Goldie tucked here and there and then let me look in the mirror and insisted I buy it.

When I dressed today though, there was about a two-inch cleavage that I couldn't tuck away. Gotta love my Goldie!

And apparently Dano couldn't help noticing too.

I felt like a naughty nurse, but leaned a bit forward. He said, "You look fine."

Fine? I gathered a statement like that coming from ER Dano could be likened to a compliment from Jagger. "Fine" was like the word "fantastic" in a normal guy's vocabulary. I had actually convinced myself that it was so.

As I had convinced myself that ER Dano and Jagger were *not* normal, run-of-the-mill guys.

Way too delicious for that!

He took a sip of his black coffee and looked at me, his eyes drifting occasionally to my chest as he spoke. "Pansy is in recovery now."

"Oh, wow. Good. Then she survived the surgery." I nodded. "That's great." How I wanted to ask if I could talk to her, but realized I would have to do it on my own. I'd snuck into places before and was getting quite good at it. Besides, who'd question me in my scrubs? Certain there'd be police guards outside her door, I'd have to come up with something. Although lying was not my strong suit, I was getting better and better at it. Hey, practice makes perfect, Stella Sokol always said. However, I'm quite certain she never meant to use it for lying.

In fact, I *know* she never meant to use it for lying. She was the main reason I stunk at lying—her and "Sister Mary I Can Get Away With Anything I Want Because I'm a Nun." I think I had her throughout all eight years of Catholic School, and still had the scars on my knuckles from the wooden ruler to prove it.

Dano sipped at his coffee, and I realized my mind wandering had caused a lull, the dead-airspace thing. Natch, he didn't fill it, but merely looked at me over the rim of his mug.

I owed Goldie for the cleavage.

"So, are you going back to the hospital to see her tonight?"

Dano looked confused, and well he should. There seemed to be no love lost between he and Pansy. Make that Pansy and any employee, so I guessed her room was not going to be filled with get-well cards, balloons or flowers.

What a sad life to be so disliked.

And, damn it, what a difficult case now, since there could possibly be a gazillion suspects! I made a mental note to ask Jagger . . . damn him . . . if he'd gotten anything from the lieutenant.

I would give Jagger credit in that he did share what he learned with me if it pertained to my case. For as competitive as he seemed, he did try to help me be the best investigator I could be. He taught me well.

But just what was he teaching Airbrush Lady?

I told myself to stop that and shoved a spoonful of my clam chowder into my mouth.

"Nice day, weather-wise," Dano said, taking me by surprise.

I nodded, yet hadn't paid attention. The day had flown by so far. When I looked out the diner's window, I noticed everyone with shorts, hats, tees or sunglasses on and a gentle breeze said it must be a gorgeous New England day. Very low humidity.

I swallowed. "You're right. It is." After several minutes, I had finished my meal pretty much in disappointing silence. ER Dano was a pip. Quite possibly harder to figure out than Jagger—which seemed like a monumental impossibility.

He paid the check even though I insisted I should, we walked out the door—with a dull disappointment in my gut—and I turned toward my Volvo.

"Give me your address, Nightingale."

I swung around, scowling. "Huh?"

"Be ready in an hour. Can't let this day go to waste." With that he turned and walked toward his white pickup truck.

Ready? Ready? How ready? "Hey, wait!"

He turned around.

"Wear what?" I shaded my eyes with my hand since the late-afternoon sun was so crisp, clear and bright. "What should I be ready for?"

He looked at me as if I should have known. "Beach."

I gave him my address and he waved away my directions and I had no doubt ER Dano could find me. And not because he drove an ambulance and knew the entire town of Hope Valley and surrounding areas.

Nope.

ER Dano *always* got what he wanted. Of that I was quite certain. Always? Hmm?

Watch out, Pauline!

"I think the pink is better than the peacock blue," Goldie said as he hustled about me, stepping over the pile of clothes on the floor. My clothes. On my bedroom floor! And me standing there in my bra and white jeans without a hint of embarrassment in front of these two jokers. I didn't even have to tell myself it was like a bathing-suit top.

Miles hurried out of my closet. "Gold . . . hon, blue has always made her pale gray eyes look more silver. More noticeable. And she needs that with her hair. You know, so light next to that skin."

Goldie leaned into me as he held up the blue spandex top close to my face. "I see what you mean, but it also makes her pale complexion look . . . well, forgive me, Suga, but paler. No. She needs more help than blue."

I grabbed the top from him. "You two busybodies are going to make me late. I'll wear *yellow*."

They both screeched.

I shook my head and laughed. "Well, it's only a trip to the beach. I'm sure we'll just walk along the boardwalk and besides; I'll need my denim jacket. With the sea breeze, it's probably cooler down there. So it almost doesn't matter what I have on underneath."

Goldie grabbed the blue top from my hands and stuck the pink one in its place. "Jacket schmacket. Make sure you wear uncovered spandex long enough for him to get a load of your perky—"

I smacked him on the arm.

"You two are pathetic." I looked Goldie in the eye.

"And stop trying to force another guy on me 'cause you don't want me interested in Jagger!"

Goldie's face dropped.

"Damn it." I hurried toward him and wrapped my arms around his gigantic frame. "Sorry. I'm sorry, Gold. I know you always have my best interest in mind and keep telling me that Jagger is addictive, like cocaine, and will mess me up. I know. I know." I felt him lift his head and in the mirror behind him, noticed him grin. I pushed him away. "You shit!"

Miles broke out into hysterical laughter, and it was at that moment that I knew I loved these two as my best friends and couldn't move out of there anytime soon. It really didn't feel as if I were an intrusion.

Besides, I couldn't freaking afford it yet.

A bad choice in cosigning a car loan for an ex-friend and a bad addiction to a shopping habit, which I'd curtailed immensely lately, would keep me there a bit longer.

"I'm gonna be late if we keep this up." I grabbed the pink top—since in reality, Goldie was the fashion expert—and said, "Gold, do my makeup. Please? I'll wear the stinking pink."

After Goldie got his hands on me, I looked into the mirror and said, "Wow. You could get a job in Hollywood with your expertise. I look better than I really am!"

The doorbell rang and suddenly my stomach dropped.

We'd had a lot of fun getting me ready—but now I was actually going out with ER Dano—*alone*!

A girl might be taking a big chance with a guy like him. . . .

* * *

"Cold?" Dano asked.

He pulled into the parking lot of the beach. We'd driven down to the Connecticut shoreline and stopped at Meig's Point in the Hammonasset Beach State Park. "Uh-uh. I'm fine for now." I could picture Goldie in my head, shaking his head at me covering up the spandex. Dano probably had been too busy driving to notice, so I'd have to tough it out for a while.

Damn. I was feeling very "naughty nurse" again.

Seems the hot, sexy, probably burned-out paramedic brought that out in me.

Consequently, no jacket schmacket for now.

He pulled the truck into a space near the brown nature-center building. Actually, we pretty much had our pick of spaces. The place wasn't very crowded, and I guessed that was because it was a weeknight. Good. *We'd have more privacy on the beach*, I thought, and then I also thought, *For what, Pauline? For what!*

Oh well, a girl could dream, and ER Dano was definitely dream material.

He got out of the truck, and I figured I'd better get out too or be left behind, but he surprised me. ER Dano actually opened the door for me! How very un-Jagger-like.

I decided right then—and having a visual of Airbrush Lady actually was the catalyst—that I was not going to think of Jagger again. Well, not tonight anyway.

I rather liked this guy. . . .

We walked toward the boardwalk that led to a pavilion on the beach, and Dano placed his hand on the small of my back. I loved that! It was such a minor little thing but said a wealth of romantic stuff in my mind. Dano wanted to make physical contact and that was fine with me, so I leaned into him a bit.

When we walked through the pavilion onto the beach, a gust of sea air tousled my hair, pushed me into Dano a bit more (really!) and made my perky you-know-whats stand out in the stupid Spandex. Oh, my.

Naughty nurse versus CSIC alumni (Catholic-school-induced conscience). Talk about being conflicted!

We walked for several minutes, and then Dano stopped, held my arm, slipped his feet out of his cowboy boots and yanked off his socks. He looked at me as if we were in the throes of passion and he was waiting for me to disrobe.

Trying to ignore how hot that made me feel, I smiled, bent down and slipped my feet out of my little white flats. No nylons. The cool sand felt gritty against the soles of my feet, but it was kinda neat to be sans shoes. Dano took them from me and with his, set them on the edge of the pavilion boardwalk.

"Look, the sunset is beautiful," I said, pointing toward the russet sky in the west.

Before I could mention the cloud formation like some dummy, his arms were around me, pulling me closer and whispering, "I'm seeing beauty all right." His lips landed on mine—not so softly, which was pure ER—while his arms tightened their hold.

All I could think of for a second was, my "perky problem" was going to be solved in this position, since I was now burning hot.

Dano kissed me for several seconds and then eased his tongue past my lips and into the warmth of my mouth. Ah. What a fantastic feeling!

I ran my hands up his back to reach his cheeks. When I stood on my tiptoes, I couldn't resist brushing back his hair with both of my hands.

He moaned.

I joined him while we kissed for several more minutes.

Without a word, he led me toward the little sand dunes filled with bushes and wild grass of sorts—a perfect spot in which to hide from the world.

I thought of the cold sand for a second, since I'd left my jacket in the car, but before I knew it, Dano had his jean jacket off, laid it down, smoothed it out best he could and waved a hand over it.

I laughed, joining the squawking gulls and crashing waves in the musical ambiance of the shore.

Dano eased me down onto the hillside of sand and joined me. I found myself moving closer, snuggling, kissing and even wrapping my leg over his. It felt . . . so right. So damn right.

Ah. . . .

Thirteen

My fantastic, larger-than-life make-out session
with ER Dano had me all hot and bothered and
not in the least in need of a jacket. With no words spoken, we
shared an intimacy that I was barely able to stop.

"Hey, there's a time and place for everything, Nightingale," he said in all his realism, yet they were the
most disappointing words I'd ever heard!

Dano leaned to the side, bent forward for a quick
kiss on the lips and then took my hand into his. "You
fit perfectly."

Wow. Nice sentiment.

"Um," I mumbled. Funny how when you click with
a guy, your intelligence sometimes bottoms out.

He was correct about the time and place, although
for a few fleeting, CSIC-less minutes, I might have gone
a bit farther if *he* hadn't stopped us.

Pauline Sokol: real naughty nurse!

For a change I'd thrown caution to the wind—and
I loved it! Hey, I told myself, this was the twenty-first
century and women were *allowed* to have sensual feelings. Even allowed to be the ones to *start* the romantic/
sensual actions.

But this really wasn't the place, so I tucked my desires into the back of my mind in a new folder called "ER Dano . . . Yum" and sat silently looking at the sunset.

We left the beach, since it closed at sunset, and he drove me home. He said good night with a decent kiss and, most important, an "I'll call you."

Now, I was no fool. Having a guy say he'd call was akin to having someone say "I'll see you" when you meet them on a vacation, they live on the other side of the world and you didn't even exchange email addresses. I'd long ago learned not to trust those words when a guy said them, so I quickly added, "When?" and Dano and I soon had a date set up for Friday night.

I mentally patted myself on the back when I went inside my condo and marked our date down on the calendar.

A light at the end of the single Pauline Sokol tunnel.

My mother would be stuffing lacy table favors with candy-coated almonds in pastel colors right now, if I told her.

No one was home, so I hugged Spanky for a bit, set him outside and pressed the PLAY button on the phone recorder.

"Pauline Sokol? This is your m-m-o-t-h-e-r-r-r-r." The last word came out in a slow, deep voice, much like Darth Vader's.

I shook my head but sat down and listened, knowing the tone was all in my mind.

"Your sister Mary is coming over for lunch tomorrow. I thought you might want to join us—"

"I'm gonna have to pass despite the tempting offer," I mumbled.

"—Oh, and Uncle Walt has to have his wisdom tooth out. Who would touch an old man's wisdom tooth? Can't they just dope him up so he's comfortable? Pauline?" Silence. "I thought I heard a click and maybe you came in and picked up the phone. Just to let you know, you are not home much lately. Well, ever since that job. You know *that* job. . . ."

I laid my head down on the counter and shut my eyes. I wanted to keep smacking my head against the counter, but that might dent the counter, and Miles would be pissed. I wasn't crazy . . . yet.

"—Okay, I guess you did not come home. From where? It is nearly eight o'clock on a Wednesday night. Where are you at this late hour?"

This time I was really tempted to slam my head into the counter—a few times. Instead I sat up and went to press the STOP button. Too much Stella Sokol at this time of the night could cause wicked nightmares.

"—Well, you call me before I go to sleep so I don't worry. It is still eight o'clock, well, four minutes after. Wait. Wait a minute. I've got five after on my watch."

I could hear she had put her hand over the phone receiver to yell, "Michael, what time do you have?" Daddy was probably asleep, so she took her hand away and said, "I go to sleep at nine sharp, Pauline."

As if I didn't know that. Creature of habit Stella Sokol had gone to bed at nine sharp and woke up at six sharp my entire life. I only hoped that as a baby, I woke her up a few times during the night.

Mentally I chastised myself and stuck my finger on the STOP button—

"Meet me at our spot at ten. . . ."

Shoot! I stopped the message before it finished, but knew full well whose voice that was and where our spot was.

Ah . . .

As I'd stripped off my beach outfit to don dark clothes, I knew Jagger had called to work on the case. My case. Our case, as it so often became. I appropriately had stuck on "investigating" clothing, along with stuffing my pockets with work tools like gloves, my camera beeper and a tissue (okay, that was mother induced, like don't leave home without going to the bathroom first or wearing clean undies).

Once dressed, out the door and into my car, I pulled into the Dunkin Donuts parking lot and into a space near the back. Soon Jagger's SUV drove up beside me. Without a word I got out and hopped into his car, and we were off without any explanations needed.

Before long, we had come to the intersection where TLC Land and Air was located. My heart started to race in anticipation of finding something, some clue, no matter how tiny, that would jump-start this case.

Because right now we had nothing.

One murder, one attempted murder and medical insurance fraud being committed. The only guarantees so far.

I looked at Jagger. "Anything on Pansy?"

He parked on a nearby side street and said, "She's in a coma."

"Damn. I was afraid of that. Her body must be in shock after the blood loss and trauma of surgery."

He looked at me, and I ignored how damn good he

looked. "What are the chances she'll pull out of it?"

"Geez, your guess is as good as mine."

"I'm not guessing, Sherlock. I'm asking your medical opinion."

My shoulders stiffened. "I *know* that, Jagger. What I meant was that no one can really say. I doubt even the surgeon would give you decent odds." With that, I got out and stood on the sidewalk.

He followed me and took my arm to lead me toward our destination. "Someone's a little testy tonight."

I pulled my arm free. How I wanted to shout something about Airbrush Lady, but was too smart to say anything. "All's fair in love and war" came to mind, and then I told myself we were not lovers, but coworkers. So I said, "Long day. Sorry."

He nodded, took my arm again and before I knew it, we were at the back door of the building where Pansy lived. The Tudor house was built amongst the other buildings as if it had been there first and everything else sprung up around it.

"B and E?" I whispered.

"Don't touch anything. Don't *take* anything," Jagger said as he placed something in the lock and fiddled with it. In a few moments it popped open, he turned the handle, looked over my shoulder and waved me through the open door.

Talk about eerie. I felt as if Pansy and Payne were standing in the hallway looking at us.

Something touched my face! I started to scream but found a gloved hand over my mouth. I swung around and found Jagger looking me in the eye. "Cobweb," he whispered. "And no great surprise," he added as he shined his flashlight across the foyer.

It looked like something out of *The Munsters*.

Dark, dank, and medieval in appearance, the place looked like a Tudor house, all right—only one that was centuries old and not cleaned since the day it was built.

"Geez," I mumbled after Jagger took his hand away.

"I'll say. But not surprising."

I was surprised, I thought as we made our way into the living room—which was as colorful as Payne's office, including fifties décor. "I love that old television," I said, looking at a pine-console TV that had to be very old. "These two were really nuts. His office taste, yet her living room. Let's go see the kitchen."

No wonder we'd all come in a different way for Pansy's after-memorial-service gig.

I followed Jagger down a dark hallway to a swinging door. He held it open so it wouldn't swing back and smack me in the face (or maybe so it wouldn't swing back and make any noise) and I walked in. "Wow."

The kitchen looked like Mother Goose had decorated it. Country/nursery rhyme was an understatement. Pots and pans hung from the ceiling. Braided rugs covered the hardwood floors and dried flowers hung from every nook and cranny possible. And if I had a nickel for every duck, goose and chicken in the room, I could quit my job.

We could only shake our heads. How sweet! Simultaneous head shaking.

Usually we'd get right down to the business of snooping, but both of us had our curiosities so piqued that we made a tour of this "fun house" before starting.

The bathrooms were decorated like the ocean,

complete with real water inside the windows, which bubbled constantly (I felt a bit seasick). Upstairs, the master bedroom was done in monochromatic black and red this time. If it weren't for the rest of the house, I would have thought Pansy had no imagination until Jagger opened the door to a spare bedroom.

Junglemania.

The entire room was done in animal prints, including a bear rug. I could only whisper, "Goldie would kill for this place," and then caught myself. "Oops. Bad choice of words."

"Yeah," Jagger said, but I noticed he was as intrigued with the place as I was and nearly speechless too. A real rarity. "We need to get going," he warned once he obviously came to his senses.

I followed him down to the living room, where he motioned for me to start looking on one side of the room. "Gloves on?"

I curled my lips at him and held my gloved hands up, wiggled my fingers and started to put all of them down except the middle one—then caught myself and made a fist instead.

"Good girl, Sherlock."

I smiled despite myself and started to open drawers—not even sure what the hell I was looking for—but knowing I'd realize it when I saw it.

After several minutes of snooping, we came up cold and headed to the other rooms. Despite the very interesting objects we'd found, including a horse's bridle and whip in her bedroom—neither of us wanted to go there—and scented soaps in male fragrances in the bathroom, we ended up in the hot African-style spare bedroom. And hot it was.

My face burned each time Jagger or I discovered some sexual device. That was what I termed everything we found. H . . . O . . . T.

Pansy was no wallflower. That was for sure.

Jagger stood in the center of the sexual jungle while I tried not to blush. He shook his head, which looked like a pissed expression in my book. Maybe he was embarrassed with all the "toys" we'd found.

Then again, this was Jagger.

If anyone would come out of this embarrassed, it would be *me*.

I started to walk toward him and tripped over a "toy" on the floor. No way was I even going to imagine how *that* thing worked. However, on the way to falling, I reached out and grabbed onto a handle on the wall.

A vine-covered, fur-covered (black leopard, I assumed) swing came out of the ceiling and smacked Jagger right in the back.

"Oh!" I shouted, steadying myself.

"Damn it," Jagger mumbled, pushed the swing to the side and went to the wall where he jiggled with the handle until the thing disappeared back into the ceiling like some snake retreating into a hole.

I could merely stand there and watch, amazed that Jagger could work the damn thing, along with amazed at what Pansy did on the thing.

Jagger motioned for me to follow him, so I figured our search here had been futile—and we weren't going to play Tarzan and Jane.

On the way out, the lounge chair (which was what I was calling it although tiger stripes and vibration did not exactly say La-Z-Boy) caught my eye.

It did look rather comfortable, yet there were no

arms to it. One could easily straddle . . . Whoops. Better not go there.

For some reason, I walked toward it though, pressed the ON button and stepped back.

The top flew open, revealing a stack of papers.

I looked at Jagger.

Jagger looked back at me.

And the papers sat there begging to be read.

Fourteen

It seemed like hours passed while Jagger and I stared at each other and then at the papers sitting inside the sex chair, which is what I now called it in my mind. *Had to be*, I thought, looking around this room.

Apparently Jagger pulled his thoughts to the present sooner than I; he stepped forward and knelt near the chair.

Whoa.

Be still my heart and hormones.

I swallowed, mentally chastised myself, relived kissing ER Dano for a few nanoseconds (reminding myself we had a date, a real date, in two days) and bent down next to Jagger. My joints would kill me if I stayed this way too long, so I joined him on the floor, totally ignoring how our shoulders touched or our knees brushed each other's. Totally.

Although I had these sensual feelings being so near a hot guy, I told myself that Jagger and I were really only coworkers. Right now, ER Dano was a front-runner.

"Anything?" I whispered.

He seemed engrossed in a paper that he'd taken off the top of the pile. It appeared as if it had been thrown into the chair without being tucked inside one of the many folders.

"TLC carried dead bodies," Jagger said.

I raised my eyebrows. Probably looking like a curious kid, I said, "They can't. They can't carry dead bodies."

Jagger looked at me. Was that an "are you stupid" kinda look? I studied him a few seconds to make up my mind, but he saved me the time when he said, "You're absolutely right, Sherlock, but look at this." He held out the paper toward me.

Thankful it wasn't an insulting look, I shined my flashlight onto the paper. "Oh, my goodness. They carried dead bodies."

"Many times."

I looked at Jagger. "Why would an undertaker call an ambulance instead of transporting the dead body themselves?"

Jagger gave me a kinda "psychiatrist" look. That was a look that said, "What do you think?" much like a shrink would do to get the patient to talk on and on until they cured themselves.

I paused to think. Why the hell . . .

"Well," I said, "if they were too busy. That's it! They must have had calls simultaneously, and if TLC didn't get their bodies for them, they'd lose that customer to a competitor. There are only three funeral homes in Hope Valley, so the competition is pretty fierce." I sat back on my heels and noticed Jagger smile in the dim lighting.

My heart danced in my chest.

"So, TLC made extra money. But what about the

EMT and paramedics? They had to be involved—"

Jagger handed me a stack of papers from the folder on top. "Check out the names."

I flipped through the fraudulent papers, noticing the same four names over and over.

"These are all *fake* names."

Jagger pulled up to the drive-in window at Dunkin Donuts and once again ordered for both of us without asking. I couldn't even complain, because tonight was a Boston Cream kinda night. I needed the chocolate—and he knew it.

Once he handed me my order, he drove us to the back, the spot where we always parked—where no one would pay much attention to us—pulled in and shut off the motor.

He took a sip of his black coffee. "You're sure none of those names struck a chord with you?"

"Did they with you?" I bit down on my donut. Cream shot out the other end, landing on Jagger's dashboard. "Whoops. Sorry." I wiped at it, furious that it was all wasted. I really needed sugar *and* chocolate.

"Nope."

"Well, we've both worked at TLC the same amount of time and both of us are attuned to noticing things—"

He turned to me.

"Shut up. We both are. You just have more experience than me." I finished off my donut before I aimed the rest of the cream at him.

Licking my fingers, I watched him take a few sips of his coffee and then set the cup in the holder. "Damn it," he said. "We have to get to Pansy before she leaves this world."

My body shivered at the thought. "True," I said,

"but whoever killed Payne and stabbed her might *also* be trying to get to her."

"Is trying to get to her. *Is* trying," Jagger corrected. He cleared his throat and looked as if he were debating whether to tell me something.

"What?"

"Hmm?"

"Come on, Jagger. Spill. You know more."

"A few hours ago, one of the cops sitting guard outside of Pansy's room was hit from behind—"

"Shit!"

"Yeah. He wasn't knocked out completely and before whoever the culprit was could finish the job, an orderly came off the elevator."

"Did they see anything? Anyone?" I moved closer and leaned toward him as if that would pull words out of Jagger's mouth. "Huh?"

"Naw. The attacker disappeared so fast, neither the injured guard nor the orderly could even say if it was a man or woman. All they agreed upon was the color of the scrubs."

"What color?"

He looked at me and said, "Blue."

I really didn't relish dealing with a murderer. This fraud stuff was bad enough, but it seemed the stakes grew higher and higher in each of my cases. Evidently greed led to more than just stealing.

It led to murder.

Yikes.

"I'd think a woman might have to smack a guy's head a few times to knock him out." I looked at Jagger—wanting agreement.

He shook his head. "Feminists would smack you for that one, but you might have a point."

I was considering the word "might" as agreement. "Yeah. Hey, what do you think of Sky?"

Jagger's eyebrows grew together.

"Oh, stop that. Yeah, he's a hunk, but I'm talking suspect here. I found him in Payne's office after the stabbing."

"What do *you* think?"

I wanted to curse at him, but this was Investigation 101, Jagger style. "I'd be surprised, since he seems like such a great guy, but that doesn't discount him. Then again, what would his motive be?"

Jagger merely looked at me.

"Right. We don't have any. But it might be worth looking into."

He didn't nod, smile or concur. That, in Jagger-ese, was affirmation enough for me.

"You get any more of those phone messages?" he asked.

I shook my head. "Maybe the caller stopped so they wouldn't get caught."

Jagger just sipped his coffee.

We finished our drinks and donuts and Jagger started the engine. I looked at my watch and wanted to say I was tired and had to get up early to do my ride along tomorrow during orientation, but knew he was correct.

No time like the present to beat the "Angel of Death."

"We'll stop by your place to change," Jagger said as we headed south out of the Dunkin Donuts parking lot.

"Change?" I looked at myself all in black and thought, not only did I look perfect for spying, but hot too. Okay, that was my opinion.

"We can't go walking around the hospital like this, Sherlock."

Duh. Damn it, I hated when he got the drop on me like that. I should have figured that out myself, and would have, if it hadn't been such a long day.

And long it was. Seemed like ages since I had "necked" on the beach with ER Dano. I sighed.

"You all right?"

Oh . . . yeah. I looked at Jagger as we stopped at my condo. "I'm fine. Just fine." How I wanted to hop into my bed when I got inside though. Suddenly I pictured Airbrush Lady. Well, that was his prerogative.

"Be quiet so we don't wake Goldie or Miles," I said to Jagger as I unlocked the door. Wasted words, sure. Jagger was never a ball of energy or a chatty kinda guy anyway.

But what a guy!

Spanky looked up from the couch and smiled sleepily at . . . Jagger. *Good*, I thought, *you little traitor*. Good that you fell asleep down here waiting for me. The little guy always slept in my bed unless I wasn't there. Served him right.

I turned on the living-room light and walked toward the stairs. "I'll only be a few minutes."

Jagger was already on the couch with Traitor Spanky fast asleep on his lap!

When I walked into my room, the bed stood out as if it'd grown a hundredfold. It *called* to me. "Pauline," I heard it say, "just sit on my edge for a second. It won't hurt to do that. Only a second. My pillows are so soft."

Trying to ignore it, I went to my closet, where I shuffled through the many sets of scrubs hanging there.

What color would be most inconspicuous? Something rather dull. Rather drab.

Gray.

I certainly wouldn't stand out in gray. It'd match my eyes and make me look pale and tired—as if I were working the night shift. Perfect. And I sure didn't want to wear blue, like the person who'd attacked the guard.

I dressed quickly and sat on the edge of the enticing bed to put on my socks and clogs. Typical nursing shoes nowadays. Had to have comfortable feet in a job where one stood so much. I leaned back to pull my sock up. . . .

"Sherlock. Sherlock."

"Hmm?" I rolled to the side and felt something solid under my hip. In my groggy state, I reached down and pulled out a clog from underneath me. Then I blinked several times in confusion, only to look up into the dark, sexy eyes of . . . Jagger.

In . . . my . . . bedroom . . .

Oh, my.

Suddenly I flew upright and shoved the clog onto my foot. "All set. I'm all set!"

"And the sun is out," he said, nodding toward the window.

"Sun? At this hour?" Not sure what the heck hour it really was, I looked at my clock. "Damn. I fell asleep and have to be at TLC in a half hour." I remained on my side of the bed. "Why didn't you wake me?"

He raised one eyebrow. "I've had more luck raising the dead on several cases." With that he turned, walked toward the door and said over his shoulder, "Be ready after work. We can't drag our feet with Pansy's condition the way it is."

"Drag our feet? Drag *our* feet? You should have woken me up!"

He merely turned around and grinned.

And for the rest of the day I'd picture that look that reminded me—Jagger had stood by my bed, watching me sleep.

And, horrified, I'd keep wondering if I . . . snored.

I'd taken my own car to work so it wouldn't look as if Jagger and I were in cahoots. That was my idea, and I was still smiling about it as I stepped out into the parking lot and saw ER Dano pulling his truck into his space.

My knees knocked. Ouch.

Taking a big deep breath, I told myself to calm down. He was just a man. A man who I'd kissed. Liked kissing and hoped to kiss more.

I gave a very casual wave, smiled nicely and walked toward the door. Dano was fast on my heels.

"Hey, Nightingale." His uniform was clean but worn and wrinkled, unlike the snap, crackle, pop of Buzz's. However, Dano looked so male and hot, no one cared about damn wrinkles.

"Morning." I kept up my pace even though I wanted to slow, turn and grab him. Get that second kiss out of the way, you know.

"We'll be doing a daily on the southern border of town today. Be prepared to sit and wait for calls. Bring a magazine or something." With that he grabbed the door handle before I could, yanked and held it just long enough for me to get through.

I smiled so he couldn't see. For some reason, I didn't

think ER Dano would want me to acknowledge any gentlemanly moves from such a macho guy.

He turned toward the guys' locker room with a quick, "Later."

Too bad he seemed so burned out. Been there. Done that.

I walked to the reception desk, where Lilla sat talking on the phone in French. "Your mom?" I asked quietly.

She winked.

"Say hi for me." I sat on the chair opposite her desk and waited, wondering if she had anything helpful for me.

Lilla held her hand over the receiver. "Fabio is asking how the case is going." She shook her head and winked at me.

I groaned. "Fantastic. Tell him fantastic."

She continued on in French at what seemed like a lot more words than my "Fantastic. Tell him fantastic," but didn't translate for me after her "*Adieu*."

Frankly I could care less about the jerk Fabio. I leaned toward her and asked, "Hey, Lilla, anything for me?"

She curled her lips. "Pansy's guard was attacked—"

"Um. I know." For a few seconds I wondered how *she* knew. Did Jagger tell her? If so, when would Jagger have seen Lilla? Maybe Buzz had told her. They seemed to have been getting along. Yeah, Buzz. I was going with Buzz.

"Morning, ladies," a deep voice said from behind.

I swung around to see Sky heading toward the lounge. I looked at Lilla. "Yum."

She giggled. Only someone dressed exclusively in black and having a face and body like her could get away with giggling and not have it be annoying. "You are special for him, *chéri*?"

"Special?"

"Interested."

"Ah. No. Actually, he's a doll and one heck of a looker, but no." Just then ER Dano walked out of the locker room, and turned toward the lounge without a word. I remained silent.

Lilla's eyebrow rose.

"What?"

"Ah. I see." She winked at me and shuffled some papers on her desk.

I got up, turned toward the lounge and then looked back. "No you don't see. You can't see. There's nothing *to* see."

She chuckled. "You have the hots, as they say here, for *Monsieur* Dano."

It wasn't a question, merely an astute observation. "Does it really show?" I asked quietly.

She touched my hand. "No. No, *chéri*. It doesn't."

"Yeah, right. Thanks for that. I'll be more careful," I said, laughing.

While the two of us continued laughing, the intercom above my head boomed, "Copter 123, report. Copter 123, report."

"That for Sky?" I asked as Lilla's phone rang.

She nodded, answered and sounded concerned.

I waited a few moments for Lilla to hang up. "You have to go, *chéri*. They need a registered nurse on this flight. The trained helicopter paramedic will be with you too."

For a second I was glad I hadn't had my morning cup of tea yet, or else it might be climbing up my throat right about now.

* * *

Out on the helipad I met Nicky Straight, the paramedic. He explained that the patient we had to pick up needed some IV meds in transport that he wasn't trained to give.

Okay, I told myself. That didn't sound too bad. IV meds I could do. Watching for signs of distress I could do.

Whirr. Whirr. The helicopter's blades started to turn.

Riding in this tin can with blades, I couldn't do. Blades held on by only one nut, I'd heard.

Sky looked out the window and gave Nicky and me a thumbs-up. For a second, I thought of Sky being a suspect. But he had no motive for crashing a helicopter with a patient on it, so I tucked that potential fear away.

We both stuck our helmets on and stepped inside. I had to. A person's life depended on it and that's why they had hired me at TLC. Even though my job was investigating medical insurance fraud, I was a nurse first.

And always would be.

Not to mention I'd be alert for murder clues too.

Sky was a hell of a pilot, was all I could think, as we landed safely on the roof of the hospital, where a group stood waiting with the patient we had to transport to a larger trauma center.

They worked quickly and in such a synchronized way that I felt much calmer and safer at the job, especially when I looked into the pale blue eyes of the woman on the stretcher. She couldn't have been older than her early twenties. Her coloring was cyanotic and those lovely blue eyes were quite glassy.

Didn't look good at all.

I said a silent prayer and she started to mumble something. I couldn't hear much with the helmet on and the blades of the helicopter whirring, but I did make out "my kids."

It didn't matter what she said, how many kids she had, how old they were. I was bound and determined to get this mother to wherever she needed to go as safely as she needed to go.

So I put all my reservations out of my head.

"You really are one hell of a pilot," I said to Sky after we landed, unloaded our patient at the destination hospital and got back inside the helicopter.

Nicky strapped himself into his seat and shut his eyes. "I had a late night, you guys."

Sky shook his head. "Night, buddy." He turned to me. "Thanks. I try. Isn't too hard really, though, when you love your job."

And I could tell he did. We took off and while I was now able to watch the scenery below, Sky's voice came over the earphones in my helmet.

"You did good, Pauline."

I smiled and nodded, giving him the thumbs-up.

He chuckled in my ears and maneuvered the helicopter as if we were in a video game.

I laughed, but my insides didn't find it too funny. When I waved at Sky to calm down, he did.

"How long have you been doing this, Sky?" I thought he'd fly safer and straighter if I kept him busy in conversation.

He chuckled. "Three years with TLC. I used to fly with a hospital out in Phoenix for a few years before that."

"Oh, what brought you to Connecticut?" Suddenly I sounded interested. Maybe it was the altitude, although, yeah, I knew we weren't much higher than the power lines (at least I hoped we were higher than the power lines). Maybe it was because Sky was a real looker and a decent pilot to boot. Or, maybe he'd say something that would help my case, or cast suspicion on himself.

I sighed. Anything was possible, and right about now I needed *anything* to get this case moving—so I wouldn't have to lie to Fabio again.

Lies always seemed to jump up and bite me in a not-so-pleasant spot.

Sky seemed to hesitate, but at the same time there was a gust of wind that had us shaking. I'd hesitate too. No, I'd land this sucker in the nearest field so the wind wouldn't blow us into any power lines. Then he said, "Came here for a change and to be with someone special. Didn't work out though."

Even through the noise of the helicopter, I could hear him sigh and hear the pain in his voice.

A woman.

Sky had moved nearly across the country for a woman and he was still single and obviously alone. Lonely, maybe.

"Sorry."

He waved a hand at me, and I worried he needed that hand to fly. "No need to be. Wasn't meant to last." He chuckled. "No big deal. I've met several since that one, and will meet a hell of a lot more. You always live here?"

I groaned. "Does it show?"

He laughed.

I told him my entire life story, and before I knew it,

we were sitting on the helipad at TLC. "Nice, smooth landing," I said.

Sky nodded at me and got up and nudged Nicky, who woke up and appeared to be rather clearheaded. If I took a quick nap, I was groggy for days. I envied him.

"We need to fill out our paperwork, Pauline," Nicky said.

"Sure. Later, Sky." We nodded at each other and I followed Nicky into the lounge, where I got a hot tea, he a coffee. In a few minutes our paperwork was done, and I wondered if the woman Sky had come here to be with had anything to do with TLC.

The entire trip took so long I hadn't realized that I'd missed lunch. Now I was famished. No one could leave the lounge area since they were all waiting for calls. I wondered where ER Dano and Jagger were. Maybe together sitting on the southern side of town—talking about me! Yikes!

No. No way.

"I'm going to get something to eat. Doesn't anyone want anything?" I asked the gang, but they all declined since they were used to bringing their own food. Since I was still on orientation, I felt certain that I could leave, so I went to tell Lilla I would be gone.

"To where, *chéri*?" Her desk was neatly cleaned off. Lilla was a heck of a worker. Just like her mom. Hopefully the powers that be wouldn't throw her back across the border. I was fairly certain someone had pulled some strings so she could work here.

Fabio? Jagger? Her mom?

"I'm going to . . . hmm. Not sure." Half of the day was shot, although the flight was rewarding in the fact that we got the patient safely to her destination, and I'd given her meds on time and without any problems. Now I had to work on my "second" job. I looked at Lilla. "The hospital cafeteria has a chicken Caesar salad to die for."

Her dark eyes widened. "Oh, *chéri*, bad choice of words," she said, grabbed her purse from her desk and took my arm. "You drive. I have to redo my makeup, and we need to stop at your place so I can borrow some scrubs or something for a disguise."

With that Lilla and I set off to my place, and then to "lunch" in the hospital—only floors below comatose Pansy Sterling.

Hmm. . . .

Fifteen

Lilla, dressed in my white lab coat with my stethoscope draped over her shoulder, and I eyed each other and then our empty Caesar salad dishes. For some reason, I knew, just knew we were thinking the same thing.

"So, how do we get in to see her?" I said.

Looking very much like a doctor and sporting my old hospital employee ID—which my friend Sara in Human Resources arranged for me to keep as a souvenir from Saint Greg's Hospital, where I'd worked—Lilla winked at me and we stood and took our trays to the conveyor belt. My heart started to race.

We could get a huge break in my case—and I'd be doing it without Jagger!

That alone was reason enough to be there.

Although, to be honest with myself, I knew Jagger was keeping up behind the scenes with Sergeant Shatley about the stabbings and as much as he could find out about the fraud.

I "borrowed" Miles's ID badge and wore it backwards as if it'd turned around on its own. Although Lilla didn't look like my picture—unfortunately, that is—I figured no one would be looking that closely at the ID badge. As evidenced by all the males in the cafeteria, they'd all be looking at Lilla's face and other more important parts and not checking her ID. Besides, she acted so nonchalant, no one seemed suspicious.

A few people recognized me though, so I claimed I was there doing part-time float-pool work, so they couldn't connect me with any unit. Each time I acted as if I were in a hurry so there'd be little chitchat with old coworkers. Damn. I was getting better and better at this stuff.

I said a silent prayer that we could get in to see Pansy and she would be out of her coma enough to give us some information. Well, I wished she'd be out permanently for her own good.

Lilla and I made our way toward the Central Supply department, as that was the least traveled route. We could have gone straight up to Pansy's floor on the elevator, but I noticed a few docs that I'd worked with near the elevators and needed to avoid them. This area was like walking in the basement of the hospital: Very few people came through here.

"You look very good, Lilla. Very real."

She smiled. "Thanks you, *chéri*."

I winked and decided not to correct her English. She was turning out to be a real asset to my case. "I'm trying to think of a reason for us to use to get into the room. Past the guard. With one being attacked already, they might be more careful. Not that they weren't before."

I stopped talking and pushed the elevator button. When nervous, I tended to ramble, and right now I felt a whopper of a ramble coming on.

"Can we say we are going in to exam her?" Lilla asked as we stepped into the empty elevator.

"Examine? Yeah, and hopefully, the guard won't ask questions. So much staff goes in and out of patients' rooms on a daily basis that I'm banking on the hopes that fake outfits and IDs will do the trick. Not to mention the fact that we need Pansy to wake up for us."

I watched the floor numbers inside the elevator light up as we passed each one. Good. No one else got on.

Suddenly it slowed, stopped and the door opened to the OR floor. Damn it. Staff was bustling about inside the OR doors. Good thing Miles was off duty for the next two days. Someone might recognize me and see his ID if it turned slightly. I looked down to make sure it hadn't flipped around.

The doors started to shut. Just as I started to take a breath in relief a hand reached out and grabbed the door.

"Damn elevator," a male voice said.

I slunk to the back of the small elevator cab and pushed Lilla to the side to kind of cover me.

The orderly pushed a stretcher in. Johnny Wakefield. Miles had dated him! The patient had on a mask. Must have been in isolation so she wouldn't be spreading germs into the air.

Germs.

Air.

Masks!

I looked at Lilla and winked. She stepped more in front of me and Johnny started rapping some song that sounded like every other rap song I'd ever heard. Well, at least he didn't turn around and see me.

The elevator opened on Pansy's floor, and Johnny didn't move. Darn it.

Lilla had the good sense to say, "Excuse us, please."

Her female pheromones were wasted on Johnny, but she didn't know, and I didn't care. He moved to the side and let us out without a word as I bent my head forward enough so that my hair pretty much covered my face.

I did, however, trip out of the elevator and landed smack into old Dr. Carrington, whom I think looked like he could have starred in *Father Knows Best*, he was that old.

"Excuse me, nurse," he said to me.

Great. I passed the incognito over-eighty-medical-staff test. Now, on to the real thing.

Lilla followed me toward the nurses' station and around the corner. I paused and looked over the receptionist's shoulder to see the room numbers of the patients on the charts in front of her.

No luck. Too far away.

Lilla murmured, "Won't her room be the one with a guard outside the door?"

I wanted to grab her and hug her. "Good going."

We walked around the unit with no one noticing while we chatted and acted as if we belonged there. I noticed a guard sitting on a straight chair outside the room at the end of the hallway. I would have thought they'd have her closer to the desk, but maybe that was all that was available. When we got closer to the guard, I paused and grabbed Lilla's arm.

"Today is our lucky day," I whispered.

We walked right up to the guard, said hello and took out masks, rubber gloves and Johnny coats from the supply stand near the door.

Pansy Sterling was in isolation!

That patient on the elevator must have been a sign from up above that it'd work out.

Everyone who entered Pansy's room had to dress disguised in these outfits so that they wouldn't spread germs to her. I felt badly that she must have developed some complications to warrant the isolation, yet I winked upward at Saint Theresa. *Good going*, I thought. *Thanks*.

I looked at Lilla. "Doctor, do you want me to assist?" I asked, hoping the guard had no medical knowledge at all.

He kept looking at a magazine in his hands and Lilla played along brilliantly with, "Of course, nurse. I'll need you the entire time." She even spoke with an American accent!

I looked at the guard. "Have a nice day, sir."

He nodded. "Yeah."

Thank goodness hospitals were filled with bustling staff during the day shift. If I'd come last night with Jagger, we'd be very noticeable. I mean I was talking, *Jagger*—in a building of predominantly female staff.

Lilla stood to the side, so I pushed at the handle on the door. It swung open—and I gasped.

Two nursing assistants were in the room with Pansy. Oh . . . my . . . gosh. For some reason, I expected an empty room except for the patient. They chatted in broken English, switching back and forth into Polish, since Hope Valley had a very large population of that nationality.

Both seemed to care less about Lilla and I. They finished fluffing Pansy's pillows, tucking one folded in half behind her back and resting her leg on another one.

Pansy didn't move.

Damn it.

When one of the assistants lifted her hand to rest it on a pillow, she got the IV tubing caught on the railing.

And Pansy moaned.

"Need any help?" I offered, but they both looked at Pansy and declined.

"She's set for now. We turn her in two hours," the nursing assistant near the window said as she walked toward the door, starting to take her gloves off already.

Thank goodness for busy medical staff. Neither woman paid us any attention, as did the guard. We were home free. I just hoped Pansy would do more than moan.

Once Lilla and I were left in the room, I adjusted the IV tubing (hey, once a nurse, always a nurse) to make sure it wouldn't get caught again if Pansy moved. It really hurt to have an IV yanked on.

Lilla and I stood there for a few seconds.

Pansy remained like a corpse. Her color was pretty much the same as prior to her surgery, but I assumed she'd had a few units of blood, which did probably help to make her lips a less lovely shade of cyanotic blue. Then again, she was fair skinned anyway.

"I hate to disturb her," I said, "and I'm not even sure we'll get anything out of her."

Lilla nodded. "Won't hurt to try though, *chéri*."

Pansy stirred.

Did she hear us? Hearing was the last sense to go— not that Pansy was going anywhere right now—so I assumed she could still hear.

I touched her hand.

She pulled back.

"Good," I said. "Pansy, this is Pauline. From work. TLC. The nurse."

Her hand remained still.

"Damn it. She isn't responding." It was a long shot trying to get information from her, but when murder was involved, I had to take a chance. I took the penlight that was next to the bed, held her eyelids open and watched her pupils dilate. "Good." I repeated it on the other side and looked at Lilla again. "Both of her eyes are equal and reactive to light, which is a good sign. They might have her heavily sedated to remain still."

I walked to the other side of the bed to check out some of the equipment. Chest tubes. A plastic container hung from the side of her bed. Evidently when stabbed, her lung must have been punctured and the chest tubes inserted to re-expand it.

The buzzing and clicking of monitors and other equipment filled the small room, and I wondered why every hospital had that same scent. Hospital scent.

I watched Pansy's monitor for a few minutes, pleased at what I saw, and then walked to the other side of the bed, where she faced.

Lilla and I tried asking Pansy question after question. A few times her hand would clench, and Lilla and I would look at each other and nod. We kept it up for several more minutes, not wanting to affect Pansy's recovery in any negative way though.

I cleared my throat and leaned close to her, thinking the noise of some of the equipment might be making it difficult for Pansy to hear me. "Pansy. Pansy, do you remember that you own TLC Land and Air?" I took her hand. "If you do, squeeze my hand."

Her hand tightened on mine.

"Good," I said, about ready to jump around for joy. But that was a far cry from getting her to respond, and

I knew that it could have been more of a reflex than her being coherent.

"Do you remember ER Dano, and Buzz . . . Jeremy, and the rest of the staff?" I asked, hoping that would bring her memory forward.

Her hand remained limp in mine.

"Shoot."

Suddenly there were voices outside the door.

I dropped Pansy's hand and looked at Lilla.

"Maybe the guards are changing shifts?" she said.

"Let's go with that. If we get caught, we get caught. We can say we are here as friends checking up on her even though visitors are restricted."

I turned back to Pansy and decided our time here was short, so I might as well go for broke. I figured she might suddenly wake up and respond. At least, that's what I hoped. "Pansy. I saw the room in your house that looks like a jungle. Neat. It is neat and love, love, love that chair."

Her eyelids fluttered.

I sucked in some air and, feeling horrible, continued, "You must have some great times there. That chair looks perfect for . . . well, you know." I forced a chuckle. "Who's your special guy?" Maybe if I found out Pansy's lover that would tie into the case. Jilted lovers often made it onto the suspect list in cases, as did disgruntled employees. Maybe there was a connection with her ex and Payne too.

Pansy's hand started to clench and unclench on its own.

Hoping it wasn't more reflexive action, I took a deep breath and asked, "Who are you involved with? Or were involved with. What is his name?"

The door started to open.

Lilla's eyes looked as horrified as mine felt.

I grabbed her arm and headed for the door before it opened all the way. Suddenly it shut. We looked at each other and let out a collective sigh.

Then the door started to open again.

I grabbed Lilla and pushed her into the bathroom with me. We shut the door just as the other one opened all at once. Apparently whoever was coming in had been talking to the guard. Maybe getting the okay to come see Pansy.

I caught the door before it clicked shut. A tiny opening remained. Not big enough for anyone to see us, but definitely big enough for us to see them. I looked, blinked, and sighed.

Buzz Lightyear.

My body relaxed. Obviously he'd come to see his employer. I looked at Lilla and winked. She held her finger to her lips to shush me, but then she winked back.

"Hey, Pansy . . . uh . . . it's me. Jeremy." He stammered a bit and tapped his fingers on the bedrail.

I almost asked "who?" and realized the kid was a nervous wreck.

Jeremy stood on the side of the bed that Pansy faced. He looked almost as white as she was, so I figured that for a young guy it was tough coming to the hospital to see someone he worked for so sick. Then I thought his mother would be proud. Kudos to Jeremy Buttman.

He stood there staring at Pansy as if waiting for her to yawn, open her eyes and say hi. But she remained still and Jeremy remained even stiller.

He finally must have pulled his thoughts together. "I hope they find who did this to you, ma'am. I really hope they do," he said as he touched her shoulder and then nonchalantly fiddled with the IV tubing.

I agreed in my head, then listened to Jeremy proceed to tell Pansy, in great boring detail, how things were going at work. He seemed much more at ease now; he even pulled up a chair and sat there talking.

He stood up and stared at the monitor beeping over Pansy's head, and then the door opened and in walked a few more isolation-clothed people. Kim Gonzalez, the RN from the ER; the receptionist, Nancy; and Jennifer Shelton, one of the EMT girls. They all said hi to Buzz and then a few words to Pansy. Nice that they realized that she could probably still hear them.

Soon Nancy said, "We should go," and the group said goodbye to Pansy and started toward the door.

But Jeremy turned back. "I have to use the john."

Lilla and I looked at each other and the only thing I could wonder was, did I look as beautiful as she did with a horrified look on my face?

This time, Lilla grabbed my arm and yanked me into the shower stall and pulled the curtain to the side. Now all I could wonder was, could someone see a shadow through a white plastic hospital curtain?

While a quick prayer flitted through my brain, I heard the door open, shut and another sound, which had Lilla and I raising our eyebrows, our only movement.

The john flushed.

The water ran in the sink.

And the door opened again.

Lilla and I let out a breath.

"Who's there?" Jeremy asked.

And I think my entire world went black.

* * *

Not even Lilla or my eyebrows moved. We remained like statues while Buzz asked nervously, "Is someone there?"

"Jeremy, come on. I have to get to duty," Kim called out.

"I thought I heard someone," he said.

Kim must have walked closer, because her voice was louder now. "With all the noise these machines make, of course you're hearing things. Let's go. Unless you think this place is haunted?"

All three women laughed, and I pictured Jeremy blushing. He'd have to leave without another word in order to save face.

Thank goodness for the male ego.

Lilla and I waited until we heard the shuffling of footsteps grow fainter, the door to the hospital room open and then shut with a click.

She started to touch the shower curtain, but I held her hand and whispered. "Not yet. They'll still be outside the door taking off their isolation garb."

She nodded.

After what seemed like a safe passing of time, we stepped out, looked cautiously around and then went to Pansy's bedside.

"I wonder if she heard all of that. Or any of that."

Pansy's eyelids fluttered. Her hands seemed clenched tighter than before—almost as if she were angry.

"She looks different," Lilla said.

I nodded. "Um. I wonder if that was too much confusing stimuli for her."

"Ah, yes. True."

"We should go," I said, and took one look at Pansy. Her lips started to twitch. Suddenly I wondered if she were about to seize. A grand mal seizure would bring a gang of staff in if her heart rate soared on the monitor. "Let's get the hell out of here." We locked arms as if that would make us invisible. When I said goodbye to Pansy, reminding her who we were, Lilla added, "Too damn bad we didn't find out whom she used that chair with. Her *lover* chair."

I opened the door, Lilla walked out first with me directly behind and still holding it open.

And Pansy mumbled, "Sky."

Sixteen

Once Lilla and I had made it safely out of Pansy's room, we hurried to the elevator and hopped in.

Simultaneously we said, "Was Pansy in love with Sky?" Only it sounded more interesting with Lilla's wonderful French-Canadian accent then my Connecticut no accent.

But I still repeated over and over. "Sky. Sky. Sky?" as the doors shut. Thank goodness we were alone. "Sky and Pansy. Eeeeeeyew." We looked at each other and made disgusting faces. Then I wondered if some lovers' spat had him trying to kill her. But why would he have killed Payne?

Mistaken identity?

I told myself that was not a very Christian attitude to have.

"Pansy certainly does not appear to be the pilot's taste," Lilla said.

I shook my head. "I know. Interesting though. Maybe he wanted a raise?" I chuckled, but Lilla just looked at me. Sometimes I forgot that foreigners did not get some Americans' sense of humor. Okay, make that my sense of humor, as evidenced by Lilla right now and many of the foreign doctors that I used to work with there.

"What does 'wanted a raise' mean, *chéri*?"

I explained that maybe Sky slept with Pansy so she'd treat him better than the other employees. Maybe he was using her. Maybe, though, they had a spat. "But what did Pansy get out of it other than . . ." My face burned. "Okay. He is one hot tamale. Guess they both had their agendas."

When the elevator stopped on the Central Supply floor, we hustled out and hurried to the exit.

"Pauline? Pauline Sokol?" I heard someone say so I grabbed Lilla by the arm and yelled, "Nope!" to Janet—who used to be my boss.

I dropped Lilla off at TLC, noticed Jagger's SUV was not in the parking lot—so he wasn't on a run with ER Dano—and decided I needed a powwow with none other than him, so I called his cell and said, "Meet me at the office," on his voice mail, which he never answered, but I knew he'd show up.

While I drove toward the old building that housed Scarpello and Tonelli Insurance Agency, a thought flitted through my brain. Was Jagger's last name really Tonelli, and did he really have any ownership in this . . . oh . . . my . . . God.

Airbrush Lady drove out of the parking lot in a hot pink Mercedes—obviously special ordered, as I'm sure the folks at Mercedes-Benz had never made that color before. Didn't seem to fit in with the original classy German style.

She didn't notice me—or maybe ignored me, was more like it—but I turned in and, fuming for no reason, pulled into a space near Goldie's yellow

Camaro. I needed a good dose of Goldie right about now.

A real big dose, since Jagger's SUV sat at the end of the parking lot.

I got out, went inside and had a quick chat with Adele, who said Jagger had stepped out for a few minutes (probably after seeing Airbrush Lady). Adele was thrilled to pieces with my praise of her daughter, Lilla, and then I slunk down the hallway to Gold's office in order not to run into Fabio.

When I opened the door, I groaned.

"Hey, doll, when the hell is that case going to crack?" Fabio asked, standing next to Goldie's glass-top desk.

Gold rolled his eyes at me and I nodded.

"Oh, Fabio. I'm so glad you are here. It is coming along so well that I will be done in . . . a very short time."

Goldie stood and took Fabio by the arm. "Isn't she just a peach?"

"Yeah, fucking peach," he mumbled while Goldie ushered him toward the door.

"You feel free to start assigning her the next case, since she's so close to cracking this one, boss," Goldie said in such a flamboyant manner, he had me choking back a laugh.

Mesmerized by Goldie, Fabio seemed speechless. Finally he muttered, "Um. Yeah. Next case. Working on it."

I wanted to shout, "What? I will have a next case? What is it?" but held my words. I wanted Fabio to leave more than I wanted to find out the case info.

Before I confessed to him that I really had nothing.

Yikes.

Once Fabio was safely out the door, Goldie shut

it with more force than needed and leaned against it, looking very much like a tortured Marilyn Monroe in his blonde curly wig, gold brocade dress with a flared bottom and his arm pressed against his forehead. "Why did his old man have to die and leave him here?"

I laughed. "I heard the father didn't make much money though."

Goldie left his post at the door, got a peach vodka on the rocks from his wet bar, handed me a diet Coke and draped himself over the leopard couch. "True. But he was a sweetie. A real human being. Fabio sucks."

I held up my drink to a toast and said, "Hey, listen to this," and told Goldie everything about Pansy, Sky and how Lilla and I were so successful.

Goldie screeched a few times (appropriately) and toasted again. As he held his glass up, a knock sounded on the door.

"Enter!" Goldie yelled and looked at me, "Hope to hell it's not Bosshole again."

"Would he knock?" I asked, causing Goldie to spit out a sip of his drink.

I kept laughing, until Goldie's face grew serious as he looked behind me. I swung around.

"Goldie. Sherlock," Jagger said, looking oh-so delicious, I took a sip of my diet Coke and thought it was jam-packed with sugar.

Thankful that I didn't spill my drink, I said, "Hey." Jagger helped himself to the beer Goldie offered and then sat opposite me on a stool resembling an elephant leg.

"Where'd you go?" he asked.

None of your business sat on the tip of my tongue, but then I remembered we were working a case.

Together.

Go figure.

"Well," I hesitated, knowing I'd have to face the fall-out of Jagger's possible wrath when I said Lilla and I had sneaked into the hospital to see Pansy. Oh, well, I decided to go for it, and what could Jagger do to me anyway?

Once I finished my story, I found out. At first he took a very long, slow sip of his beer. Occasionally he looked from Goldie to me and back.

Poor Goldie looked as if he'd seen a spider—and everyone knew that gay guys couldn't really handle spiders very well, as evidenced by Miles and Goldie found up on a chair in the kitchen when one ventured in when Spanky stepped out last summer.

I could take Jagger, but it wasn't fair to upset Goldie, so I said, "Come on. Get it over with. Give me your two cents' lecture so we can move on."

Goldie gasped. I think he wanted to jump up to protect me, but this was Goldie. Poor guy didn't do too well with brute force or anything that might break a nail.

Still in no hurry, Jagger sipped even more slowly.

"Stop that before Goldie has a stroke!"

Jagger smiled at Goldie. "Why would he?"

I set my glass down on the desktop with a thump and a splash. "Because you are going to chastise me, and he's my friend and you nearly have him suffering apoplexy!"

Goldie said, "Apo—"

"Spitting mad, Gold. Give it up, Jagger. You've held us in suspense all along. What about my investigating without you?"

He set his beer down next to mine without a sound or a splash. "Excellent."

My jaw did its "amazed at Jagger" routine, land-ing wide open and nearly at chest level. Excellent? Was there really such a word in Jagger's vocabulary? I was ready to say, "Says you, Jag." Then I'd follow it with, "And *I* think I did a great job," but I no longer needed those words, and I didn't have any backup ones ready.

Goldie and I exchanged glances and smiled.

Since Jagger and I needed to get back to TLC and ex-plain our "absence," we drove from the office parking lot to TLC in record time. When I parked, I noticed Buzz Lightyear walking toward the building.

His shift wasn't over yet, so I wondered what he was doing there. I followed him to the entrance, and had to bite my tongue when I was tempted to say, "Didn't Pansy look pale?"

Instead I shifted my thoughts. "Hey, Jeremy, have you heard any news about how Pansy is doing?"

His hand tightened on the door handle. Poor kid. He'd had a rough day and I was making him relive it.

"I hear she's still in a coma," he said and walked briskly into the building.

You heard? You *saw*, Buzz. You saw her today and why would you keep that a secret?

I shook my head. I likened him to one of my younger brothers. If he told me about being there with three women, and him being the one who looked even paler than the patient, he'd look bad in front of a girl. I smiled to myself. Yeah, poor kid.

As I was headed into the lounge to see who was there, I was paged over the intercom. "Pauline Sokol, to the helipad."

Oh, great. Another dizzying helicopter ride to make my day.

Proud of myself for not getting nauseous and for stabilizing an unstable patient midair, I sat next to Sky on the ride back to Hope Valley, mentally patting myself on the back.

Only thing was, it was damn difficult not to ask about him and Pansy.

I managed to make small talk and learned Sky was an only child who had grown up in an orphanage. How sad, yet he seemed to think it was an okay upbringing.

"Well, look where it got you," I said. "Great job and a great guy."

He chuckled in the earphones of my helmet and asked me to tell him more about myself. Yikes. I had to give him the edited version, leaving out that I was an investigator.

Trust no one, I could hear Jagger whisper in my ear. Okay, due to the noise of this flying tin can, it was more a shout than a whisper.

But it was in Jagger's voice and helped to keep me calm.

"How'd you come to work for TLC?" Sky asked.

Whoops. Hadn't ever planned out a lie for that one. Never really expected someone would ask. I paused for a few seconds and looked out the window.

The TLC helipad was in view. If I bought myself time I wouldn't have to lie, since I sucked at that. So, I looked around as if I hadn't heard Sky's question.

"Hey, Pauline. I asked how you came to work at TLC. Someone recommend it to you?"

Hmm. That would have been a good answer unless

he asked me who had. I pretended to be interested in the terrain below.

I was contemplating why Sky would ask *me* that question. Small talk? Or trying to find out who knew about him being a possible suspect?

Sky leaned toward me and tapped my helmet. "You hear me?"

"What?"

"Your system out?"

"If you are talking to me, I think my system is out." Damn. I should have used another term, but he didn't seem suspicious as he gently set the helicopter down.

"Nice landing," I said as I took off my helmet and got out before, Mario, who'd been riding with us and taking a nap like Nicky had, stepped out. I handed him the helmet.

"Have the system on that thing checked out, Mar," Sky said.

Whoops. Oh well, if need be, I could say I had wax in my ears.

Back in the lounge, while several of the other staff busied themselves I poured milk into my cup of hot tea and started to plan out my evening. Evening? Geez. It seemed ages since I'd come on duty here today. This job was as demanding as most nursing positions were. Proud of my accomplishments on my two helicopter runs, I took a sip of tea and decided I needed the down time.

"Four five six, possible Eighty-four at 333 Oak Street, third floor," came over the intercom.

Buzz flew from his seat. "Let's go, Pauline!"

"Pauline?" I said, tea sloshing around in my mug as I set it down on the table.

"Yeah, didn't you hear your name called? ER Dano is already in the ambulance. Let's go!" Buzz adjusted his crisp white shirt as if that would make him look more professional to a patient suffering an Eighty-four, whatever that was.

In my relaxed mood I hadn't, in fact, heard my name being called, but I trusted Buzz (and decided he was more a Buzz than a Jeremy since disturbing my down time) so I rushed out behind him.

ER Dano was at the wheel. "Shotgun for you this time, Sparkie. Sokol, you got the back."

The experienced paramedics—well ER Dano anyway—called the overeager EMTs who always wanted to drive "Sparkie."

Neither Buzz nor I argued, since a person's life might be on the line—even though I hated riding in the back. Jagger wasn't on this call; he must have been used on another run where a paramedic was needed.

I sat in the back while ER zoomed the ambulance out of the driveway with the lights and sirens going.

Adrenaline was a powerful hormone, I thought as it surged throughout me, waking me up so I'd be ready for anything.

But when we reached 333 Oak Street, I really wasn't ready.

We flew out of the ambulance, Dano cursing a few times. He ordered Buzz Lightyear to get the bag—which pleased Buzz to no end. I could tell he felt very important carrying all the equipment. Almost as important as ER felt, amused that he didn't have to carry it.

We got to the rickety front porch of the green, white and dirty brown three-story house. The door was left open so ER Dano led the way, mumbling,

"The damn fat lady always lives on the third floor."

I figured he wasn't talking to anyone, but the poor ambulance crews really did have a physically demanding job—and hopefully, this patient would not be too heavy to carry down these stairs. They wound around corners with triangle steps at each curve and because of the narrowness of the stairway, I wondered how anyone got any furniture up there.

"Hurry up!" sounded a young voice. I couldn't tell if it was female or male, but it was frantic.

Then we reached the top floor and I saw a girl. Really just a girl. Maybe seventeen or close to it. Dressed all in black and with bright yellow hair, she stood there waving her hands and yelling, "He needs help! He needs help! Don't let Slick die!"

Buzz stiffened in what I think he thought was a very professional manner. "We are here, ma'am. No need to panic. We'll do our best—"

ER Dano pushed Buzz to the side. "Get the hell out of the way. Where is he?" he asked the girl.

She pointed to the open door at the end of the hallway.

I stopped short at the bedroom where the girl, who said her name was Chloe, had pointed.

Sitting in an old, ripped Hunter green stuffed chair was Slick—whose face was a metallic shade of silver. The Tin Man came to mind, only Slick wasn't in the best of health.

"Shit," ER Dano said. "He been huffing?" he asked Chloe, who nodded as if to say, "Of course, what else?"

Buzz opened the bag and started to take out equipment. I helped with whatever Dano told us to do while he called into Saint Greg's ER.

Slick's eyes were red, with a dazed look in the darkness. He started to mumble but sounded very drunk, although I'm sure the inhaling of metallic paint was the cause, as Dano found the can next to Slick's leg and shoved it into the ambulance bag.

Chloe stood very still to the side of Slick, and I thought I saw a tear sneak out. She tried to remain stoic, but then she started to lose it. When she broke down, Slick's eyes flickered and his arm swung out, landing smack-dab in ER Dano's face—and then Slick kept punching.

ER fell backward with a curse and then a smash when his head hit the leg of an end table—and he remained motionless on the torn, stained braided rug.

"No!" I shouted as Buzz tried to hold Slick back. Apparently huffers could become very violent, as evidenced by his flailing arms, cuffed fists and smacks and jabs at everyone.

Slick hit me in the back of the head when I bent to check out ER Dano. "Ouch!" I yelled, and when I turned around to say something I swear Stella Sokol's voice came out of my mouth: "Do that again, and I'll clock you. Stop it, NOW!" Not the exact words she'd use, but my tone was right on the money.

Despite the inhalant causing Slick to act out, he slowed, settled back and remained still—but only for a few seconds.

Suddenly he was up and swinging again. Chloe was bobbing and weaving (looking very used to having to do that) and before I knew it, Buzz had tackled Slick to the ground.

I'm not sure what shocked me more: Slick being out of control, or Buzz Lightyear's strength! The quiet, accident-prone EMT slammed a fist into Slick's shoulder, which made him scream out in pain. It worked, as Buzz was able to restrain him long enough for me to call the police on Dano's radio.

Before they got there, Slick calmed down enough for Buzz's weight to hold him still.

"Stick an IV in his arm," I ordered Buzz while I bent down to ER Dano's shoulder and called dispatch on his radio.

Since Slick looked more annoyed than about to kick the bucket, I turned my full attention to ER Dano, who had barely stirred. First I checked my ABCs and when I tilted his forehead back, I found his airway patent (open). Then I held my hand over his nose to feel the warm breaths, to make sure he was breathing all right, and last, I noted his color—a bit pale but not cyanotic, and he wasn't coughing.

I grabbed the ambulance bag and took out sterile gauze, which I applied to the gash on the back of his head. Despite the numerous stains on the rug, I knew the bright red spot behind Dano's head was from him. I reminded myself how head wounds bled a lot and sometimes looked worse than they were.

The cops arrived, and not any too soon, since Slick once again became combative as Buzz tried to start the IV. Since he had no luck, and I wasn't surprised, I had to do it for him. When I looked at the silver face of Slick and then at Dano, I wanted to shove the needle . . . but I didn't. With the IV running, I told Buzz to stay near the jerk and sat by Dano's side.

He still didn't open his eyes so I stuck an IV in his arm too. He'd kill me if he woke up then.

It seemed like hours before we had backup help—

although it had to be only a few minutes. Every ambulance at TLC would rush to the aid of the craggy, negative ER Dano—I just knew it.

Jennifer, one of the EMTs, and Jagger, thank goodness, appeared at the door with a stretcher.

Dano had started to stir. His eyes opened and he looked at me. "What the hell did you do to me?"

"I . . . you . . . nothing! Huffer Slick slugged you and you hit your head."

He tried to turn, but groaned at the movement.

"Stay still," I said. "They've got Slick down in the ambulance. You're next."

"Like hell." He tried to get up, but I firmly pushed him down. He looked at the tubing coming out of his arm. "What the . . . this had to be your idea, Nightingale." He tried to get up again.

"Like hell you are getting up," I said. "And, by the way, I enjoyed every minute of sticking you with the IV needle. I was going to use the largest bore needle, the size of a freaking garden hose, but Buzz wouldn't let me."

He growled at me and tried to get up once more, but I was relentless in my effort, and ER Dano didn't stand a chance. "You think you are fine?" I asked.

He glared at me—a not-too-pleasant glare in fact. "Absolutely."

"Then how is it that a girl like me can hold you down?"

"Shit," he muttered, just as Jagger and Buzz came into the room with another stretcher.

Chloe had stayed by Slick's side after numerous apologies to us all for what Silver Streak had done to ER Dano.

I had to shake my head and say a little prayer for

the two sad young people, whose lives were obviously owned by inhalants, pot and probably alcohol. What a waste.

Dano continued to sputter and curse until the guys had him on the stairway—with a few close calls of him nearly sliding feet to head with Jagger. When they got to the lowest landing and had to make a narrow turn, I heard a *smack*.

Buzz Lightyear lay sprawled out on the landing.

"Oh, Lord!" I yelled, but before I could get to him, Buzz was up again and grabbing the stretcher, while Dano muttered some curses.

I shook my head at the thought that these things always happened to the poor kid. He shook his head a few times as if that would help take away any pain.

"You all right, hon?" I asked.

"Yes, Ms. Pauline. I'm fine."

Dano looked up. "You look like shit. You should be on this ironing board instead of me." He shut his eyes and said, "Get me the hell out of here before one of us gets killed."

Once he was safely out and tucked into the second ambulance, Dano ordered, "Go get in Four five six with your patient, Nightingale."

I took his hand and held it, all the while sneaking a feel of his pulse. "There's been a change of assignments. Jennifer's crew took Slick so we can transport you."

Dano looked at me questioningly.

I nodded. "Yep, Buzz too. He didn't want to leave you. Isn't that sweet?" As soon as the words came out I knew I should have chosen more wisely.

"Ef'n sweet," he said. "All I need is a good stiff drink to get rid of this headache."

"And about seven stitches," I added as we pulled up to the ER at Saint Gregory's Hospital.

Suddenly I felt something on my hand. ER Dano was holding it!

He winked, despite the pain it must have caused as evidenced by the wince that followed. "Then I'm glad you'll be with me, Nightingale."

And my heart fluttered.

Wow.

Seventeen

"Well, they didn't get to fix the giant hole in your head, but they did a decent job with the small gash," I said to ER Dano as we walked out of the emergency room.

He grunted.

Buzz was behind the wheel of #456, and I know ER Dano would not want any other transportation back to TLC. How fitting.

We climbed into the back and sat on the bench. Buzz turned around, gave ER a thumbs-up and then pulled slowly out of the driveway.

I felt Dano's knees bump against mine as the ambulance took several turns. Yum. I shouldn't be ogling an injured guy like this, but damn, I felt something. ER Dano had made a darn lousy first impression—and I am sure an impression that he thrived upon—but in the end, a different guy came through—and I liked him!

I had a sobering thought. Hopefully, he wasn't involved in the fraud or . . . the stabbings, and damn, but I had a gut feeling that the two crimes were related.

In my heart I didn't believe it was true about Dano, so I had to trust my instincts yet again. And this one was the clincher: Jagger wasn't keeping me away from him. If anyone suspected ER Dano of anything nefarious, Jagger would know, and I sure wouldn't be sitting here!

The ambulance stopped and before I could say a word, the back door was flung open and Buzz stood there as if he'd just stepped out of a brand-new toy box I could swear he was made out of plastic, the way he held his shoulders straight in that crisp uniform, legs apart as if at attention. And such a serious look on his face.

"Need any help?" he asked Dano, who looked at him and groaned. "Okay, sir. I'll be here if you need me."

I had to smile to myself as Dano stepped to the side, then turned and hurried to open the door. I leaned toward Dano and said, "He was only trying to help. Cut him some slack."

"Cutting a kid like that slack is not going to get him skilled in this profession, Nightingale. He has to toughen up. One time he was about to zap a patient with the cardiac defibrillator, and I had to point out to him that she was still holding onto his leg. Does the term 'clear' mean anything to you?"

I wanted to say, "But he's such a sweetie," but realized Dano was correct. Buzz obviously had to toughen up. I remembered the look on his face when he'd seen Pansy.

I tried not to feel negative about his future, but I wondered how long Jeremy would last as an EMT at TLC.

* * *

Since our duty day was nearly over, I sat back on the couch in the lounge and sipped my tea while everyone fawned over ER Dano—from a distance. Obviously they were not stupid people. I saw him wince a few times, and I guessed it wasn't from pain.

"What the hell are you smiling about, Nightingale?" he said.

"Hmm? Oh, nothing." I hadn't realized I was.

He eased away from Jennifer and Lilla and straddled a chair from the table in front of me. "Yeah, right. You're loving this."

This time I chuckled. "Okay. You got me."

He kicked my foot with his. Just a gentle touch. A sensual touch even through my shoe. Wow.

It wasn't easy to rein in my thoughts, when I had to work with him so near. I sighed.

He looked at me.

Damn. He knew. He knew that he was causing a reaction—the bad boy! And, the worst part was, I was losing control of my reactions.

Buzz came over to ER Dano with a cup of black coffee. "Here ya go. How you feeling?"

Whoops. I thought Dano was going to fling the mug at the poor kid. But he did take it and mumble something. I was going with "thanks."

Dano took a few sips and then shut his eyes.

Dear Buzz could not take a hint, I thought as I bit my tongue.

"So, you know the ER doc, Dr. Richard Pringle, does not want you alone tonight. He said you need someone to check up on you," Buzz said, clearing his throat. "Someone has to keep waking you up in case you have a concussion."

Oh, boy. I started to send mental notes to Buzz to

shut up, and even used my facial expressions to try to capture his attention before he ended up wearing Dano's coffee; but darling Buzz kept up. Being zapped by a defibrillator would be nothing compared to what Dano might do to him.

"So, I will volunteer. I can bunk at your place, boss, and wake you up every hour or so. You know. Ask you what day it is. Who the president is—"

Before Buzz could keep rambling on, ER Dano was up and out of his seat and had Buzz's unwrinkled tie in his hand—I think, about to yank. But Dano staggered and had to let go. He dropped back to his seat with a thud and a curse that would make a longshoreman blush.

The room hushed.

Buzz swallowed and turned pale.

And I sat motionless, waiting for my mind to catch up to the scene that had just played out in front of me.

Sheepishly and yes, foolishly, Buzz said, "Someone has to be there for you, Dan."

Yikes! I started to get up to run interference should Dano attempt another attack, but he merely looked at Buzz and said, "*She's* doing it."

I looked around the room to see who'd gotten the short straw and was going to have to stay the night at ER Dano's place, taking her life into her hands by waking *him* up? Ready to offer moral support and sympathy, I noticed that everyone in the room, including ER Dano, was staring at . . . *me*.

Oh . . . my . . . God.

My attempts to get out of the job of "nursing" ER Dano had failed miserably, and here I sat in my car, on my way to his place with a stop off at mine for some clothes, makeup and a check of my phone recorder (no more riddle threats for days now)—and him sitting next to me since he couldn't drive.

Not that I needed much in the line of clothes or makeup, as Dano was not one to be impressed, but I was one to feel more comfortable, and any reason to get out of my scrubs was a good one.

I pulled into my assigned space, got out and said I'd be right back. Before I made it up my front steps, he was right behind me.

"I need a drink," he said. "Damn shit they gave me in the ER made me thirsty."

I paused to try and choose the right words and then thought, *Oh, hell.* "You shouldn't be drinking with a head injury. You know that."

He looked at me and kind of grinned.

Phew.

"Nightingale, I'm talking water here, and don't try to nurse me. The last woman that attempted ended up . . ." He grinned again.

My heart did a tiny dance, and I smiled and opened the door to Spanky, who ran up to me and looked behind me. I think the little creature was looking for Jagger!

But the dog settled for ER Dano, who growled a bit that he wasn't a pet lover, and the next thing I knew, he was sitting on the couch with ice water in hand and Spanky on a pillow nearby. Dano did not, however, pet him, but just sitting there gave Dano a more human quality.

And a rather tasty one at that!

I looked at the pile of clothing on my floor and felt like a teenager. Then again, what I wore was important tonight because I didn't want to look too sexy—since I was only there as a friend and nurse. And, I didn't want to look not sexy because, well, I was going to be there—and I was a red-blooded, single, thirty-something woman!

After much contemplation, trying on things I hadn't worn in a while and wishing my roomies were home to give their expert opinions, I settled on jeans and an aqua long-sleeve top and stuck some toiletries into my makeup bag. I decided my slip-ons would be most like slippers and the jeans weren't too tight, so I could sleep in them.

Because no way was I parading around ER Dano's place in my nightie.

ER Dano's place?

I flopped onto the end of the bed and in my wildest imagination could not think of what it would look like. That'd be one step below figuring out what Jagger's place looked like. That is, if Jagger really lived someplace and didn't simply drive around in his SUV.

My thoughts were that Dano's place would have chrome and glass, and be dark, rather scary, and . . . male.

Since I had a "job" to do, I pushed any Jagger thoughts out of my head, took my scrubs and shoes for tomorrow and stuck it all into my gym bag. My suitcase looked too girly. Too purple. I couldn't do purple girly in front of such a guy as Dano.

Brown paper bag might do it though.

When I walked down the stairs, Spanky was not on his pillow any longer. And he wasn't on Dano's lap as I'd expected. Evidently Jagger was the only one Spanky had taken a liking to other than myself, Goldie and Miles.

"All set?" I asked.

"Um." Dano stood, wobbled a bit, and steadied himself on the couch's arm. "Hold on."

"Wha--"

He was out the door and into the kitchen before I could finish.

"What the heck?" I muttered, and followed.

There near the back door was Spanky eating out of his dog food dish. But not his dry food. Nope. Dano had raided our refrigerator and helped himself to morsels of leftovers that he'd given to the dog.

After my attack of muteness left, I said, "He has to watch his weight. If he gets another pound heavier, his little kneecap goes out of joint."

Dano looked at me and then Spanky. "He needed a treat. That's about as low-cal and wholesome as you can get." With that he turned and walked back out toward the front.

Spanky gave me a quick look, as if agreeing with Dano.

"Shut up," I said to him, gave him a pat on the head, looked to see no phone messages, and left. By the time I got out to my car, Dano was in the passenger seat, eyes shut and occasionally wincing.

The tough guy was in pain and despite how he felt, he had taken care of an eight-pound dog.

Eighteen

Life has never ceased to amaze me. My mother used to tell me things that I never believed unless I saw them for myself. "Doubting Thomas," she and my sister used to call me, after the apostle who didn't believe that Jesus had been crucified and had risen from the dead.

Well, no one could have prepared me for this.

ER Dano's house.

Yeah, *house*. First of all I was expecting an apartment, or condo at the very most. But nope. He lived— and owned, I'd learned—an old Victorian house on the west side of Hope Valley, in one of the finer, older neighborhoods.

Bachelor: grumpy at times, grouchy at others. House: burned-out-bachelor pad, it was not.

As I followed him up the pink flower-bordered walkway, I couldn't even speak. Without a green thumb on either hand, I knew nothing about the flowers other than that they were pink and pretty, and that Dano must either live with someone or had hired someone to landscape. Yet, what would make him do that?

Then he bent to pick a brown leaf off one of the plants and I mumbled, "He planted them."

"I planted them. Don't sound so shocked. Did all the landscaping myself. Good therapy to empty my bucket of ambulance runs when I need to forget," he said, and opened the large, dark paneled wood front door with a leaded and frosted glass window in the center.

"Oh," was all I could manage until I stepped inside and added, "Oh, my." Oh, again.

Dano appeared to ignore me as he pointed out, "Here's the living room, the john's in there and you can stay upstairs in the room to the left of the railing. When you try to wake me, don't get close."

I wanted to ask why, but figured he must have been a deep sleeper and would probably clock me if I startled him.

We went into the kitchen, which had copper pots hanging from the ceiling, large tomato plants growing in pots by the bay windows and old large-plank hardwood floors. At a white enamel sink, he took a glass from a cabinet, filled it and drank it down in one swallow.

"This place is neat," I said, sitting down at the white wooden kitchen table. There were even crocheted doilies on the table as placemats.

"My grandmother made those," was all he said when he noticed me noticing them.

"Ah. That's nice. Look, Dano, I'm here to help you. Let me get you whatever you want while you sit and take it easy. I don't want your head to start hurting."

He looked at me.

Gulp.

Damn. The guy had a way of looking that I *felt*. Actually felt.

"Already hurts like hell. I'd go to bed now, but then I'd be up all night long . . . thinking."

There was pain in his voice, and I knew ER Dano had really been on the job far too long. It'd taken a toll on him, and grabbed his life without releasing. I could sense that he didn't like to go to sleep—obviously since job-demon dreams awaited him.

So I sat there staring at him in the little Victorian kitchen, which looked more like a librarian lived here than a macho paramedic, thinking, *What the hell am I going to do?* when the urge to kiss him shocked the hell out of me.

I made some excuse about seeing the rest of the house. At least it was an interesting place, and he bought my reasoning for taking the unguided tour while he rested. Naturally Dano had not volunteered to show me around, but had merely shrugged and sat himself at the kitchen table to read the daily newspaper.

Since he hadn't seemed to mind, I walked through the dining room, which had old mahogany furniture, chairs with needlepoint mauve roses, lacy curtains that looked genuine and antiques—in the corner was an old China tea set on a lace-covered pedestal table.

I had to shake my head. There was an air to the house of antiquity, yet it was freshly kept up and not musty, as one might expect. He had to have inherited this place. For the life of me, I couldn't imagine Dano decorating in this taste. Then again, he lived here without changing anything. Hmm.

ER Dano was one hell of a dichotomy.

In the living room, I sat on the rose-colored Victorian couch. It wasn't the most comfortable thing; as a matter of fact it made me think of how prim and proper ladies must have been in the Victorian era. They had to be, to sit this straight. White porcelain vases holding silken floral arrangements sat on the sideboards. Wait a minute. I got up and walked to them and ran a finger along the petals, which came off in my hands.

Real flowers.

Real flowers? Dano had real flowers in his house? Man. This was almost creepy. I turned to see him standing in the doorway. Whoops.

"Hey," I mumbled.

He nodded. "I'm beat. Going up to bed. Remember, not too close when you annoy the hell out of me."

I smiled. "Um, Dan. These flowers are beautiful. Did you arrange them?" Now if there was one thing I just knew ER Dano would not want to talk about, it would be flowers.

But he looked at them and said, "My therapist had me take a freaking course in floral arrangement."

I laughed. "Yeah, right. Really. Did you do them?"

He walked over to them and poignantly took a brown petal from a rose much like he'd done outside. "My old lady had a greenhouse. She taught my sister, and I used to watch—as a kid. And, the therapist part is true." He turned and looked past me as if his mom and maybe sister were in the doorway. "Helps. They help." With that he walked out of the room and up the staircase.

I stood there and thought, *I'll bet it does.* Anything to take his mind off the daily tragedies of life that ER and the crew of TLC faced.

* * *

My eyelids fluttered. The annoying buzzing tickled my ears, and I opened one eye to look at the digital clock on the bedside table. Midnight. Geez. I thought it was time to get up for work. I turned over and shut my eyes—then realized this wasn't my bed.

I sat bolt upright and I looked around the old Victorian room where I'd been sleeping. Oh, right. D-day. Time to take my life into my hands and check on Dano. I'd peeked in on him just before I'd gone to sleep myself, but he'd been awake and growled the date and time as I'd said good night.

As I rolled out of bed and slipped on my shoes, I had to smile. I'm sure he was fine, since his attitude never adjusted one second.

When I padded down the short hallway, I noticed light coming from under his door. Hmm. Maybe Dano couldn't sleep and was up reading. I slowly eased the door open despite the squeaking sound the old thing made.

Dano was fast asleep. The Tiffany lamp on his bedside table was still lit. Oh well. Guess he dozed off and forgot to shut it off. I only hoped he hadn't gotten too tired because of the head injury. Purposely I walked to the edge of the bed, reminding myself of my nursing days. It almost felt as if I were making my rounds on the unit where I used to work.

"Ah. No. No!" Dano mumbled.

"Are you—" I started to say until I realized he was sound asleep.

Dano talked in his sleep. But the thing was, he sounded disturbed by something. Suddenly he lashed out with a left jab.

I stepped back. Geez! He could have knocked me

out with that one. I remembered what he'd said about not getting close. Dano must have known that he was a restless sleeper. A very restless sleeper.

He tossed and turned, still mumbling, so I got as close as I could, thinking I could move back fast if need be, and said, "Dano. Dan, it's Pauline."

I stepped back as Dano suddenly sat upright.

"Dan?" I asked.

But he merely looked my way in a glassy stare. Not a word, and he was out of bed and walking toward the door. Dressed in black boxers and no tee shirt, Dano looked hunky, but when I realized he was sleepwalking, I had other things on my mind other than how hot he looked.

What should I do?

My sister Mary had a child who walked in his sleep and the doctor had told her never to try and wake him. Dano was out the door already! So I hurried to follow him but found him standing in the hallway, rubbing his head as if in pain.

"No. No. I should have. I should have given the epi. She died because of . . ." His eyes locked on me. He paused, blinked. "What the hell?"

Dano had woken himself up with some nightmare that sounded like an ambulance run gone bad. It wasn't any that I'd been on with him, as I didn't remember a patient needing epinephrine. No. Dano must have relived a case from the past.

Standing there, looking at this hunk of a guy appearing so confused and upset, I had to wonder how long it had taken for him to burn out from such a stressful job.

Soon enough to commit fraud for money?

"I'm fine," he growled and headed into his room.

When I went to the doorway, he was already under the sheets with eyes shut. "Good," I said.

"Thursday. It's freaking Thursday, Nightingale. Go to sleep."

I nodded and mumbled, "Technically, it's already Friday."

"Semantics," he said, and I knew his head was fine.

But what demons did ER Dano face on a nightly basis?

I tossed and turned in the bed with the too-soft mattress, knowing that I couldn't fall into a deep sleep, or I might not get up to check on Dano. Then again, I also knew he might show up at my doorway in a sleep-walking state.

That one kept me awake the longest.

But I reminded myself that I worked tomorrow, or later today, and had to get some rest or not be in any shape to assess or treat patients. With my luck, I'd get a helicopter run.

"Aye!"

I flew up to the sound of shouting coming from ER Dano's room. Damn! Thank goodness I'd had the common sense to wear real clothes and not pajamas. I jumped out of bed and ran down the hallway.

He wasn't up but was flailing back and forth in the bed, arms swinging as if in a fight, and pillows flying.

"Oomph!" One hit me in the stomach and, if it were heavier, it would have knocked me over. As it was, it knocked the wind out of me. The damn feather pillow weighed more than Spanky!

Dano continued on until I could no longer stand watching. I cautiously stepped forward, remembering how the patient had hit him today. If I got knocked out, I'd be no good to Dano.

"Hey. Dan. I'm here. It's all right. You're dreaming," I said in the softest yet clearest voice I could manage. Enough to wake him up, yet quiet enough not to startle him.

I knew I had to rescue ER Dano from his dreams, his nightmares . . . himself.

I got close enough to touch his arm, all the while using soft words to calm him down. I grabbed it until he quieted and stopped fighting me.

As if a switch turned him off, he stopped immediately, looked me in the eyes and shut his.

He was awake.

I sat on the edge of the bed and said, "You're all right now. It was only a dream."

His opened his eyes again. "A dream? It was a freaking nightmare, Nightingale. A nightmare. A nightmare that comes each time I go to sleep."

Not being able to help myself, I sat on the edge of the bed, wrapping my arms around his shoulders and hugging him to my chest.

Dano was apparently fine as far as the head injury was concerned, but his mental-health status was in question as long as he worked his job, tried to save lives and sometimes lost them.

He moved closer to me, his head pressed against my chest, and I tightened my arms around him. It seemed like hours that we lay there, me trying to comfort him yet knowing that I couldn't do anything to release the demons from his memory.

I brushed his hair back behind his ears and he looked up at me. Not sure exactly what happened next, but knowing his head was fine, I gave in to his lips when they touched mine.

And we kissed as if starving for each other.

"I'm all right. Just a nightly occurrence, Nightingale. I'm all right," he repeated.

I returned his kisses, and with my lips pressed against his cheek managed to say, "I know you are fine. I'm glad."

With one swift motion he'd reversed our positions, and now I was lying next to him, his arms straddling mine, and his lips covering mine—and it felt so good.

Dano slid his hand beneath my top, running his hands across my breasts—and I was so glad I could never sleep with a bra on. When he touched my hardened nipples, I moaned.

He then lifted my top over my head and the last coherent thought that I had was, *we are two adults*. Two consenting adults, sex was a natural desire and . . . oh, man, did I want to consent to ER Dano.

So I did.

Since we both needed some semblance of sleep, I went back to the guest room, telling myself I'd be *able* to sleep. Ha! After such a pleasurable ride, I could barely shut my eyes without reliving parts of it—no, all of it.

This was going to be a futile effort, I told myself, until I felt my eyelids close.

When I opened my eyes to the sound of the shower running, it again took several seconds to orient myself to my surroundings.

ER Dano's guest bedroom.

Yikes. Was that a fantastic dream that I'd had or the real thing? I turned over, hugged the pillow and smiled.

Then I looked at the alarm clock and groaned. Damn.

A half hour to get to work, so I jumped up and grabbed my makeup kit. I'd at least get my teeth brushed in the downstairs bathroom until he was done with the shower. Ignoring the fact that I could join him . . . but knowing there wasn't time, I hurried out—and told myself to stop those kinds of thoughts.

Thank goodness the stairs were carpeted, as I'd forgotten to shove on my clogs and hated walking barefoot. At the bottom of the stairs, I stopped at the end table and noticed myself in the mirror.

Raccoon eyes. Smudged mascara. Great. Did I look like this last night when . . . ? Naw. Besides, it was dark. Still, I couldn't go to work like this, so I reached into my bag for a tissue. Stella Sokol would be shaking her head right now. No tissue. Here I'd broken one of her golden bring-a-tissue, go-to-the-bathroom, and make-sure-to-wear-clean-underwear rules.

I chuckled, as I'd often wondered if the ER staff really cared or noticed anyone's clean undies. Still in the afterglow of last night, I walked much lighter, nearly prancing, and headed into the bathroom. No tissues there either. Apparently ER Dano's mom did not practice the same words of wisdom as Stella Sokol.

Laughing, I walked into the kitchen to look around, as there wasn't even toilet tissue in the bathroom. Despite the Victorian setting, this was still a guy's house. On the counter was a tissue box—empty.

"Damn." There might be some in the cabinet above, so I opened it—to a pile of papers that cascaded out at me.

I shook my head and started to grab them to shove back in when the words caught my eye. TLC. Overcharge. Carry deceased. The fake list of EMT and paramedic's names were listed as receiving cash from the undertakers, and no real names were given.

My eyes blurred. I didn't need to read any further.

ER Dano had the papers that proved the fraud at Tender Loving Care Land and Air so nonchalantly piled up in his kitchen cabinet—as if he didn't give a care in the world about them.

Dano was involved in the fraud.

Nineteen

After my "find" at ER Dano's house, and knowing he was physically all right—after he insisted as much—I had showered, dressed and headed off to work, where the first thing I did, even before my morning tea, was to seek out Jagger. I found him sipping his coffee in the parking lot.

Jagger leaned back on the hood of his SUV. When I told him about my discovery and that I had been there to nurse Dano, he said, "Interesting."

"Interesting? That's all you've got? Interesting?" I leaned against the fender, as my lack of sleep was already taking a toll on me. "Come on, Jagger. Obviously ER Dano is involved. He was hiding evidence in his kitchen cabinets!" And damn, how I hated that. I mean the sex was great (great!) and I really cared for him—however, those words would never pass my lips to Jagger's ears.

"If you talk a bit louder, all the employees will be able to hear," he said.

I curled my lips. "I'm just so pissed." I was really pissed at fate. Here I find a hot guy I liked, who seemed to like me, and he's a criminal. I looked up to

the clouds and shook my head. Saint Theresa must
have been very busy last night and my "needs" didn't
qualify for prayer answering.

Jagger said, "Look, you don't have any proof of why
they were there. We need that."

I bit my lips. "Are you saying you don't think Dano
is guilty? That he's not covering up the fraud?" *Please.
Please say it because I believe whatever you say since it's
always true.*

But Jagger merely responded, "I'm saying we need
proof. Can't close a case on assumptions. Right ones or
wrong ones." He looked past me. "Here he comes now.
You'll need to get into his house again tonight and find
out more. I'll go with you."

"No!" I said way too loudly. He glared at me. "No
need. I can handle Dano. You maybe should go see if
Pansy's any more alert."

Suddenly I wished I could have swallowed those
words.

Had I really just given Jagger an assignment? An order? Or something close to being an order?

Yikes!

He looked at me, got up off the car and walked
away.

I watched his butt moving from side to side as he
swaggered off, and I didn't even get hot. Okay, I did
get a wee bit warm.

I had way too much on my mind between fraud and
getting back to ER Dano's house, where who knew
what would happen . . . again.

I hoped to hell that I wouldn't get hot at some inop-
portune time.

Heading for the entrance I wondered if Jagger had
agreed to my "order," or would he show up tonight?

* * *

Dano smiled at me as we poured ourselves the usual morning drinks. The tea bags at TLC always tasted a bit stale, but I chalked that up to cheap management.

"Any word on Pansy?" I asked Dano.

He shook his head and winced.

"You shouldn't move like that." I sipped my tea and then *I* winced. Really stale.

"Damn it. I'm fine. Just the external shit hurts when I move too much. No mental problems, Nightingale." He leaned closer. "But thanks for last night," he said way too loudly.

Everyone in the room gave a collective stare!

I muttered, "Last night . . . we . . . Dano . . . ER Dano . . . Dan . . . I . . ." After a fast sip, which now tasted delicious, I said firmly, "You all know I had to wake him up to check his pupils and sanity." I turned to walk out of the room and over my shoulder said, "That last part is still in question."

The room roared.

As I reached the door I heard Dano growl—in an amazingly sensual way.

In order to get away from the embarrassment, I had headed for Lilla's desk.

She sat there filing her nails, and I knew that all her work was already done and now her day would consist of answering the phone, directing visitors and snooping. Lilla was a dream!

"Hey," I said, sitting down opposite her. "What's going on?"

"Morning, *chéri*." She leaned closer and smiled. Very sexy, but I knew it wasn't as if she were flirting with me. Nope. It was more as if she *knew* something.

"What? What's going on? You have some info?" I set my tea on the edge of her desk.

"No, but *you* do."

"Hmm? What do you mean, Lilla?"

With her sexy smile switching to a sexy grin, she whispered, "I see you have made love."

I blinked. Had to. Maybe her accent was confusing me, so I chuckled. "This is funny. I thought you just said I'd had sex—"

Waving a bright red polished handful of long nails in the air, she said, "You heard correctly, my *chéri*. Which one?"

"Huh?"

"Dano or Jagger?"

I choked on nothing. My hands, sans any long nails or bordello polish, flailed in the air, sending my tea mug spilling over. "Geez! Sorry!"

Lilla laughed, pulled several tissues from her container and said, "Relax. It only shows to women like *moi*, who are astute in those matters."

"Oh, yeah. That makes me feel much better." I took some tissue and wiped the desk. Luckily the mug had only been half full and there were no papers nearby to get soaked. The closest one only got a beige splash of a stain. "Sorry." I picked it up and couldn't help but glance at it. Oh, boy. I was correct.

Dano had a similar run sheet to this one—only a few of the medication charges were different—and I could swear the date, times and names were the same. I explained what I'd found to Lilla, and she showed me all the papers that recently had come in to be filed.

One more was the same. Identical information except for the final numbers—so one had to have been doctored.

"I have to go back to Dano's tonight—"

Before I could finish, Lilla was up and wiping vigorously at my scrub's top, which wasn't even wet.

"What are you—" I asked.

"Don't worry, *chéri*, that will come out. You use some . . ."

I know she kept talking, kinda wildly actually, but then I looked up to see a reflection in the glass partition behind Lilla's desk.

"That'd be okay with Dano," ER Dano said, standing behind me, "but he wonders what for."

Oh, no! I smiled, Lilla wiped and then I said, "We had a date, silly, or did you forget?"

Thank goodness for Lilla's fast actions and my quick mind!

I slowly turned around, pushed Lilla's hand away because she was so flustered she kept wiping at nothing, and I didn't want Dano to notice. "Oh, hey. I'll bring dinner. How's that? Sure. I'll bring the eats."

That implied I'd cook it, but before I could clarify it'd be takeout, Dano agreed and hurried past us.

I flopped backward in my chair and said, "I have to call my mother to make my dinner."

Lilla laughed, but I wasn't feeling very jovial.

I sat in the back of #456 while Buzz drove at top speed. Premature labor. That was the call, and I prayed the baby would calm down and decide a Friday was not a good day to be born. Specifically *this* Friday.

At least I'd had some time to call Stella Sokol before we got the call. It took several minutes to clarify that I didn't have time to stay and eat, but would she make me a take-out dinner for two? Mom made the same menu on the same day of the week forever. Even before I was born. That's how far back forever went.

Since today was Friday, my mother was making potato pancakes. Not exactly a sensual gourmet aphrodisiac.

I looked up toward the window between the cab and the back of the ambulance and noticed Dano's hair just about touching his neckline. Damn. He looked hot even from the back.

I really wished he wasn't involved in the fraud or . . . gulp . . . the stabbings.

Relying on gut instinct had gotten me through years of nursing and saving lives. Right now my gut said Dano wasn't involved. I decided I'd be looking for evidence to clear his name instead of convicting him.

And besides my gut—I had Jagger.

If he'd thought Dano was guilty or a threat, he wouldn't let me go in alone. I'd convinced myself of that.

So, if he thought so, it would be revealed tonight, *if* Jagger showed up.

Dano had joined me in the back of the ambulance, since the patient really did appear to be in labor. Her husband was at work, so before we left, I had called him to tell him to meet us at Saint Greg's while Dano and Buzz worked on Angie in her living room. We'd called the ER, gotten orders from Dr. Pringle and were now following them as best we could.

However, I knew these little ones could have a mind of their own.

Dano adjusted the IV while Buzz pulled the ambulance out of the parking lot of the condo complex where the woman, Angie, lived.

Her eyes glistened with tears as she looked up at

Dano and asked, "Is my baby . . . my baby going to—"

Dano touched her arm. "Naw. I'm taking over. This kid is going to stop running the show and let us pros call the shots from now on."

Tears formed in my eyes. Not only did the gruff, burned-out paramedic do his medical treatments to perfection, but also, when push came to shove, his bedside manner adjusted to meet the needs of, and to calm and relax, the patients. I could still hear the ER nurses fawning over how he always put in the IV with a saline lock, his paperwork was always in order and he taped the IV with a "V" shaped piece of tape—all of which made their jobs easier.

What a guy.

He couldn't be involved. Just couldn't be.

Angie smiled, and then grimaced. "Oh. Oh. Oh, God."

"What?" Dano asked, feeling her abdomen and listening to the fetal heartbeat. He turned his head to the side, so she couldn't hear, and cursed. "What is it, Angie?"

"I think, well, I've never had a baby before, but I think my water broke."

Dano and I looked at each other. I'm sure a similar curse word came to both of our minds, but we held back.

Dano banged on the window to Buzz. "Step on it!"

"Right, boss," he said, and swerved so hard, I toppled into Dano's shoulder.

But neither of us could say a thing because, with Dano's hand still on Angie's abdomen, and with her facial expression, I knew she was heavily contracting.

Just like I knew this baby was going to be born today—soon.

"Hold on, honey." Dano assured Angie.

She looked from him to me and said, "I can't."

Dano kept talking softly to her, getting her to pant through contractions so she wouldn't push, and checking the fetal heartbeat.

I examined her to see if there was any sign of the baby and looked up at Dano.

"Black hair," I said so only he could hear. "I see a bit of head crowning."

"Shit," he mouthed and before I knew it, he was banging on the window ordering Buzz Lightyear to pull over to the side of the road.

And then the fun began.

Buzz hurried to the back of the ambulance, but it proved to be too close quarters for him to get near Angie too. Besides, Dano said there wasn't anything for him to do other than radio the hospital and be the go-between.

At first Buzz looked pissed. I guessed he wanted in on the excitement of a delivery, but since I'd worked OB for many years, Dano kept me assisting.

I followed his instructions of what to grab from where. Although I'd been in delivery for hundreds of babies, I didn't know the setup of the ambulance well enough yet, and this little one might be way too little without any NICU (Neonatal Intensive Care Unit) equipment or staff here.

The only thing going for us was that Angie's abdomen was a good size, so I silently prayed her calculated date wasn't correct, and the baby would have already developed lungs enough to survive.

Please, Saint Theresa.

"Angie," I asked, "who is your doctor?"

"Greenberg," she managed through heavy breaths.

I wrinkled my forehead and looked at Dano. Dr. Greenberg was a general practitioner and not even in a family practice business. "I mean your OB doctor, hon. Who has been seeing you since you became pregnant?"

Angie's eyes spilled over. "My husband lost his job and we didn't have any insurance. We couldn't afford it. So—"

I patted her hand. "No problem. This little one is going to be fine," I lied. Geez. She didn't have any prenatal care, went into premature labor (maybe) and couldn't afford the impending hospital bills *or* this ambulance ride to boot.

Damn insurance again.

Buzz had stayed outside the back door to direct traffic away and prevent rubbernecking. He'd pulled the ambulance into a scenic overlook off the highway, but cars still slowed when they noticed us. Every once in a while he'd come to the door and ask how things were going until Dano growled at him that we'd let him know when we needed to.

Angie began to scream.

Dano lifted the blankets from her, and we both looked to see the black hair very obvious now. I thought the head looked much bigger than a preemie's and again hoped Angie had been wrong on her due date.

"It looks a decent size," I whispered to him, close to his ear as a matter of fact, since Angie was now in such pain and yelling.

"Let's hope," he added.

Dano explained to Angie that we couldn't give her anything for pain and instructed her again on breathing. I stuck on a pair of rubber gloves and assisted Dano as he told me what to do.

Even though I handled emergencies very well, he had a way of calming me, and thank goodness it also worked on Angie. Her hysteria turned into compliance and she followed his instructions.

"I want my baby to live," she repeated several times.

I winked at her. "It will. Don't worry. Just do as we say and things will be fine."

I looked down to see Dano grimace and wondered if his head hurt. Then I noticed the baby's head was out—and the cord wrapped tightly around its neck.

Damn!

"Don't push," he ordered, and the seriousness in his voice had Angie panting instead.

"Good girl. That's right. Don't push right now," I kept saying until Dano had the cord eased off from around the baby's neck after several tugs.

"It has lots of black hair, Angie." I smiled at her. "Does your husband have black hair?" I asked, to keep her mind off of things.

Dano gave some information to Buzz to tell the ER while I made small talk with Angie to keep her from listening.

"Push!" Dano ordered.

I got close to her ear and guided her through every step. ER Dano, Angie and I worked as a well-oiled machine (he just couldn't be involved in the fraud or stabbings) until the pain became too much for Angie.

"I can't!" she cried out several times.

Dano leaned over and looked her in the eye. "Stop that!" he ordered, like a verbal slap.

And Angie stopped.

Then he told her what to do, and I placed her hand on the railing of the stretcher so she could squeeze. I'd remembered from my nursing days that you never let a patient hold your hand when they were in pain because they could break your fingers.

By the grip Angie had on the railing, I was glad I'd remembered that.

Dano told her when to push and when to stop.

"You're doing great," I'd add and I looked to see Dano, pulling and tugging one shoulder and then the other until the baby came out in a *whoosh* of amniotic fluid.

He wasn't any preemie was my first thought, and *Thank you, God*, my second.

"It's a boy," Dano said in a very matter-of-fact tone.

At first I was disappointed that he wasn't more excited, but—the baby hadn't made a sound.

Dano was yelling at Buzz to tell the ER things.

I kept talking to Angie so she wouldn't hear, but *I* heard.

Cyanotic. That dusky bluish-gray color. Dano had said the baby was cyanotic. By now he should have taken a few breaths and pinked up. "Apgar, four," he said as he grabbed the blue bulb syringe and started to suction out the baby's mouth.

Four. Not good, with ten being the best on the scale that measured a newborn's condition at birth, but it was only the first scoring, at the one-minute point.

I held an oxygen mask near the baby's face as Dano worked on him. It seemed like hours although it was only a few minutes. He suctioned so much amniotic fluid out of the baby's mouth that I wondered if this little one really would make it.

Angie started screaming that she didn't hear the baby.

I kept trying to reassure her, and Dano suctioned the

baby, held him downward and ran his finger along the baby's foot until he let out a sound.

A sound!

The baby started to make occasional whimpers, although still a bit weak, but with the oxygen and Dano's treatments, the little boy soon really started to cry.

Angie broke out into tears and Dano wrapped the baby up and held him out to his mother. She took him and held him while the placenta was delivered, and before we knew it, we were on our way after informing the ER that the baby now had an Apgar of seven.

Dano and I sat next to Angie and son, exhausted and exhilarated.

"Birth is just amazing," came out of my mouth before I realized that I'd spoken my thoughts out loud.

Dano reached over and took my hand into his. "You did good, Nightingale. Real good."

I turned and saw something in his eyes that I really couldn't identify, yet in that instant I knew, just knew—that ER Dano was not guilty of anything except being a super grouch—but a hot, sexy one.

And being a grouch was not illegal.

Twenty

We dropped Angie and baby off at the ER, had baby pronounced healthy and met the proud daddy. As we got ready to restock and head back out, I noticed ER Dano standing at the nurses' station, where he'd been filling out the paperwork on Angie.

When he talked to the father and heard that they wouldn't have insurance for several more months since he was new at his job, Dano tore up some paperwork and threw it in the trash.

He'd just given Angie and family a free ride.

Speechless, I robotically moved into the back of the ambulance and sat there staring.

He better not be a criminal, was all I could think. He was too damn nice for that.

We pulled into TLC's driveway and I took a deep breath. For some reason—maybe what we'd just been through—I felt as if I were betraying Dan. Even though I'd found those papers in his cabinet, it still felt wrong to accuse him of anything.

The guy was a fantastic paramedic and understandably burned out of a high-emotion, high-stress and physically demanding job that I surmised he lived for.

ER Dano was not a nine to fiver.

The back door opened, and Buzz stood there. I turned and saw Dano still in his seat up front.

I looked at Buzz. "Is he all right?"

Buzz shrugged. "Told me to get the hell out and not to ask questions. He said he'd do all the paperwork. Guess he's fine. Himself."

I patted Buzz on the arm. Dano didn't want anyone to know that he'd broken some TLC rule that patients pay for their services, and I had to agree with him on this one.

The day dragged on, as we didn't get any more exciting calls. Twice we had to move patients from the hospital back to the nursing home, but none were emergencies. Now I sat in the lounge sipping the rotten tea and occasionally looking at ER Dano on the couch, his eyes shut and oh-so relaxed.

In a short time, we'd be dining together at his house, and then I was somehow going to manage to snoop around.

I felt sick to my stomach.

Jeremy had asked me to play a game of cards to pass the time, so he, Jennifer, Marty—another EMT—and I played Texas Hold 'em poker, with me winning the fake jackpot.

Soon the shift ended, everyone said their goodbyes and I walked out the back door.

"See you in a few, Nightingale," Dano said from behind.

Exhausted, I waved my hand in the air. "Be there around sixish." I wanted to turn around and see him, but told myself I needed to go home, unwind and get the food or else die of embarrassment when I arrived empty-handed.

* * *

I should have arrived at Dano's empty-handed. Dying of embarrassment in front of a hunk would have been a welcome relief, as opposed to sitting in Stella Sokol's kitchen—and getting the maternal third degree.

And no one, *no one*, did the maternal third degree like my mother.

"So, Pauline, why two dinners?" My mother turned away from the frying pan, which held the fantastic potato delicacies, and waved the spatula at me as if ready to use it. "And I still don't understand why you can't stay and eat with us. The family that eats together stays together."

"That's prays together," I mumbled, and then shook my head, sipped my tea to buy time (mom's tea bags were so fresh, I think she grew the herb and made them herself). "I'm . . . I'll need them for leftovers. You know how I love the pancakes with eggs the next morning. So does Goldie."

She spun around and turned the golden brown potato pancakes over. "Goldie. What kind of name is that, and where are my boys?"

"Both working, Ma." She hated when I called her that but now I was so tired and crabby from her questions that I did it on purpose. I did have to smile at the way she called my roommates "her boys." I'd grown very protective of the two of them, and was always thankful that someone like my mother could be so accepting of them.

"Working. Like you should be," she said, taking the first batch of pancakes out and setting them on a paper-towel-covered dish, which she then stuck in the oven.

"You don't have to keep mine warm." I got up and

made myself another cup of tea. I'd be in the bathroom all night, but that might be just the excuse I'd need to get away from Dano in his own house. "I won't be eating them right away."

She shut the oven door and looked at me. "Yes, they need to be kept warm anyway, and you ignored my statement about working. You should be working at Saint Gregory's Hospital, like Miles. There is a nursing shortage, Pauline."

"There's been a nursing shortage, Ma, since the days of Clara Barton."

She clucked her tongue at me.

I had to say, watching Stella Sokol work her magic around the kitchen was like watching Donna Reed in color. Stella even wore the button-down housedresses, aprons, and sensible shoes that were so popular in the fifties. She seemed to draw the line at pearls though, which she only wore on special occasions, like weddings and funerals.

Why anyone tied those two together, I never knew.

I shook my head as I stuck my mug into the microwave and realized I'd never seen my mother in pants. "Do you own a pair of pants, Mother?"

"Women should dress like women. And who makes tea in a microwave? Use the stove to boil the water."

"I hate my tea so hot, and I *do* work, Ma."

"Stop calling me that." She ladled spoonfuls of pancake batter into the hot oil. A crackling and sizzling sound filled the kitchen, along with the delicious scent of the potatoes and onions to which she always added just the correct amount of salt.

Now the nostalgic aroma had me leaning against the peacock-blue Formica countertop and remembering my childhood, which was damn good considering

Stella Sokol raised us kids. As a matter of fact, when she wielded the spatula at me, I had another déjà vu kinda moment. Mom always waved some kind of kitchen utensil at us kids to make her point, but she never actually hit us. She left that up to the wooden-ruler-wielding nuns. I figured mom's weapon of choice always came from the kitchen because that's where she spent her entire life.

"Okay, Pauline, we are back to my original question. Why two meals, and don't give me any malarkey about leftovers. You never liked leftovers. Even as a child you were finicky about eating something that was made on a different day."

I felt myself shrink down to the age of five. No, make that seven. The age of reason, when I realized there was no reasoning with my mother. "That was before the dawn of the microwave. Now I love leftovers," I lied.

"Baloney. Why two meals?"

"I have a date!" flew out of my mouth in the most childish voice.

Mother swung around, sending a drip of grease flying onto the sparkling black-and-white-checked linoleum flooring. While she vigorously wiped it up, she said, "A date. A date? A date!"

I shook my head at her excitement. Or, was that her *amazement*? Damn. "Don't sound so surprised, Maaaaa."

Once again she waved the spatula at me, but this time she quickly wiped it with the paper towel first. "Stop that, or I won't feed you."

My favorite uncle, Uncle Walt, walked in. "Not feed her? Yowza, Pauline. What the hell did you do?" He and I chuckled.

Mother gave him a stern look. "Don't use such language in front of her, Walter."

He shrugged. "Maybe I won't get fed tonight." Then he winked at me, kissed me on the cheek and hurried out.

I guess he figured he'd better get the hell out of Dodge, or she really wouldn't let him eat.

"Ma, Uncle Walt's language is fine." I wanted to say she should hear the guys I hung around with curse, but thought better than to share that. I really wanted my food soon. She finished taking out the rest of the pancakes from the frying pan, and I went to her and put my arm around her shoulder. "I do work, Mother. You know I'm doing very well as an insurance investigator. We're needed too. People cheat the companies out of millions and that makes the premiums go up for everyone."

I decided to go for broke, so I told her about Angie, the baby, and no insurance. Before I finished, my mother was making the sign of the cross and saying an Our Father for Angie and her family.

Now I had her.

"So, let me package up mine now. I have to get going."

"Where?" She took out a plastic container and lined it with several paper towels.

"My date. I told you." I got out a bag from the cabinet and the applesauce and sour cream from the fridge. Both went great with my mother's homemade potato pancakes.

"Yes, you did say a date." She carefully laid one pancake atop the others as if making a gift basket. "But, Pauline, you didn't say—actually I think you are trying not to say—where." She swung around and glared at me. "Are you having a man over to your condominium?"

Age seven started to resurface again, but I held my head up and said, "Nope." Then I stuck the rest of the applesauce and sour cream back into the refrigerator. "Okay, Mom." I kissed her cheek. "This is great. It all smells great. I appreciate it. Great. Great. Great."

She grabbed my arm. "*His* house? You are going to a *man's* house?"

Even though I'd never been good at reading body language, mother's eyes were wild, accusing, sneaky and probing. Before I knew it, I'd be telling her that I'd had sex with ER Dano! So, telling her I was going to his house was mild in comparison. If I stuck around though, she'd have me confessing he also might be a murderer. I had to pull my face away so she couldn't use her motherly interrogation techniques on me.

"Well, gotta run." I made it to the doorway, but her voice yanked me back. I swung around just in time to hear her say, "You're in your thirties, Pauline. For God's sake, wear a thong."

Once in my car and on the road, I could barely drive after the verbal shock Stella Sokol had given me.

And yet, I still loved her.

I kept the potato pancakes in the oven on low and hoped to hell they wouldn't dry out. Mother's never did, but that didn't mean a thing, considering my cooking skills.

After my shower, I headed to my room to get dressed. When I opened the dresser drawer, I noticed a thong she'd left there—amid the rest of my undies, which I'd promptly replaced with bikinis and even some briefs that I only wore to work. Hey, I didn't want any panty lines on my scrubs.

When I went to get a bikini pair, my hand—all by itself, mind you—drifted over and picked up the yellow thong. I held it up to figure out how women actually put the damn things on when from behind me a voice said, "Yellow is your color, Sherlock."

I shoved the thong behind my back and swung around. "You . . . what are you—"

Jagger stood in the doorway, looking at my robe, which had now fallen open a tad, revealing some cleavage.

I yanked it shut, but when I did, the thong swung around in my hand. Turning, I threw it into the drawer and decided not to try to explain that my mother had bought it.

"Goldie let me in." He leaned against the wall, looking oh-so delicious.

"Oh." I held the robe for dear life. "Wait. Goldie isn't even home!"

Jagger waved his hand as if he had no intention of explaining how he got in and, frankly, I didn't care. When I looked at him standing there, my first thought was—*he came. He's going to ER Dano's with me.*

Jagger thinks Dano is guilty.

While hugging my robe, I felt my heart plummet in my chest. Shit. I didn't want that to be true. "You think Dano is guilty, then?"

Jagger curled his lips. "One of these days you're going to have to explain how your mind works. I mean, one moment you're ogling sexy lingerie and the next, you're making statements out of left field. What the hell are you asking?" He sauntered in and sat on the edge of my bed.

Yeah, I was in real good condition to explain things now. Even *I* didn't know what the hell I was thinking. I looked at Jagger and then at the door, hoping Goldie or Miles would come in. After a few seconds, traitor Spanky walked in and directly up to Jagger, who lifted the dog up onto the bed.

What an adorable sight!

But I had work to do and part of that was to get dressed. So, I summoned my logical thoughts and said, "If you come with me to Dano's, then you must think he's guilty and are worried about my safety."

Jagger looked at me. "I don't think. I do." With that he scooped up Spanky, and walked out the door. "Get dressed."

I stuck my hands on my hips and then realized how childish that must look, so instead I stuck my tongue out at his back.

I wore the yellow thong.

That thought stuck in my head as I walked down the stairs in my condo to go to the kitchen. Jagger was seated on the couch, watching CNN. Without looking, he said, "Shatley said the two stabbings are related. Not that we didn't know that."

"Did he say anything about Sky?"

"Nope."

"Oh." I continued on toward the kitchen.

Suddenly I could feel him glaring at me, and I could swear he knew, just knew, that I had on the thong.

"Shut up," I said and walked by.

He scowled as if genuinely confused. But instead of admitting something like that, he said, "Call me as soon as you've found out what you need to know." He got up, walked to the door and left.

My mouth hung open for a few seconds, I looked at Spanky and said, "Shut up," and then hurried into the kitchen, where I packaged up our meal. I had fifteen minutes to get to Dano's or be late. I hated being late and prided myself in being on time.

On the way out the door I had a thought: *our* meal. I'd thought *our meal*, but it could be the last if I found anything suspicious in Dano's cabinets—or if I found out the reason the papers were there.

Then again, Jagger wasn't coming.

Jagger *wasn't* coming!

Twenty-One

"You are one hell of a cook, Nightingale," Dano said as he took another bite of potato pancake. "Damn. I'm impressed."

My CSIC (Catholic-school-induced conscience) said I should tell him the truth, but for the moment, I reveled in the compliment and thought, hell, he might be lying about something much more serious than potato pancakes, so why not let him believe the cooking was mine?

I really didn't want to like him. I really didn't want to think of this as a date. I really didn't *want* him to be guilty!

"Thanks," I muttered and stuffed my mouth with a glob of sour cream. Yuck! I cut a piece of pancake and ate it to wash down the sour cream.

Dano looked at me, rather oddly, I might add. "What's wrong?"

I waved my hand and took a sip of wine. "Oh, nothing. Just too much sour cream."

"That's not what I mean, and you know it."

He almost sounded angry. At least he did sound serious. Wow. Suddenly my mind snapped to attention, and I touched my finger to the pink locket—which I'd used once already on this case—hanging around my neck. A Jagger present. A very appropriate, albeit not romantic, present. Pepper spray. The locket contained pepper spray for me to use on my cases. Yes, Jagger did not trust me with a gun. Something about my foot and shots being fired—by me.

But one of these days . . .

While fingering the locket, I also ran through the self-defense moves Jagger had taught me. I only hoped I wouldn't have to use them on Dano, since we'd done other moves that were much more pleasant. . . . Geez. Just my luck.

If I didn't keep reminding myself that Jagger wasn't here—he actually didn't come—then I might start to get a bit frightened. When I looked across the table with the handmade crocheted tablecloth, I found it hard to believe this guy could be a criminal, much less a murderer.

"How's Pansy?" I asked.

Dano hesitated.

Why? What made him do that? I headed into investigative mode and decided no matter how hot he was or how much I liked this guy, I had to find out the truth very soon.

He looked at his food. "She's had a setback."

Damn! "What kind?"

"Fever. The report is that she started talking, but with her temp 103, seemed she wasn't making any sense." He took a sip of his wine and looked at me.

To whom? Maybe what Pansy was saying made perfect sense to my case. "Interesting. What was she saying?"

"Jennifer went to visit her and said she kept repeating Sky's name over and over."

Gulp. I wished I could share what I knew about Sky

and Pansy with Dano. Maybe he even knew about it or knew something that would make sense. "Hmm. That doesn't make sense to me. Does it to you?"

Dano sipped his wine and shrugged. "Guess it might."

Bingo. "Might? How's that?"

"Well, he worked for her. Sky's only been at TLC a few years, but he used to take Pansy on helicopter rides. She was interested in flying them."

That's not all she was interested in.

"Hmm. Maybe she was interested in Sky too." I forced a chuckle.

Dano didn't join me, but said, "Naw. Pansy's not interested in boys."

"She's gay?" I nearly choked on my wine. What about the sex chair and the fact that she'd mentioned Sky's name to Lilla and I?

"Not gay. I think neither. She's never really had a life outside of work." He wiped a dollop of applesauce up with the remainder of the potato pancake and stuffed it into his mouth. Stella Sokol would be thrilled to see a guy enjoying her work of art like that.

"Neither? How can you be sure?"

He wiped a napkin briskly across his lips. "I'm not. Just guessing, and frankly, Nightingale, I couldn't give a shit."

Well, *I* certainly could!

Damn, but it was romantic cleaning up after our meal. Dano was cute and said whoever cooked shouldn't clean, but in my gut I knew I should be helping. So, we did it together and now we sat on the couch in the living room with some soft piano music playing in the background. Romantic? Yeah. Did I wish I didn't keep noticing that stupid cabinet in the kitchen while cleaning up? Damn it. Yeah.

I had to go check it out soon or my hormones might betray me. Hey, I was human and didn't feel as if Dano was really a threat. However, I drew the line at making out with a possible criminal, so I had to get myself into gear so I could shift into another kind of gear.

Dano reached over to put his arm around me. With the other hand he touched my cheek very gently, running his finger down to my lips, which he encircled.

Oh, boy. . . .

"Hey, I have to use the little girls' room." I removed his hand reluctantly and got up.

"No problem. I have a few phone calls to make anyway." He got up and walked to the front door.

"Where are you going?"

"Oh, this thing doesn't get very good reception in this old place." He held out his cell phone. "Gotta go outside each time I want a clear, uninterrupted call. Take your time. Help yourself to more wine too, and feel free to refill mine."

When he stepped out and closed the door, I looked up to heaven and winked. "If only you'd make each and every case this easy." With that, I hurried into the kitchen to the cabinet—that could make or break my night.

Or, make that more than just this one night.

I kept looking at the front door to make sure that Dano hadn't popped back in. Certainly he didn't suspect me of anything. Of that much I was sure. Because if ER Dano had suspected me of being about to snoop, he wouldn't have left me alone in the house. Nope. I never got any sense of suspicion on his part.

Since the coast looked clear, I hurried into the kitchen,

propping the swinging door open a crack in order to hear the front door open. The whiteness of the place gave an eerie feeling, whereas when I first saw it, it looked as if it belonged in a featured article of *House Beautiful*.

Had to be my CSIC acting up, but since I had a job to do, I pretended I'd gone to public school as a kid and was Lutheran. That helped a bit as I walked to the cabinet where the papers had been stashed.

When I touched the cabinet's door handle, I half expected the papers to be gone when I opened it.

But there they sat. All in a messed-up pile, but still there. Dano really hadn't suspected me of anything and must not have known that I'd already seen them.

I looked toward the door and listened for a few seconds. Nothing except the grandfather clock's gongs signaling the hour. It had been dark outside for a bit, so I realized that anyone walking by the bay windows could clearly see inside the kitchen. Realizing that gave me pause, but I turned back to the matter at hand, deciding I had to take chances in this business.

The papers on the top were all about overcharged payments made by TLC. Things like extra charges for oxygen or nurse transport when other documentation showed that these were not the case. Plus, I knew the ambulance charge was a flat rate and it was against the law to charge for some things individually.

I read through several more papers and found out that Sky's flights were making much more money than they should. Hmm. Insurance companies were being charged for ground miles, which included every twist and turn through the streets, instead of air miles, which were direct shots through the air.

Yep. A big difference.

Sky's signature was on several of these forms.

I leaned against the counter to digest this information. My potato pancakes started to rise in my throat. Was Sky somehow involved? Did he fall in love with Pansy and then decide he wanted to get ownership of TLC by using her—and she found out?

Jilted lovers again.

They made great suspects.

A few of the other papers had notes in the margins. Handwritten notes that I would bet my life were in Dano's handwriting. I'd read some of his daily run sheets, and the writing looked the same, as far as I remembered. Only on these, he'd explained how medications could be double charged. When the paramedic cracked open the glass vial of a medication to give to a patient, the half-full vial was to be turned in to the ER nurse for replacement.

But Dano's note said some of the medication could have been replaced with saline and when the nurse went to discard it, she'd never know. The patient would be charged for the medication, and the paramedic could have used the rest on him or herself or sold it in one of the crack houses over on Lincoln Street. Lord knew those poor souls would buy just about anything.

After going through everything that I read, I really wasn't convinced of anything. As a matter of fact, I was more confused. Dano's notes almost sounded as if he were—

"What the hell are you doing with those?" he said from behind. "Geez. Damn. Now what, Pauline?"

The hair on the back of my neck stood up. My heart started to race. In the glass of the cabinet door, I could see the serious, almost threatening face of a very pissed ER Dano. And in his hand was a shiny metal object.

A knife. A *knife*!

Twenty-Two

"No!" I screamed and swung around to defend myself against the knife-wielding ER Dano. Although my instincts had been wrong about him, I wasn't going to let my feelings get in the way.

My life depended on it.

After all, he'd killed Payne, stabbed Pansy and hidden the fraud evidence in his house!

Without another thought and in only a few seconds, I had the pink pepper spray locket in my hands, aimed and sprayed.

"Aye!" he screamed and dropped his knife.

I went to kick it to the side, but Dano grabbed me by the shoulders.

"What the hell? That feels like a freaking Habanera pepper in my face! Goddamn! Even my ears burn. Jesus! What the hell are you—" He nearly shook me so hard I was about to knee him in the groin when I caught a glimpse of the knife near the kitchen table.

I blinked.

Then blinked again.

Cell phone.

Dano's cell phone lay on the floor.

He'd let me go and hurried to the sink to run water over his face. Between breaths and gurgles, he cursed at me and asked over and over why the hell I sprayed him.

I couldn't take my eyes off the phone.

Dano didn't have a knife. But did that make him any less guilty of something else?

I hurried to his side and grabbed the water sprayer to help. "I thought you . . . you had a knife. I thought you were going to . . . what the hell are you doing with all those papers, Dan?" I kept spraying until he pushed my hands away, grabbed a towel and stood up.

His face was brighter than a boiled lobster.

"You're gonna have to explain that one, Nightingale. That is, if I live. My eyes are crying like a damn baby's. My mouth is drooling like a freaking waterfall!"

"Oh, geez. And your nose is running like a sick kid's. I am so sorry!" Despite the look he tried to give me through his pain, I said, "Get your shirt off. The effects won't be as bad." I grabbed his shirt and tugged.

"Yeah, not as bad," he muttered.

The spray obviously caused the mucus membranes of his nose and throat to swell, which made it difficult for him to breathe. His eyes had swollen shut, and I knew beneath the reddened lids they were as bloodshot as if he'd drunk a case of tequila.

He kept cursing and mentioning my name over and over.

"Get to the shower!" I yelled, half pushing him toward the downstairs bathroom that did, in fact, have a shower hose attached to it despite the claw-foot antique tub.

"Did you kill Payne?" came flying out of my mouth as I undid Dano's belt buckle.

Dano managed to open one tiny slit of his left eye and somehow glared at me. "What the hell is wrong with you tonight? No, I *didn't* kill anyone." He stood closer to me, probably to see me better. "But the thought did cross my mind this very second."

I fingered the locket.

He grabbed my hand and yanked it off, breaking the clasp. "You can't be trusted with that thing. Thank God you don't carry a gun. I still want to know what the hell you are up to!" He shoved off his jeans and stood there in his boxers.

I stood my ground instead of giving into the flight-or-fight response that my adrenaline was pumping out. Actually, my first choice was the flight one. Okay, the *very* first one had something to do with seeing him in his boxers. "I need to know. Are you involved in the fraud at TLC?"

He hesitated. My mouth went dry.

"How do you know about that?" he asked, very seriously.

"It . . . doesn't matter. *Are* you?" My nurse's nature made me want to gently wipe the water from his eyes and face. He looked so miserable—and I had caused it. But I held back, remembering Jagger's words. "And don't go nursing the criminals," he'd once said to me.

But I couldn't believe I was standing here with a criminal.

It seemed like hours that I stood in the kitchen grilling ER Dano, sans clothes and now only with a towel wrapped around his waist, until he finally started to recover from the pepper spray. I knew if he'd meant to harm me, he could have done so a long time ago.

Had to be a good sign.

Actually, he became very cooperative about the questioning and made sense a few times, but right when I thought I'd figured him out, he'd get back on the "What the hell are you up to?" line of questioning.

"Make me some tea to ease this feeling in my throat," he said. It really wasn't a gruff order, but then again he didn't say please either.

When I went to put a tea bag in a mug and pour tap water into it, he said from behind, "Don't you know how to make proper tea? Boil it."

Shades of Stella Sokol.

I boiled his and nuked mine and in a few minutes we were sitting at the table. His face looked much better, although still a bit pinkish.

And there I sat, not sure if I should feel badly or not.

Dano took a sip of tea and looked me in the eye. "Who do you work for, Pauline?"

Yikes. He'd used my first name as Jagger always did with his no-nonsense voice. As I sat there contemplating a lie, I realized there wasn't a scared bone in my body.

ER Dano had to be clean. I just felt it.

"The more important question, Dan, is why do you have all that evidence of fraud at TLC?"

He didn't even look surprised, which surprised the hell out of me—and maybe did scare me a bit. Then again, a con man usually could play a poker face like a gambling Vegas billionaire.

I sipped and swallowed and sipped then swallowed and sipped a few more times. When I looked him in the eyes, I said, "It shouldn't take so long to answer truthfully."

Dano chuckled, and then started to laugh. "You are one hell of a woman, Nightingale."

Now I've faced murderers before, several times, as a matter of fact, and even had them make attempts on my life, and with my limited knowledge of psych, I could sense the nefarious personalities of these folk when it came right down to it.

And I didn't sense it now.

Dano's laughter wasn't eerie or scary or nefarious. It seemed to come from deep within him and from humor.

"What is so funny?" I had to ask.

"It just dawned on me. You think I'm involved in the fraud and the stabbings."

"And that is funny *because*?"

"Because, granted, I'm a burned-out paramedic, suffer nightmares from the job, don't put up with any crap from anyone. Anyone. And have little patience for the newbies, although I always get assigned them, but I am not a killer or a thief."

He has me convinced was my first thought; however, logically, I knew I couldn't just believe his words. Probably I wanted to believe them and that was confusing me. But I looked him directly in the eyes and said, "Prove it. I need proof."

Dano glared at me for a few moments.

I swallowed several times and fidgeted with my tea mug, feeling like a bug under a microscope. I also fidgeted in my chair. Finally I said, "Stop that! Tell me the truth now."

He calmly got up and went to the cabinet that I'd been snooping in. When he pulled out the rest of the papers, he shuffled through them and handed me several. "Read."

I read all right and had to push my jaw back up off my chest several times. Slowly I set them down.

"Then who killed Payne and stabbed Pansy?" the stupid question came out before I could think, since I was so delighted (and, yes, relieved) that Dano was not guilty of anything other than gathering inside information for one Global Carrier Insurance Company—the biggest one that Fabio dealt with in his agency.

Dano shook his head. "I thought you cared about me."

Oops. "I did . . . *do*." I set the papers down, got up and went to place my arms around his neck. "You have to believe me that I never wanted you to be involved."

And his kiss said more, a hell of a lot more than any words could.

He started to nuzzle my neck. "If I knew who hurt Pansy and killed Payne, don't you think I'd tell the cops?"

Preoccupied by his hands running over my body in oh-so delicious places, I barely remembered what he was talking about. In a few seconds I leaned back, looked him in the eyes and said, "Yes, I do."

"Then sex isn't out of the question, once I recover from your attack?"

Thank goodness he was smiling his dynamite ER Dano, sexy, girls-can't-keep-their-hands-off-me smile.

I ran my fingers down his chest to grab onto the towel. "Not at all."

His lips covered mine, and despite his earlier "discomforts" he lifted me up and carried me into the living room, where soon my clothing lay in a pile on the floor—right after I'd yanked off Dano's damp towel.

* * *

It didn't take me long to forget my concerns about Dano. As he ran his hands across my breasts so very gently in the afterglow of our lovemaking, it seemed like a dream. Well, this very moment seemed like a sexy, unbelievable dream, but any thoughts that he was a criminal seemed like ages ago and not very real.

I turned toward him, taking his now very pale pink cheeks in my hands and kissing his lips with purpose. "I am so sorry."

He kissed me back, running his tongue inside my mouth until I thought we could do ... it ... again. "Fagetaboutit. You've worn me out." He playfully pinched my nipple.

"I really do want to forget it all but need to make it clear. The job stuff. Not the sex. I'm sure you're wondering who I am."

He wrapped his leg across mine. "Nope. I know you rather intimately now."

I smacked his hard chest. "Ouch. Well, I need to make it all clear." And I really did. I couldn't start a relationship on a lie, so I told ER Dano who I really was and who I worked for, leaving out Jagger's identity—or what little I knew about it.

Dano leaned back, looked at me and smiled. "I was wondering when you'd get around to all that."

I felt my eyes widen a hundred times larger. "You ... were wondering?" I wrinkled my forehead. "I'm not following." But my investigative abilities were sending out signals that said, *He knew. He knew. He knew all along!*

He leaned over and kissed my forehead. "We're straight now, Nightingale. Straight."

When he held me closer, I wanted to go on and on

asking questions, but this felt so right that I shut my mouth. But in my mind I screamed, *Jagger!*

Jagger had to have already told him.

Of course, Jagger always managed to finagle us into getting jobs in the companies that we were investigating, and it made sense that one of the employees would have to know who we were.

While Dano kissed me deeply, sensually and well, damn hotly—the last thought on my mind was *I'm going to kill Jagger*.

Twenty-Three

Dano and I were dressed and heading out the door when my cell phone rang. I opened it and brought it to my ear.

"Pansy's awake. Meet me there." Then Jagger hung up before I could scream at him about the Dano situation. In my mind though, I knew Jagger always had my back. He never would have let me come here tonight alone if he didn't really know who ER Dano was.

But did Jagger really know what Dano and I had done?

Yikes. I hoped to hell he couldn't tell about my "glow" like perceptive Lilla could. Naw. Guys were not perceptive.

"We need to get to the hospital. Pansy woke up." Pansy woke up. Perfect.

Dano turned to look at me. "That Jagger?"

Oh, yeah. Jagger had known. I'd kill him for sure and not with a cell phone but a real knife!

"Yep," I said as Dano threw his keys at me.

"You drive. I'm indisposed as far as night vision. My truck will get us there faster than your yuppie Volvo."

I wanted to argue that it was not yuppie, but that'd

be a losing battle since my car, in fact, was. Hey, I bought it secondhand from a financial advisor in suburban Glastonbury, CT. Couldn't get any more yuppie than that.

On the way to the hospital, I kept apologizing to Dano about the pepper spray until he made me pull over and said, "Stop that. You did the right thing. I wouldn't have expected any less out of you, Nightingale. You've got guts and chutzpah. That, my dear, is why you make a fantastic nurse, investigator, and . . . sex—"

"I get it. Thanks." Phew. I really didn't want him going into *that*—even if it sounded like a good compliment coming on. There was that Catholic-school-induced-conscience thing, and once you heard something out *loud*, it became all too real.

Premarital sex. Or pre no-plans-for-marriage sex. Yikes.

We drove off and soon were pulling into the parking lot of Saint Greg's.

"There's Jagger's SUV," Dano said, pointing to the left side of the parking lot.

At first it surprised me that Dano would recognize Jagger's SUV, but working with Jagger, I'd learned not to be bowled over by Jagger-induced shockers any longer, and that obviously pertained to Dano-induced shockers too. "Let's see if he waited for us in it."

I opened my own door since even after having sex with ER Dano I wasn't expecting any changes. Truthfully, I didn't want any. He was hot and perfect the way he was and there was enough chemistry between us to blow up a small building. Nope. I liked ER "as is" and no amount of wishing and hoping could produce that amount of chemistry—and apparently, I liked it.

And, hey, since he was still talking to me after pepper spraying him—he had to feel something close to it too.

Jagger got out and walked toward us.

I could swear he looked at me as if he *knew* about . . . you know. But then I told myself that was my stupid conscience acting up again. No way could he tell—but when we got closer, he stepped next to me and touched my arm. "Let's go inside," he said.

Wow.

Was that a possessive kind of touch?

I decided to concentrate on the case at hand and not try to figure out my romantic involvements/non-involvements. Besides, a thirty-something who up until now hadn't had a date or sex in X (truthfully I didn't want to know the real number because it'd be too embarrassing) number of months was in no position to figure anything out.

Walking between these two, though, proved more difficult than I thought—especially when they both went to put their arms around my shoulders—at the same time!

We made it up to Pansy's floor without any more physical contact on anyone's part, and not a word of explanation either.

I, however, smiled to myself all the way up on the elevator.

We stopped at the desk, and ER Dano explained that we were all employees who had come to visit their boss.

The stern-looking nurse glared at me.

Geez! At first I worried that she might have recognized me as a past employee from there. But she didn't look familiar. I let my hair slip forward to partially cover my face and took a step backward.

As if he read my mind, Jagger leaned forward until I was nearly hidden from Nurse Ratched's view. She did have a similar-looking expression to the nasty nurse in the movie *One Flew Over the Cuckoo's Nest*.

"Visiting hours are over." She stepped back and folded her arms across her chest.

I started to turn around, but both Jagger and Dano pulled out the charm—nonstop—and before I knew it—and in quite a whirlwind of confusion—we were walking down the hallway to where the guard sat.

I could only shake my head in amazement at these two hunks.

Not only could these two hunks sweet-talk their way into a patient's room after visiting hours, but also they could talk an armed guard into letting us get by.

I figured he knew who Jagger was anyway, so this time I didn't let myself get too impressed.

"Lieutenant Shatley's in there," the guard said, mostly to Jagger, who nodded.

"Maybe we should wait?" I suggested.

But they were both putting on their isolation outfits and damn, but they both looked so tasty in Johnny coats (unfortunately over their clothes) and masks.

Couldn't decide whose eyes were sexier.

Then I concluded—both were.

"Okay. Okay." I dressed up and followed them into the room, certain they didn't want any discussion out in the hallway and in front of Barney Fife.

When Jagger stepped aside and Dano walked toward the bed, I got a glimpse of Pansy. Yikes. She looked awful. Then again she had been stabbed, suffered quite a blood loss, survived surgery and a whopper of an infection and a temperature, not to mention the trauma her body had endured.

What struck me most was the glassy look in her eyes. For some reason, Pansy didn't look back to normal. Normal for her, that is. She and her brother were pips and often had the most unusual looks on their faces. Ones that no one got except them. I chalked it up to "twin telepathy."

Right now she was glaring at . . . me!

I moved to the side behind the lieutenant. "Hey," I said.

He nodded and turned toward Jagger, who was next to me. "Not much useful stuff yet. She's hopped up on meds, is my guess."

Or hiding something, was mine. But I didn't want to say anything that was accusatory, as I really didn't have any evidence. I looked around the room of masked professionals and decided I'd need ironclad proof for this gang.

Jagger stepped forward. "Hey, Pansy. Jagger here. Remember me?"

She nodded, but I don't think she meant it, and I'm sure Jagger realized that. "Jagger."

"Yeah, I'm a new paramedic, Pansy. I'm still on orientation." He touched her hand, which was holding onto the side rail.

Actually, I wondered what she was thinking with this group in here. Pansy probably was frightened. Yeah, that made sense, when I looked at her face.

I walked next to Jagger. "Hi, Pansy," I said in my softest, friendliest voice. I'd reverted back to my old nursing tricks and before long, I seemed to have her trusting me. At least she held my hand instead of the railing. I let her, thinking she wasn't going to have a baby right now like Angie, so I was safe as far as a broken hand went.

Jagger started to talk more about work, trying to get her mind into focus, I assumed.

Every time she answered, she looked at me.

I caught Lieutenant Shatley looking at me and winking. He wanted me to get her into my confidence. Okay. I could do that. I'd worked psych before. And I'd worked neuro, so between the two, I should be able to get Pansy's mind off the gang in the room and get her to tell us something.

Dano made a kind of groaning sound as if irritated, or more like it, impatient. I looked to see him edge his way toward the bed, kinda pushing Jagger out of the way.

Oh . . . my . . . God.

They looked at each other and remained calm, although *I* felt the tension.

"Hey, Pansy. It's me, Dano. ER Dano."

Suddenly I felt as if Pansy had just returned from Oz and the Tin Man, the Scarecrow and Lion Jagger were all re-introducing themselves to gain her confidence. Only thing was, in Oz Pansy would've only had to worry about a "non-waterproof" witch, where in Hope Valley, there was a potential killer on the loose.

She kept looking at me as she spoke, and I had to admit, she got a hundred percent of the answers—wrong. Didn't know who the president was. Said the year was 1951, and although the guy was an enigma, she really didn't know who ER Dano was, despite the longevity of his employment with TLC.

I looked at the men in the room and we collectively frowned. A few of them cursed.

"Pansy, do you know where you are?" I asked, hoping my femaleness might give me an upper hand over the guys.

She made a coughing noise. I checked her monitor and her heart rate and respirations were okay, although a little fast, which I chalked up to stress. Who wouldn't be stressed with this gang in their room interrogating them right after they'd woken up from a few days of a deep sleep?

I waited until she calmed down and said, "That's all right. How do you feel?"

She looked at me. "I'm fine, Pauline."

My eyes widened at that lucid statement! Everyone in the room looked hopeful, so I continued on with my line of questioning. "Do you remember what happened to you?"

"Of course. What the hell are you all doing in those stupid outfits? Is it Halloween?" She started to chuckle and it turned into a cackle.

The hairs on my neck stood on end.

I gulped and felt myself being nudged from behind. Jagger. Natch. He'd had my back all right, but was pushing me forward as if the woman in the bed was some sweet young thing who'd just awakened like a harmless Sleeping Beauty.

I think the only time Jagger touched my back was to push me into something or someone.

I looked at Pansy, and her face contorted into a shape that made me remember the witch with the poison apple in *Snow White*.

Jagger nudged.

I turned around and said, "Stop that!" Again, Stella Sokol's tone.

He didn't look as if he were smiling under the mask. "Ask her."

Oh, great. He wanted me to ask her who had stabbed her, which was the same as asking who had killed her precious clone of a brother. Yeah, right. My luck would be that Pansy would drift off into a self-induced coma in fear of her life.

So, I chatted more until she answered a few questions correctly. However, Dano looked at me and said, "Those are pretty generic. She could be just mumbling."

"She might be," Jagger interrupted with, "but we have nothing else. Go for it, Pauline. We could lose her again."

Whoops. Pauline. Pauline. There it was. The serious tone. The serious name. The one word that got my knees knocking, and I stepped forward in some out-of-body experience and asked, "Who stabbed you, Pansy?"

She looked horrified. Then she turned toward me and spat!

Thank goodness for masks, I thought. "I didn't mean to upset you, Pansy."

She started to babble, and often I wasn't even sure it was English. Visions of the Exorcist came to mind. She yelled. She screamed, and then she whimpered like a little child, all the while thrashing about and yanking on the IV tubing.

Tears streamed from her eyes, and she babbled on for a few more minutes.

I grabbed her hand and released the IV tubing so she wouldn't pull it out. "We need to leave," I said, so the patient wouldn't relapse in front of our eyes and it'd be my fault. "Someone get the nurse," I ordered and Jagger pushed the call button.

Then Pansy started to say random names. They all

seemed to be either employees or family, which was only Payne, come to think of it. She repeated his name over and over.

The door opened and in walked Nurse Ratched, who gave us all the evil eye. It didn't take us long before we were hurrying out the door and disrobing from our isolation garb.

I breathed a sigh. I felt relieved to get the hell out of there, until the nurse opened the door while we were disrobing isolation gear and asked, "Which one of you is Pauline?"

I curled my lips at her since I was the only female there and raised my hand and waved it at her. "That'd be me."

"Well, she said she wants to talk to you and—" She stuck her head back into the room and asked Pansy, "Who?"

"Jeremy."

Twenty-Four

"Oh, Lord," I said to Dano. "Buzz will pass out if he has to deal with *that* Pansy, the evil incarnate, who's in there."

Dano chuckled.

"It's not funny. He's such a wimp. Why on earth would she want to talk to him? Why would she want to talk to me?" I asked.

"I'm guessing she just relates to you as a female that she knows works for her. A nurse. A new hire, so not involved in the politics of the company," he said.

Sounded plausible.

"They're pretty tight, Pansy and Buzz," he said. "She hired him and kinda took him under her wing. Like a mother figure, if you can believe a Sterling having maternal feelings." That's why he was upset when he visited her, I figured.

"Ah."

Before I could say anything more, Dano had his cell phone out and was ordering Buzz to get his ass over here.

I looked at Jagger. "What?"

He was smiling. "This is gonna be better than Leno's monologue."

I punched his arm, turned and punched Dano. "You were thinking the same thing," I said when he looked all confused.

But in the back of my mind, I worried that poor Buzz Lightyear would not survive on his own.

I needn't have worried about dear Buzz last night, I thought as I fixed my horrible tea in the TLC lounge. By the time he'd gotten to the hospital—looking much paler than Pansy herself—curiously enough, she'd slipped back into a coma.

Self-induced? Or new complication?

No one could be sure, but darling Buzz and I were off the hook.

Jagger, Dano and I had waited to go in with him and when he came down the hallway with tears in his eyes, I was glad we all had. Those guys were shits at times, but each had a heart of gold, and both would rather kill themselves than admit it.

"Morning, Pauline," Buzz said, coming up from behind me.

I touched his arm. "Oh, hey, how are you today?"

"I'm fine, ma'am." He spilled a droplet of coffee on my clog.

We both looked down at the same time to see it spread out like a California wildfire on my white shoe. Before he could do his usual apology, I said, "Don't worry about it," but in seconds he was down on all fours wiping away.

Yes, I felt stupid and sorry for him all at the same time.

"Bu . . . Jeremy." I touched his shoulder.

He stood up and threw the paper towel toward the trash can.

It landed on ER Dano's foot.

Yikes. I hurried over and said, "Hey, morning," so he wouldn't take it out on poor Buzz, who was now bending down to pick it off Dano's very worn black boot. Those boots had character and, I'm sure, some stories to tell.

Thank goodness Lilla sashayed into the room at that very moment, before Dano could punt Buzz across the room.

She gave Buzz a big smile.

He seemed more nervous than usual, but they sat down together.

"Talk about the odd couple," Dano muttered.

I slugged his arm and said, "Shut up," just as Ambulance #456 was called over the intercom. "Ten fifty-four on 442 Lincoln Street.

Dano, Buzz and I left our mugs on the table and hurried out. Lilla wished us luck (and with her Canadian accent I thought she sounded so cool).

Buzz was blushing from ear to ear when we got to the ambulance, where we all stuck on raingear, since a monsoon had decided the flowers needed watering. Dano insisted on driving—with me up front.

Darling Buzz didn't argue, and if I wasn't mistaken, I think the sweetie actually winked at me!

Dano drove #456 like it was a multimillion dollar Rolls. No one could take corners as smoothly or get us to our destination as quickly. On the way, he'd explained to me that the call was a teenager who supposedly was having a panic attack of some sort, according to the caller, a neighbor.

"Might be drugs," Dano said as we pulled down Lincoln Street.

"Over there," I said, pointing to an old green-and-beige three-story house with two cop cars parked in front. "Cops?"

Dano jumped out and Buzz already was there, getting the bag. "Neighbors didn't tell dispatch everything," he growled.

We ran toward the back of the house where two cops were standing. Just our luck. The rain seemed to pour harder, which seemed impossible. I could barely see with the hood of my yellow slicker up and no windshield wipers to keep my vision clear.

Dano yelled to the cop nearest the door. "What's up?"

He pointed toward the house. "She's in there. Be careful."

Careful? Did he mean that she was in such bad shape that we had to take care not to let her die, or—

Suddenly, a blood-curdling scream followed by ripe cursing came from the house.

Dano shook his head, "Shit. Nutcase."

I wanted to chastise him, but we didn't have time. First he yelled to the cops to stay out in front in case any family members came home or neighbors came by to gawk. Then we all went in, slipping and sliding on the hardwood floors.

"You fuckers get the hell out of my house!" The voice came from what must have been the bathroom, because there seemed to be a shower running.

"You think she's going to commit suicide?" Buzz asked.

Dano looked at him for a second. "If I could see through the freaking walls, I'd let you know."

The female voice said, "It's the end."

Hearing that Dano ran down the hallway and shoved the bathroom door open, shouting, "What's wrong, ma'am?"

Dano's shoulder must have hurt, was all I could think as he broke the door open, sending pieces of the frame flying. Damn, but that always looked easier to do on TV.

We all took a step forward and stopped.

There, standing in the middle of the tub with steaming-hot water pulsating down on her, was a teenage girl, about fifteen or sixteen, with her underwear on. She was holding a soggy stuffed Snoopy doll in one hand. Her legs were beet red from the heat. In the other hand she held a knife.

God, how I hated knives. But this one looked like a butter knife, which made me feel a lot better. In seconds, Dano had it out of her hand, and her out of the shower. As I reached over to turn it off, she kicked and screamed, nearly shoving me into the tub, which had the stopper in and was full of hot water.

A hand touched my back and I felt Buzz pulling me up. "You all right, Miss Pauline?"

"Fine." Just then the girl slugged Dano in the groin and he yelped and let her go—so she took off running down the hallway.

Dano looked at me. "Shit. Why is it that I always attract the whackos?"

Since I didn't have time to agree with Dano (although I did), we ran out, following Buzz, who was following the patient. I wanted to throw a robe on her, since her underwear had now become quite transparent.

When we got to the back door, there was no sign of the cops. Dano muttered a few curses and said they'd better just be out in front somewhere, where he'd told them to wait.

Buzz was out front running and sliding in the wet grass after the girl like Bambi on ice. The girl, however, seemed to have better traction with her bare feet, which I guessed were very used to going without shoes. Calluses probably helped.

"Leave me the hell alone!" she shouted.

Several neighbors came to the fence and one yelled, "Rebecca is not supposed to even be here. Her old man took her to the mental hospital yesterday. Guess she got out."

Dano and I looked at each other.

"You go left," he ordered.

I followed his suggestion, but when I got close enough to grab her, I ended up in a heap on top of Buzz, not even sure what went wrong other than "Rebecca" was slick. And not just because she was wet.

I could see Dano get close enough to her to grab her, but he hesitated. No loose clothing to grab onto. The underwear clung like a second skin and obviously Dano didn't want to grab just *anything*.

"Can't you get one little lady?" the burly cop rounding the corner of the house called out to Dano.

I heard a new curse word this time from Dano and thought the cop was taking his own life into his hands, and I wouldn't want to be in his black boots once Dano had Rebecca secure on the stretcher.

The other cop came up behind the first one and they started laughing. Dano and Buzz kept trying to grab the girl to no avail—she was like the proverbial greased pig.

"Come on, Nightingale. Get your ass over here!" Dano shouted.

I got up, couldn't help but wipe some recently cut grass from my raincoat, and ran toward where he pointed, trying to ignore the *squish* of my shoes and the mud that dotted my outfit. We'd tackled each other numerous times, as if in the fourth quarter of a football game, until we finally came at Rebecca from three directions and all landed in a heap on top of her in the middle of the backyard.

She looked at me and said, "Hey, my name is Rebecca. What's yours?"

I bit my tongue while Dano took off his raincoat to cover the girl.

Wow. How sweet.

And my heart did a little end-zone touchdown happy dance.

Rebecca had chosen me instead of the males in the group to talk to, just as Pansy had.

We got Rebecca safely to the hospital. Dano followed the ER doctor's orders en route to medicate her since she'd freaked out. Dano and I took her in while Buzz stayed to clean up the ambulance. While we stood talking to the doctor, he came in and turned in the remaining half vial of medication that had been used on Rebecca, then went back out to the ambulance.

I watched the nurse throw what was left out and give Dano the replacement medication to put in his box. I could hear poor Rebecca screaming in Exam Room 3, and I wanted to go hug her. I did step in and tried to talk to her, but she tried to bite me. With that I looked at the staff, wished them well and was out the door to find the guys.

"Got a chest pain," Buzz yelled in the doorway.

Dano and I flew out the doorway and off on another

run. This job was truly exhausting, and I could see how someone in it year after year could burn out. I'd been there, done that in medicine myself.

One could only take watching the suffering of human beings for so long.

Still, as evidenced by Dano covering up Rebecca, the guy had kept his smarts about him and his heart.

If he stayed at TLC much longer . . . who knew what he'd end up like?

Thank goodness Jagger had drifted toward helping Lieutenant Shatley with Payne's homicide and the attempt on Pansy's life, since I kept getting so tied up on real life-and-death situations. Leaving me to deal with the insurance fraud made sense.

Buzz seemed delighted to be driving, and when we got to the address of the eighty-four-year-old woman with chest pain, he went to call in on the radio. Dano and I jumped out and raced to the front door where an elderly man stood—nearly in tears.

We worked on Helen, the lovely woman who didn't seem to be in any real distress. I gathered her chest pain was muscular, not cardiac, and the monitor said the same. But we started an IV, gave her oxygen and got her into the ambulance with the cardiac monitor attached.

Helen was a peach. She giggled like she was back in the thirties. After she said the pain was gone, she talked nonstop in the sweetest little-old-lady voice.

And she had a penchant for Dano.

I winked at him a few times while he carried on a conversation with the darling woman.

Thump!

Dano and I looked toward the back, where the sound had come from.

"What the hell?" he said, staring.

A sparrow glared back at him.

Dano and I looked at each other, then at the bird whose wing must have gotten caught in the crack of the doors.Dano banged on the window and told Buzz to stop for a second. Thank goodness Helen didn't look to be in any distress.

"What's wrong, Boss?" Buzz asked.

"Stop this thing. There's a bird caught in the door."

Dano and I must have thought of the absurdity of the scene at the same time, because we both suddenly broke out into laughter. The bird, too, didn't seem to be in any distress. I think it grinned.

As usual, Buzz kept up his questioning.

"How do you know?" Buzz asked, still not pulling over. He always had to find out details. Well, I guessed, being a detail man was good for this profession, but I also wondered again if Buzz would survive it.

I thought Dano would explode. "'Cause it's looking right at me!" he shouted, and then he and I started to laugh uncontrollably again.

Suddenly Helen waved a knobby finger at the two of us. "You two should be ashamed!" She went into a tirade about how we shouldn't find it humorous that one of God's creatures was stuck in the door.

Even when I tried to assure her that the bird didn't look injured, she spat words at me that I don't think ER Dano even knew. After a few minutes I was ready to medicate Helen with whatever Dano had given Rebecca, just to shut Helen up.

Buzz pulled over.

Dano opened the door.

The sparrow happily flew away.

And we hit the siren and lights to get Helen to the hospital ASAP—or I think Dano would have slugged her.

The sweet little old lady had turned into a tyrant right before our eyes. We dropped her off, restocked, didn't go say goodbye to her for fear we'd upset her more and headed back to TLC—where I fixed myself a much-needed cup of stale tea.

And when I sat down to sip it, I realized that life was strange, people even stranger, and looking over the room of paramedics and EMTs, I wondered if there was a murderer among us.

Dano, Buzz and I had the worst day on record. After two more calls—one for a child who had a toy hatchet stuck up his nose and couldn't breathe well, and the other for a construction worker who fell off some scaffolding and broke his back—we drove down through the worst section of Hope Valley with Buzz at the wheel.

He'd bothered Dano so much about being allowed to drive that Dano gave in, I'm sure just to shut up the eager "Sparkie."

I leaned against the back wall of the ambulance and shut my eyes, trying to think out the case. This one had turned out to be a doozy. Way too many types of fraud to pinpoint anyone right off the bat. And I knew, just knew, that the murder and the attempt on Pansy's life were related. I also knew money had to be the root of it all. Why else commit the fraud?

I tried to think of what I knew about the employees at TLC and if anyone had new "toys," like a car, etcetera, that would warrant looking into. Just then, the ambulance lurched and hit something, and my head was jolted forward and back, smacking the wall as we stopped suddenly. "Ouch!"

Buzz's voice came through the open window. "Did you see that oil truck pull out in front of me?"

"It's parked, you jerk!" Dano yelled, disgusted.

"Oh," Buzz mumbled.

I had to smile to myself, knowing we were all right. Dano was already outside looking at the front of the ambulance to assess the damage, so I joined him. I gave him a weak smile, hoping that would help, yet not knowing how the heck it would.

"Just a minor scratch. Get in," Dano muttered.

We looked around.

No Buzz Lightyear.

"Where the f—?"

I pointed at the house we'd stopped in front of. Through a curtainless window we could see three disreputable-looking guys—and sparkling, wrinkle-free Buzz Lightyear—in what was obviously the "house of crack."

"Oh, Jesus," Dano muttered, "they'll surely kill him once he opens his mouth." He headed toward the house. "Stay in the back," he ordered, and I sure didn't want to get on his bad side right now, so I stayed put.

Soon Buzz, looking very sheepish, came out with Dano right behind, looking as if he wanted to smack Buzz in the back of the head like a father would an unruly son.

Once they were inside the ambulance Dano said, "Why the hell did you go into a crack house?"

"To use the phone." Buzz sounded as if what he'd just said made perfect sense.

Dano shook his head and decided finally to let it go. "We have a radio in here," was all he said.

Buzz hesitated.

"What!" Dano said. "Get going! Drive!"

"I can't just pull out. I need to back up."

"Then back the hell up," Dano said.

"The rule is that you—the passenger—are supposed to get out and guide me."

Oh, boy. I had to give Buzz credit for having the guts to stand up to ER Dano, who wasn't in a very good mood. Buzz was correct. The other person was supposed to get out to guide the driver.

But Dano turned to him and in a very threatening voice said, "Back this f'n thing up and let's get back so we can go home *today*. That's what you have side-view mirrors for. You need to learn if you're gonna continue in this job."

Buzz put the ambulance in reverse.

I looked out the back window to see if I could help. Nothing. Coast clear. Thank the good Lord.

Smash!

There was a moment of silence from the cab of the ambulance. I stood to look out the window, flabbergasted that Buzz had managed to find a cement bollard—like the ones used to tie horses up to in the olden days—and that it was now melded with the back of the ambulance. It had been much lower than my sight line—and obviously Buzz's too.

I couldn't even imagine what would happen next.

Once the wrecker got the ambulance free and we were picked up by Ambulance #277, we headed back to TLC. I sat in the lounge waiting for Dano—having second thoughts about it. Maybe I should get the hell out of there before he came out, since I was sure he wasn't going to be his jolly self.

"Don't even get close to me," I heard Dano say.

But—and it didn't surprise me—I heard Buzz respond, "You didn't have to do that for me. I'm touched."

Yikes!

I hurried out into the hallway before Dano *really* "touched" Buzz.

Dano looked at me. "I'll call you." And then he was out the door.

I looked at Buzz. He never took his eyes off Dano's retreating back. He said, "He covered for me. He said it was his fault, so I wouldn't get in trouble." Buzz turned to me. "I've had a few close calls before."

I wanted to say, "Gee, what a surprise," but knew better. Besides, the kid needed to vent.

"So what happens to him?" I asked.

"He's so senior around here, they only gave him a day off . . . without pay."

Oh . . . my . . . God.

Twenty-Five

Buzz was so upset that he couldn't drive home. Dano had peeled out of the parking lot at high speed and neither Jagger nor Lilla were in sight, so I volunteered to give Buzz a lift. The poor guy needed a friend, and I was like a flame to a moth for poor souls. My darn nurturing nurse's nature kicked in, and I found myself sitting in the driveway of an adorable little yellow Victorian house with white trim.

"You wanna come in?" Buzz asked.

I did, but only out of curiosity—like a rubbernecker. What kind of house would Buzz Lightyear live in? Thinking it rude though, I said, "No, hon. I'm tired. Better get home."

Buzz turned to me. I'd seen that look before in the eyes of my nephews when I'd disappointed them—mostly by buying the wrong toys as Christmas presents. Hey, I was childless!

Before I knew it, I was standing in the foyer of the house from *Leave It to Beaver*, only much smaller and in color—a bit brighter but nonetheless odd and bordering on retro.

Buzz offered me a glass of iced tea, which I politely

accepted. He brought me a pink glass, and the iced tea looked pink too. I only hoped Red #40 food dye didn't cause me to become hyper.

"Here you go," Buzz said.

"Thanks. I really can't stay long."

I wondered if I could drink with my mouth agape. Looking around this place caused just that.

Then a woman came in the back door. "Hello, my honey!" she called in a bright voice.

"Hi, Mommy. I'm home with a friend."

If I'd been in mid-swallow, I'd have spewed tea out on the braided rug beneath my feet. *A friend! Mommy!* "Hey, don't want to make Lilla jealous," I teased.

Buzz looked rather serious. "She is a *friend* too."

Whoa, boy. Must have been trouble in Eden. I smiled and followed him into the kitchen. Now, I really wasn't one to judge, since Stella Sokol's kitchen was a retro throwback, but this place, all done in pink, and I mean *all* done in pink, was circa 1960. And all the pink was plastic. The blender. The phone and its cord, and the toaster. Pink. Pink. Pink.

I vowed I would never wear pink or take Pepto-Bismol again.

"Did you show your friend your room?" Buzz's mother asked.

What? Actually, she hadn't said it in any sexual way. Nope. It was more like we'd come home for recess and my buddy Buzz would show me his prize trophies.

Well, I wasn't far off, I thought, when Buzz led me to his room.

It was small, with a single bed with a brown plaid bedspread, but what struck me most were the walls. They were covered in posters of ambulances. On one bookshelf was a stack of EMT magazines—well read

I might add—and there were little ambulances on all the other shelves.

I looked at the window and noticed the tiny red crosses on the curtains.

"What do you think, Miss Pauline?"

"Wow," was all I could manage, and then quickly came to my senses and looked at my watch. "Oh, geez. I have to run. This place is great! You're great!"

Before he could say a word, I was out of there, and I think I forgot to say goodbye to his mom, and I still had the glass of tea in my hand.

I spent the evening with Goldie and Miles, who kept insisting that I'd made up all the stories of the day. I told them that I really wanted Buzz to succeed as an EMT but had my doubts, and that my imagination wasn't *so* good that I could make all that up.

Buzz was a veritable magnet for accidents, as ER Dano was a magnet for whacko patients, we'd all concluded. Then again, only Dano could handle some of them.

After much consideration, I decided not to call Dano, but to give him his space. He didn't phone me either, so I went to sleep with a rather empty feeling inside; but when I woke and dressed for a new day, I decided Dano could probably use the rest anyway, and I'm sure a day without pay wouldn't affect him as it would have affected Buzz, who would have lost his job.

I had more respect for Dano now, and a bit more feelings too. I could feel myself blush as I walked into the lounge at TLC.

Jagger was sitting on the couch with Jennifer. My mind tried to head toward jealousy, but then I thought of Dano, and that Jagger and I were coworkers and there was damn Airbrush Lady to think about. Guess I'd purposely put her out of my mind.

Suddenly my name was called over the intercom. I had a helicopter run to take. Almost glad that it'd get me out of here and my mind off Dano's absence, I waved to Jagger and walked out the door.

At the helipad, I put on my helmet and noticed someone already in the back, strapped in. Mario, taking a catnap yet again.

Sky was at the controls and turned to wave at me as I got in. Over the microphone he told me about the case, and I stepped into the back and sat down, grabbing my harness from the wall. With Mario along, I figured I need not worry about Sky's guilt or no guilt.

We picked up the patient at Saint Greg's and safely dropped him off at Yale New Haven Hospital.

Mario never took his helmet off, and I guessed he was now fast asleep next to me. A little nap wasn't such a bad idea. But then I saw him looking at me, and I gave him a thumbs-up.

Wait a minute. Mario didn't have such long skinny legs. He was more muscular. Hmm. I leaned over to him. "Hey," I said into my microphone.

"Hello, Miss Pauline."

Buzz Lightyear.

Oh, geez. I only hoped this wasn't going to be a repeat of yesterday. I mean, bumping a cement bollard with an ambulance was one thing, but would darling Buzz bring bad luck to a flying tin can that had rotary blades only held on by one "Jesus nut?"

Thank goodness we'd gotten the patient safely to his destination. I had no idea that Buzz did helicopter runs, but figured, what did I know? I hadn't been at TLC all that long.

After a few prayers that we'd stay airborne, I leaned back in my seat and shut my eyes. A seemingly uneventful trip, even with Buzz Lightyear aboard. I started to relax.

While in my groggy state, I felt a thud. My eyelids flew open and my heart now thudded. "What's going on?" I yelled.

But Sky didn't answer. He didn't say a thing as to why we had just landed on a beach. It looked like Long Island Sound!

For a few seconds, I sat there and told myself I must be dreaming. I blinked several times and the scenery didn't change.

The helicopter, in fact, sat on a beach. I knew it was Long Island Sound now, but a rather secluded section. No cottages nearby. No boardwalk like at Hammonasset State Beach. Not sure where we were or why, I unhooked myself and saw the door already open.

I stepped out onto the sand and called, "Sky? Buzz? Sky? Did we break down or something?"

Over my helmet microphone I heard, "You had to ruin everything. She was going to make me rich. She owed me."

What the hell?

Despite the static, I figured out the voice belonged to Buzz. Rich? She?

"And how the hell . . . What the hell did you do to Mario?" Sky asked.

I froze.

"Just a matter of a little left-over medication from a psych teen yesterday. He'll sleep it off in the locker room." Buzz laughed . . . eerily. "No one will pay attention since Mario sleeps so much."

Oh . . . my . . . God!

I got back in the helicopter to call 911 on the radio. When I grabbed the microphone, the entire wiring system came with it.

Someone had pulled it out.

Buzz.

I grabbed my cell phone from my pocket, but it said No SERVICE. I frantically pushed buttons to no avail. Shoot!

"Sky?" I yelled. I started to take off my helmet so could go find someone to help. But before I lifted it all the way off, I recognized Sky's voice again.

"I loved her, you loser. She'd never do shit for you. She should have given you up for adoption at birth. You loser—"

I heard shuffling and no more voices. Before I could turn and run, I noticed Sky and Buzz near a sand dune. Buzz had something that sparkled in his hand, and ran toward them and screamed, "No!"

And while they scuffled, he plunged it into Sky's back!

"Stop that!" I picked up a piece of driftwood and ran at him swinging it like a star baseball player. "Leave him alone! What is wrong with you, Buzz?"

When he turned, I knew.

It was clearly in his eyes. Hatred. Mental illness. A mind that had snapped.

The clumsy, lovable Buzz Lightyear had turned into a monster. The crisp, clean-cut guy who had looked as if he'd stepped out of a brand-new toy box had vanished, and now a villain stood holding a bloody knife—and Sky lay on the ground.

From here I couldn't tell if he was breathing, but the wound was in his shoulder, much higher than any vial organs. Hopefully he was just playing dead or had passed out from shock and pain.

Buzz was on me in seconds. He tackled me to the ground and held the knife at my throat before I could run for help.

I had this thing about anyone touching my throat.

I hated it.

Just as much as I hated *knives*.

And now I knew that I hated a knife at my throat.

"Buzz, hon, let me get up and help Sky. I'm sure it was just an accident. Like the ambulance yesterday. No one will blame you." That is if I lived to tell them.

He looked at me and laughed. "You are one smart nurse, Sokol, but dumb as shit for a broad."

I lifted my knee with as much force as I could, landing it in his groin, but he merely cursed and pulled the knife across my neck.

"Oh!" The pain wasn't as bad as the fear. My first instinct was to reach up and touch the cut, which was merely a flesh wound. But I felt the warm blood and trembled. He could have cut deeper, but didn't. Most likely to just scare me.

Buzz Lightyear was no one to take lightly.

And, yeah, I was scared out of my mind, but knew I had to keep in control of myself in order to live and save Sky.

"You killed Payne," I said, learning from past cases that the murderer always liked to brag before he . . . finished off his victim.

Buzz laughed. "The asshole deserved it. He was never the father he should have been."

Father. *Father*? "Payne was your father?"

"And Pansy, the sicko, my mother. She'll rot in hell with him when I get done with her."

He was so nervous at the hospital because he mus
have come there to finish her off. That's why he'
stayed behind. When Lilla and I had made a noise,
scared him off and saved Pansy's life.

"But the woman at your house—" I said, trying t
distract him and get as much information out of hir
that I could. I only prayed that I'd be alive to tell som
one.

"She's my housekeeper. I pay her extra to play th
role of mommy. She gets a kick out of it—if you know
what I mean." He grinned. An evil grin.

I swallowed hard despite my neck and thought tha
human behavior would never cease to amaze me.

Evil was pure evil.

"But Pansy and Payne were brother and sister." A
if that'd make it impossible to have a child. Well, in m
Catholic conscience it did.

He looked at me. "Don't be stupid, Sokol. Incest be
tween those two crazies was a given. I mean, they wei
like shadows of each other. No wonder they produce
a weirdo like me!" He laughed.

But I felt his pain. What a life it must have bee
for him growing up. The theory that siblings produc
mentally challenged offspring was valid in my eye
no matter what the studies said.

"But why kill them?"

"I didn't kill Mommy . . . yet." He pushed the knif
into my neck a bit more.

"Did you make threatening phone calls to me?"

He laughed. "I used you as a guinea pig since yo
were new, but then I lost interest when the opportunit
arose for me to complete my plan. I told Mommy yo
were bad and that you knew about the fraud. That
why she didn't trust you."

When he leaned closer, I noticed the radio on his shoulder and started to scream. It might cost me another scratch but maybe save Sky and I in the end. I flailed my arms about and hit the button as I did.

Saint T was with me. Not noticing the microphone was on, Buzz kept shouting louder and louder. I heard the static and started to shout our location, that Buzz was the killer and to send help, but I said it all in a way as if repeating his words so he wouldn't be suspicious and kill me right then.

The more I fought him, the angrier he grew, and suddenly I realized—it wasn't aimed at me.

Buzz began to go on about his childhood, and how could I do that to him and why didn't I abort him. And if he couldn't have love, he'd have money. All of it.

He'd envisioned me now as Pansy, his mother, and began to confess how he set up all the fraud at TLC to make a fortune—but Daddy got greedy and was going to cut into Buzz's profits, so he had to be taken care of.

Buzz was not immune to murder, I reminded myself.

I kept repeating our location, what was happening and that Sky was down. Buzz, now in his own world, didn't pay me any attention. He merely remained above me.

Hope Valley was only a half-hour drive from the shoreline, so the local police could drive to the beach in minutes, and hopefully, Jagger and Lieutenant Shatley could fly down soon after. I knew Jagger would have everything under control when he realized how late we were in getting back and when dispatch heard my frantic, albeit confusing, radio calls.

I decided to use my nurturing nurse's nature on Buzz although I would rather have kicked him where it hurt several times. I knew he had me in the weight and strength department, so I had to go with my brains, since, being injured, I wasn't sure I had the strength to use my self-defense techniques. Especially since he had me pinned down and the knife still near my throat.

Sky was starting to stir. Once he looked at me in a very painful, groggy stare. I winked at him and motioned for him to stay put.

Hopefully he wouldn't try to be a macho pilot.

I'm sure he wanted to get up and kick the shit out of Buzz, since Sky apparently did love Pansy and hopefully to help me .

Oh what a tangled web we weave. . . .

I leaned back in the helicopter and Jagger put his arm around me. Sky lay on the stretcher and crazy, pathetic handcuffed Buzz had been taken back to Hope Valley in the police cruiser. The helicopter was flown by one of the part-time pilots.

"How sad," I muttered.

Jagger looked at me.

"I know. I know. I can't do my job if I feel sorry for the criminals."

"Yep. No matter how nice they appear, how interesting or sad their lives are or how beautiful they are, they are still criminals."

My forehead wrinkled. "Beautiful?"

His hold tightened. "Oh, I wrapped up a case yesterday. Real looker. Real con artist."

"He was?"

"*She* was. You saw us at dinner the other night. Remember?"

Airbrush Lady! Jagger hadn't been on a date, but working another case. Oh, how Jaggerlike.

And apparently oh-how Pauline-like to suspect that a guy was bowled over by a pretty face.

Guess I'd forgotten this was Jagger I was talking about. Now it made sense that he wasn't around as much as usual. He had been helping Shatley, but also working another case and keeping tabs on me trying to solve mine.

"Interesting. But, in Buzz's case, I do feel sorry that a life was so wasted because two people made a mistake."

Jagger made some kind of guttural sound. "A big mistake."

It was disgusting to think about, yet sad too. Pansy and Payne were products of their environment. Sky had told us that the two grew up without any friends or other family around. They'd pretty much been ostracized by all the kids because they looked so much alike and were so weird to boot.

Without any choice, they were kinda thrown together. Almost molded into one. Twins had special bonds, but these two were something very different. Their parents had messed them up good by treating them like clones.

It seemed as if they were going to make a go of TLC once they'd inherited it, but that's when Buzz, who'd apparently trained as an EMT just to get the job, came back into their lives with his plan for revenge and money. Probably Buzz had lived away from Hope Valley but came back when he saw the big news about them inheriting TLC. Pansy had felt guilty and hired him, but wouldn't let him live with her. Thus the housekeeper "mommy."

I wondered if Buzz's clumsy behavior was phony, but Sky assured me the guy couldn't fake all that had happened to him. He just drew problems to himself. And these last ones were doozies.

Sky had insisted that he really did love Pansy, and it wasn't just an affair. She'd always presented herself as asexual, which she had been after she and Payne had conceived Buzz. But Sky'd gotten her to open her heart just a bit. . . . then it was too late. Sheepishly he'd admitted he'd gotten her what I called the "sex chair" on a trip he'd taken over to Europe—and it had helped—so they designed the room for . . . themselves.

Jagger suddenly tugged at my arm. We'd landed at Saint Greg's. Sky, who would be fine, was taken off the copter by the staff, and we flew back to TLC.

When the helicopter set down, I got up and stepped out. ER Dano stood by the helipad, waiting. The police must have called him. I felt something touch my back.

A gentle nudge from . . . Jagger.

At first a thread of disappointment spread throughout me. He had pushed me forward. Jagger had actually pushed me *toward Dano*.

But in a heartbeat I found my way into Dano's arms.

He held me tightly and over his shoulder I could see Jagger standing there. . . . and, in that moment, that horrible moment, I realized he *hadn't* nudged me forward at all. . . .

Epilogue

I stood in the back of the park where the ceremony was about to begin—and sighed.

Damn, but life took interesting twists and turns. After Fabio had given me my well-deserved bonus for case #6 of my newfound career, I realized that my life had really changed.

And for the better.

No longer was I the newbie Fabio had once called me. Nope. I had managed to solve a case or two on my very own. A feeling of pride surged through me, and then I looked up at the "altar."

Wow.

Nothing could have prepared me for the sight I now faced.

In the distance, a mere fifty feet away, stood the man who had brought me to this point in my life. The gentle summer's breeze tousled his dark hair. Occasionally, he'd run a hand through it, and I'd sigh again. Damn, would I ever stop reacting to him this way?

Guess he really had a great influence on me—and my libido. Then again, no. It really wasn't true. *He* hadn't brought me here, to this point in my life, at all.

Watching him. Feeling my insides flutter as usual and trying to think rationally, I finally realized—it was all *my* doing.

If nothing else, I had managed to switch from a very successful, yet truly stressful nursing career, to become a top-notch investigator for Scarpello and Tonelli insurance company. All right. All right. Top-notch might be a bit overboard, but I had grown and learned over the past six months.

The small all-guy quartet, suited in white tuxedos, started to play and my eyes began to tear up. Nothing like a wedding to bring out all the emotions of our lives.

Watching from nearby, sat my parents.

Daddy remained very stoic in his black tux, which Goldie and Miles had helped rent for him. Daddy could only have looked more handsome at his own wedding. I caught his gaze, and he winked at me.

Enough to make me want to break out in tears.

Stella Sokol had already married off four of her five children, so a wedding was nothing to her. Actually, no gala event that involved food was too much for her. Yet, right now, she couldn't have looked more full of pride in her yellow "mother of the bride" gown, which Goldie himself had designed, and had assisted in every aspect of its creation. Mother looked proud, pleased, and probably thankful all at the same time.

While the quartet played something I'm sure was by Beethoven, I wiped a few tears from my cheeks, hoping I wasn't painting raccoon eyes with my mascara, and scanned the crowd.

Small, yet personal. Friends each and every one, all decked out in their finest rose, yellow or white outfits—per the wedding planner's suggestion. *What a cool idea*, I thought, as I decided that the entire setting could have been the centerfold for *Bride* magazine.

Lilla, in low-cut rose, and her mom, Adele, in skin-tight white with matching gloves, sat near the front next to, of all people, Nick Caruso, my first mentor on the job. Damn but he still looked good and I made a mental note to ask why he hadn't taken a case lately.

Despite the special day, even Fabio had been seated near them. Thank goodness he didn't wear brown polyester and was not smoking a cigar at the moment.

Oh, well, guess I had to be charitable for the special day.

My dearest uncle Walt had forgone his brown suit, too, to don a handsome black tuxedo. A "lady friend" of his, who sat next to him in her yellow dress, nudged him to look up at the sky.

Every floral arrangement boasted the same color palette as the guests, while the trellis on the "altar" had been painted white and yellow with matching roses (my Saint Theresa was never far away). Flocks of white doves seemed to hover in the air as if waiting for their cue.

Even I felt as if this day would never come, never have been able to come, if fate hadn't shoved me out of my nursing career and into the insurance investigative field.

I actually giggled. Geez. So very unlike me, but when I looked up to see my buddy, Goldie, I had to smile.

For this very special day, Goldie had relinquished his oh-so-stylish penchant for lace and crinoline and had chosen instead what I assumed was Armani—pants—men's. There was no doubt that the black tuxedo fit Gold to a tee and made him look more handsome than even I could have pictured. A boyish look on his face, yet a deeply loving look, added an extra zing to my Gold. Our gazes met, and we both let out a chuckle of friendship and best wishes.

No better friends could there be except for Miles being thrown into the equation. He, too, wore a dark black tux, but a different cut that made my dear friend look exactly as if I would have pictured him.

While the music slowed, I looked ahead through the center aisle, set off by white wooden chairs, to notice Jagger in his tux.

I can't even explain how delicious he looked; I smiled at him and nodded to Miles, who stood nearby.

Finally!

On this perfect midsummer's day, the lives of two people would be joined forever in heart, soul and legal union.

When I sniffled, I felt a hand on mine and looked down to see Goldie's perfectly manicured hand resting, no, *squeezing* mine. "Hey," was all I could say.

"Suga." Now he sniffled. "I never thought this day would come."

"You and I both. Or is it me and you?" We both laughed, held tighter, and suddenly paused.

The music had transitioned in tune. Something I called "the wedding march" in my head filled the park, the air and my heart.

Both of my parents soon stood next to me. I linked my arm in my father's on one side, Goldie's on the other, and as planned, my mother walked next to my dad.

And my heart soared in the ambiance of the fantastic occasion.

When we reached the end of the aisle, my parents walked to their seats, I proceeded to the center and stood next to Jagger. Ah.

Goldie stood next to Miles, and the ceremony, the real thing, the life-changing moment, began.

As if from a distance, yet only a few feet away, I heard, "Dearly beloved, we are gathered here today, in this most lovely setting, I might add . . ."

Through teary eyes I looked at Jagger—and felt my heart swell.

" . . . In the presence of these witnesses . . ." The officiate waved his hands in the air to encompass the entire crowd. "To join . . ."

I'd never stood in this situation before and realized it was a once-in-a-lifetime moment. Truly one I would treasure forever.

The officiate cleared his throat. "To join in holy matrimony . . . Goldie Perlman and Miles Scarpello . . ."

And I thought . . . *someday* . . . *someday*. . . .